'Are you indeed certain you wish to wed me?'

'It is the only way I can keep you safe,' he said. 'As my betrothed wife I put my seal on you. Any man who tries to take you from me will know they become my mortal enemy.'

Rosamunde glanced away. Her heart was racing. She had agreed to wed him, and she sensed—felt—the passion in him. Raphael wanted her, but he had made it clear that he could never love her. He had obviously loved his wife greatly, but she was in her grave. He was only marrying Rosamunde to protect her. He considered it his duty to care for her, and she knew he would keep her safe—but she wanted more from her marriage than that.

AUTHOR NOTE

I hope you will enjoy this medieval story about a young woman who is sent as a hostage in her cousin's place, to pay her uncle's debt. At the very least she expects to be disparaged and returned to her family in disgrace, but what else can she do but obey her cousin? Her father has given all his money away and no longer cares about life. How can Rosamunde find a new life for them when she will lose both her honour and her chance of ever finding a husband?

Raphael has returned from the crusades a rich man, but he carries the memory of the woman he married there and her terrible death. When he discovers what his father has been doing while he was away he is ashamed, and determined to set an example to his men—but the latest hostage is beautiful, and her eyes seem to call to him. If he sets her free she might just be taken hostage again to satisfy Prince John's greed.

Somehow he must find a way to make sure his lovely prisoner is cared for—for the rest of her life—but she thinks he is his father, a man lost to honour and reputation. How can he forget the shadows that haunt him and convince her that her happiness lies with him?

I know many of you love tales of knights and their ladies. I loved writing this one and hope you will find pleasure in reading it.

HOSTAGE BRIDE

Anne Herries

First published in Great Britain 2011
by Mills & Boon, an imprint of Harlequin (UK) Limited.
Large Print edition 2012
Harlequin (UK) Limited, Eton House, 18-24 Paradise Road,
Richmond, Surrey TW9 1SR

© Anne Herries 2011

ISBN: 978 0 263 22509 9

Harlequin (UK) policy is to use papers that are natural, renewable and recyclable products and made from wood grown in sustainable forests. The logging and manufacturing process conform to the legal environmental regulations of the country of origin.

Printed and bound in Great Britain

Anne Herries lives in Cambridgeshire, where she is fond of watching wildlife, and spoils the birds and squirrels that are frequent visitors to her garden. Anne loves to write about the beauty of nature, and sometimes puts a little into her books—although they are mostly about love and romance. She writes for her own enjoyment, and to give pleasure to her readers. She is a winner of the Romantic Novelists' Association Romance Prize. She invites readers to contact her on her website at www.lindasole.co.uk

Previous novels by the same author:

MARRYING CAPTAIN JACK
THE UNKNOWN HEIR
THE HOMELESS HEIRESS
THE RAKE'S REBELLIOUS LADY
A COUNTRY MISS IN HANOVER SQUARE*
AN INNOCENT DEBUTANTE IN
  HANOVER SQUARE*
THE MISTRESS OF HANOVER SQUARE*
FORBIDDEN LADY†
THE LORD'S FORCED BRIDE†
THE PIRATE'S WILLING CAPTIVE†
HER DARK AND DANGEROUS LORD†
BOUGHT FOR THE HAREM

A Season in Town trilogy
†*The Melford Dynasty*

And in the Regency series
***The Steepwood Scandal*:**

LORD RAVENSDEN'S MARRIAGE
COUNTERFEIT EARL

And in *The Hellfire Mysteries*:

AN IMPROPER COMPANION
A WEALTHY WIDOW
A WORTHY GENTLEMAN

Prologue

In the year of our Lord 1189

Rosamunde looked down from the solar at the top of the tower, watching the activity in the court-yard below. The compound was filled with men, horses and dogs because the hunting party had just returned. The huntsmen seemed to have been successful and there was evidence of more than one kill. That meant that Lady Meldreth and her women would be busy for a few days salting the flesh of wild boar into barrels for the winter. Most of the game and venison would be roasted for the feast the next day.

She was not yet thirteen years of age, but Rosa-munde was accustomed to helping her mother in her still room; she kept accounts and embroidered hangings to keep the chill from the stone walls of her father's keep. She was wise beyond her years and knew that Sir Randolph Meldreth was not as rich and successful as some of the knights he was entertaining. Behind her, she could hear her mother complaining.

'If you do not watch your spending, husband, you will ruin us,' she scolded. 'The King is off to the Crusades and you will earn no favours by entertaining him and his knights with a lavish feast. You would do better to save our money and wait until you see which way the wind blows. Prince John is to be regent in Richard's place and it is he you should seek to please now.'

'Hush, woman. Richard asked me to entertain his friends for a few days,' Sir Randolph replied in his cheerful, easy manner. 'It is an honour, wife. Besides, I cannot refuse. If my health did not prevent it, I should offer my sword to this holy cause and go with the King.'

'Then I must thank God that you have the agues and cannot ride for days and weeks at a time.' Lady Meldreth's mouth turned down sourly. 'The King may be gone for years and only God knows if he and his knights will ever return.'

Unwilling to listen to yet another quarrel between her parents, Rosamunde went quietly from the room. She walked down the narrow spiral-staircase to the great hall below the solar. Some of the men were already spilling into the large room, laughing and talking excitedly as they boasted to one another of the day's exploits. One of them had brought his dogs in with him and they were sniffing at the rushes, yelping and growling as they hunted for scraps that might have been tossed to the floor.

Suddenly, a small kitten rushed at one of the hounds and scratched its nose; it had obviously been startled by the arrival of the dogs and had lashed out in fright. The great hound stared at it for a moment then growled and pounced, intending to crush it between its heavy jaws.

'No, please, do not let the dog harm my kitty!' Rosamunde cried and rushed towards them. Somehow the kitten had avoided capture thus far and Rosamunde flung herself on it, clutching it to her breast as the dog snarled and jumped at her, trying to reach its prey, its sharp teeth snapping inches from her face. 'Get down, you brute. Leave my poor kitty alone.'

The dog saw only the kitten. It reared up on its

hind legs to growl and bark as it attempted to grab its prey from her. Rosamunde screamed as the dog's saliva dripped on her and its yellow fangs scraped her hand.

'Down, you cur,' a voice cried and then a youth, dressed in a short parti-tunic of blue and silver over black hose, caught hold of its collar and dragged it off her. The dog snarled and fought but the youth hauled it to the door and thrust it outside, where it could be heard barking fiercely.

Rosamunde ran to a corner of the hall and sat down on the stone floor, hunching her knees to her chest and hugging the terrified kitten. Tears trickled down her cheeks because she was frightened, and her hand hurt where the dog's fangs had scraped her skin.

'Are you hurt, little mistress?'

Rosamunde glanced up as the youth spoke. He was perhaps sixteen or so and handsome, with dark-blond hair and blue eyes. His mouth was wide and generous and there was concern in his eyes as he looked at her.

'I thought he would kill my kitten,' she said and wiped her hand over her cheek. 'I'm not frightened for myself.'

'Of course not,' he said and smiled. 'Did the dog's teeth break the skin?'

Rosamunde showed him her hand. His fingers were gentle as they examined the red marks the dog's fangs had made.

'The brute has not drawn blood. I think you will not take harm from it.'

'You were in time to save me,' she said. 'I thank you, sir. What is your name? Are you here because you're going to the Crusades?'

'Aye, that is my reason for being here.' His eyes lit up. 'It is a wonderful chance for me to win glory and fame, and perhaps a knighthood. My father will not join the King's cause but I think it an honour.'

'Shall you fight the Saracens? My mother says they are fierce fighters and many will die in a foolish cause.'

'We fight for a holy cause, little mistress,' he said. 'Your mother does not understand that men will gladly risk everything for such honour and glory.'

'I do not think I should like you to be killed,' Rosamunde said, looking at him shyly. 'You are so brave. The hound could have bitten you but you did not think of yourself.'

'It was nothing. I knew the dog was too strong for you. He would not have stopped until he had the kitten and, since you would not let go, you could have been seriously injured.'

'Raphael. Here to me, sirrah. I need you.'

'My master calls me,' Raphael said. 'Sir Harold of Fernshaw trained me as his squire and I owe him allegiance. If it were not for him, I should not have this opportunity. Excuse me, little mistress. I have work to do.'

'My name is Rosamunde,' she whispered but she did not know if he heard her. 'When you return to England, visit us again, sir. I shall be here waiting for you.'

The young man turned his head and smiled at her once more. Rosamunde's heart raced, her breath quickening. She was only a child, but the men would be many years at the Crusades and by the time they returned she would be a woman.

Would Raphael remember her? She would never forget him but perhaps he believed her merely a child. His thoughts were only of the Holy Land and the adventures he would discover there.

'Come back safely,' she murmured as she stroked the kitten and kissed its soft head. 'I shall not forget you, Raphael. One day I pray we shall meet again.'

Chapter One

In the year of our Lord 1193

'Messalina! God help me…' Raphael awoke from the nightmare, his body dripping with perspiration. Putting out his hand, he discovered that the bed beside him was empty and cold. He had been dreaming of his late wife, of the terrible day a few months ago when he'd discovered that she was dead, lost to him for all time. 'Forgive me. I should have been there. I should have protected you, my dear one.'

He moaned as the agony swept over him. His beautiful, young and lovely wife was dead and it was his fault. She'd begged him not to leave her that fateful night, but he had unwound her soft white arms from about his neck and told her he must go.

'This is war, Messalina. I have been summoned by King Richard to a meeting and must obey his orders. Things do not go as well as Richard would have liked and we may have to leave the Holy Land without gaining all we came for.'

'Leave? You speak of leaving, of returning to your own land?' Messalina's eyes filled with tears. 'Will you leave without me?'

'You are my wife. When I return to England you will come with me.'

'What of my father? How can I leave him here alone to face his last years without his daughter?'

'I shall speak to your father tomorrow when I know more of the King's plans,' he'd promised— but in the morning both his wife and her father were dead, murdered by renegade Saracens.

His guilt lay heavy on his conscience for he knew that he need not have attended the meeting but had gone because he wanted to spend a little time with the knights who were his friends that night. Messalina was beautiful and he had been fond of her, like a man might be fond of a spaniel puppy, but she had clung to him and wept, and soon after wedding her he had realised that he did not love her as he ought.

He was not sure why he'd wed her, except that
her father had offered her to him, and her shy smile
had been appealing to a young man flushed with
success from fighting a holy war. He had rescued
both her and her father from ruffians who had
sought to rob the wealthy merchant, and their gratitude had been flattering. Jacob had begged him
to give them his protection and take his daughter
and her fortune as his reward. He had wanted to
protect both Messalina and her father and now felt
that he had betrayed them. Yet it was more than
that. Perhaps he was not capable of giving the deep
love Messalina had needed, but he had genuinely
cared for her, and now that she was dead his guilt
haunted him day and night.

Leaving his bed, Raphael found cold water in the
ewer and washed his face and body. His skin was
bronzed by the sun of the Holy Land, his muscles
honed by years of fighting and training in the art
of warfare. The scars he'd received in battle had
faded with time. He was drying himself when
the door of his chamber opened and his servant
Janquil entered.

'Yes?' he barked and then checked himself for
he alone was to blame for the betrayal of Messa-

lina. Janquil held no blame of any kin
news?'

'We have discovered the goldsmith you seek, my lord. It is but a day's ride across the border into Normandy.'

'Then we shall leave as soon as the others are ready. I must settle this business and then perhaps I shall have peace.'

The squire inclined his head, his dark eyes inscrutable. Raphael knew that the man was part-Saracen and part-Jew, a combination that had led to him being reviled and spat upon by the people of Acre. His mother's people hated him for being the son of a Muslim and his father's people thought him unworthy to be one of them. His parents had lived as outcasts in their village and when they had died of a virulent fever Janquil had sought work in Acre. For some years he'd worked as a house servant to a wealthy Jew but when Saladin took the city his master had been murdered.

When King Richard recaptured the city, Raphael had found the young man shivering and ill, near to starving. He had taken him to his quarters, nursed him and fed him, refusing to give him up as a pris-

...er. Janquil declined to leave after he recovered, saying that his life belonged to Raphael.

When Raphael and his friends had decided to make the long journey back to England, Janquil had asked to accompany him.

'My country is very different to yours. You may wish you had stayed here, my friend.'

'My life is yours. If I cannot serve you there is no purpose for me.'

Raphael put the memories to one side. He had become wealthy in the Holy Land, as had some of his friends, but there was also a fortune in Normandy lodged with a Jew his late father-in-law had trusted. Jacob would expect Raphael to claim it; they had been friends, and more than friends—almost as father and son. It was because Raphael had saved Jacob's life that he had given him his most precious treasure—his daughter, Messalina.

Perhaps if he settled his business the nightmares would leave him to rest in peace.

Rosamunde was mending a tunic. It was her second best and she had torn it while out gathering herbs and berries for her cures. Her stitches were neat and she could not afford cloth to make a new one, because she would not ask her father for money. He had none to give her and would merely be distressed that she was in need.

Sir Randolph had almost beggared himself entertaining the King and his knights before they had gone on the third crusade. Since then he had contributed generously by sending young men from his manor to join Richard in the Holy Land, and he had recently given three-hundred gold talents towards paying the huge ransom demanded for Richard's release.

When Sir Randolph had finally discovered that his debts were too deep to allow for a decent life for his daughter, he had decided that she must enter her cousin Angelina's service. So Rosamunde had been sent to her uncle, Count Torrs, only to discover that he was leaving England for the Low Countries. The count had accepted his late sister's daughter and Angelina had taken her into her service. Angelina was to stay with her uncle in Normandy until such time as her father returned from his travels, and so Rosamunde had travelled to France with her cousin.

At first, Rosamunde's life had not been too bad, but as time passed Angelina seemed to dislike Rosamunde and gave her all the tedious tasks to perform. Rosamunde knew that her father had hoped she would make a life for herself in her kinswoman's service, because there was little for her at home. She had no dowry to give to a husband and it was unlikely that anyone would offer for her without at least a small portion. Since coming to France, she had tried very hard to please her cousin, but Angelina was selfish and uncaring, and Rosamunde found it more and more difficult to accept her life. If she had not believed that her father would find her a burden to support, she would have returned home months ago.

Her only hope lay in King Richard's return. If he were restored to his throne, he might find it in his heart to reward her father for past loyalty. A small pension would make all the difference and then perhaps Rosamunde could return to her home.

Sighing, she placed the tunic she'd been mending in her coffer and then went to look out of the narrow window. Since Rosamunde had no further work to occupy her, she might as well go in search of their hostess, Lady Saxenburg, and enquire if she could be of assistance to her.

About to leave on her errand, she was surprised

when the door of her chamber opened and Angelina entered. Rosamunde felt a prickling sensation at the nape of her neck. It was not often that her cousin came to find Rosamunde; she was normally sent for by one of the other serving women.

'Cousin, may I do something for you? I was looking for work since I have finished all the mending.'

'You will be pleased to know we are to journey to England,' Angelina said. 'You should pack your things, Rosamunde, and then come to help me. I have set my other ladies to packing my things but only Margaret is to accompany us. Sir Thomas, who is a family friend, and his men will be our escorts.'

'England?' Rosamunde's spirits lifted. 'I am so glad, cousin. Perhaps I shall find time to visit my father. Do we go to your father's home? Has his mission in the Low Countries been successful?'

'We go on my father's behalf,' Angelina said. 'It may be that you will have time to visit your father, but we shall speak of this when we reach England.'

'I cannot thank you enough. Your uncle and aunt have made us welcome here in Normandy, but

I prefer England. You must be glad to be going home too?'

'I have no choice in the matter.' Angelina's gaze went over her. 'That tunic is shabby, Rosamunde. Have you no others?'

'This is the tunic I use for every day but I have two others.'

Angelina's eyes narrowed. 'You have grown shabbier; I had not noticed. I shall make you a gift of three tunics and a surcoat. You cannot attend me looking as you do, cousin. You will have time on the ship to make any adjustments you need.'

'Cousin…' Rosamunde's cheeks stung. Angelina's gift was generous but made in such a way that it humiliated her. 'I… You are generous.'

Why was her cousin being so generous to her? Angelina had made it plain from the start that she did not like her cousin or wish to have her as one of her ladies—so why this sudden kindness? Something was not quite right.

'I wish you to look well, cousin. We shall pass your home on our journey. You may visit your father, but remember your loyalty is to me. Perhaps if you serve me as I wish a marriage might be arranged for you. I dare say a knight might be found to wed you for fifty gold talents.'

'I do not have even ten gold talents, cousin.'

'No, but I may have.' Angelina's eyes glittered. 'I cannot tell you just yet, but soon I shall ask a service of you and, if you please me, I may arrange something for you.'

'What kind of a service, cousin?'

'I cannot tell you yet—but it is important to me and my father.'

'I am always willing to serve you and my uncle if I can, Angelina.'

Rosamunde could not help but be suspicious. Angelina always had a reason for what she did. If she was giving Rosamunde such a costly gift it must mean she wanted something from her in return.

'Yes, perhaps. See to your packing. We leave within the hour.'

Rosamunde took her leave of the lord and lady of Saxenburg, thanking them for their hospitality, and then went up the twisting stair to her cousin's chamber at the top of the tower. The door was open and as she paused she heard voices—Ange-

lina and Sir Thomas. Without meaning to eaves-
drop, she heard their words clearly.

'What are we to do? My father is a prisoner of
his enemy, Lord Mornay, and he demands one
thousand gold pieces as a ransom to release him...'

'It is an iniquitous sum. But the ransom must
be paid or Mornay will not release his hostage. I
have heard of this man, and I fear for Count Torrs
if Mornay's demands are not met.'

'But you do not know it all,' Angelina cried in
a wailing tone. 'He is not content with ruining
my father by demanding this huge sum—he also
wants me to take him the ransom myself.'

'You cannot. I shall not allow it. You are promised to me, Angelina. Had your father not been
captured in England we should have been wed
before this,' the man responded.

'My uncle says that I must go to England and
take the ransom, for if my father is not released
his lands will be forfeit and he will have nothing
left—and that means we cannot marry, Thomas,
unless our plan works,' Angelina said.

'Your cousin suspects nothing?'

'She is a fool and will do as I tell her,' Angelina
said scornfully. 'But I still do not see how sending

Rosamunde in my place will help us to recover my dowry.'

'Listen and I shall explain once more...'

Shocked to the core at what she had heard, Rosamunde turned away, sick to the stomach and unwilling to hear more. Now she understood the reasons for the new gowns: her cousin meant to send her to this Lord Mornay in Angelina's place.

Trembling, she ran back down to her own chamber. What was she to do? She had no money of her own and there was no way that she could return to England without her cousin.

How could Angelina plan such a terrible thing? She had always known her cousin was selfish but this was beyond anything. Rosamunde was distressed and angry. She would not go to this man in her cousin's place—but for the moment she had no choice but to hold her peace. Perhaps when she was in England she could go to her father and ask for his protection.

It was some ten minutes later that she followed her cousin down to the waiting horses. Angelina was to ride her own white palfrey, but Rosamunde had ridden pillion behind one of her uncle's men-at-arms when they had come here and expected to ride that way once more. However, to her surprise, Sir Thomas led a lovely chestnut mare forward.

'I believe you can ride, lady?'

'Yes, sir. Is this fine mare for my use?'

'Yes, if you can manage her.' He smiled but something in his manner caused a shiver at Rosamunde's nape. Had she not overheard their plan, she would have wondered why she was being so favoured. Now she understood why she was being given new clothes and a horse to ride. She must look the part of the count's real daughter to fool the evil Lord Mornay.

Rosamunde longed to tell them that she knew what they planned, but her only chance was to reach England and her father. If he knew that she was being sacrificed to save her cousin from shame, he would surely not allow it. So, steeling herself not to flinch, she took Sir Thomas's hand and allowed him to help her mount.

Rosamunde took the reins. Despite her anger, she felt a surge of pleasure at being able to ride independently. Not since her mother's death had she had the joy of riding her own horse. Until that unhappy day her father had kept horses for both

Rosamunde and her mother's use, but afterwards he had sold them in an effort to stave off ruin.

Rosamunde took her place amongst Sir Thomas's train. She saw that Angelina's maid, Margaret, was riding pillion behind one of the grooms. The men-at-arms rode at the head and tail of the small procession, guarding their lord and his promised bride. Rosamunde followed just behind her cousin. It was a lovely warm afternoon and pleasant for riding. A few hours in the saddle would bring them to the coast where the ship would be waiting. How much she would have enjoyed the prospect, had she not understood what awaited her when they reached England.

Somehow she must find a way to get away from them once they reached England. Surely her father would be pleased to see her and would protect her?

Sir Raphael de Valmont sat his horse and looked out to sea. The ship that was to have taken him and his companions from France to England had been battered by a storm in mid-ocean and its mainmast was now being repaired. Unless he could find another vessel with space for five passengers, he might be forced to linger here another week.

'The *Southern Star* sails with the morning tide,' a voice said to his left and he turned to look at his friend Broderick. 'But her captain says he has been asked to take a knight and his entourage to England and there is no room for us.'

'Would he not let us find a corner of the deck on which to sit?'

'He says that if we wait until the knight comes he will enquire how many there are in his party. Should there be room he might allow us to sleep on deck.'

Raphael nodded, his gaze brooding as he saw a party of horsemen arriving. His journey had become urgent ever since the news of his father's illness had reached him as he had journeyed through France.

'I believe the knight has arrived,' Raphael said, his eyes narrowed, intent. 'There are three ladies, a knight and ten men-at-arms, besides some five servants. The *Southern Star* is not large enough to take us all as well. We should search elsewhere.'

'I've been told there is a cove just down the coast and two merchant ships are in port,' Jonathan de Vere said as he rode up to them. 'It will take us no more than thirty minutes to ride there. If we cannot find a berth for us all there, you must go on alone, Raphael.'

'We vowed we would stay together until we reached England.' Raphael's mouth was unsmiling as he looked at his four friends: Sir Broderick, Sir Jonathan de Vere, Sir Michael Borthwick and Janquil. He had been some months on the journey from the Holy Land to Normandy, for it had now been a year since Messalina's death. His friends had pledged to journey with him so that he might place his claim to recover from the goldsmith what should now have been his. In return, Raphael had promised that he would take them all into his service if he became rich.

They had eventually found the wealthy but elusive goldsmith. Markoff had at first been reluctant to part with the money and jewels lodged with him, but after verifying Raphael's proof of marriage and the subsequent death of the whole family had admitted that he was the rightful owner. Raphael had considered making his home in Normandy, where he had purchased an estate, but then a message had reached him: his father was very ill and wished to see his son as soon as possible.

'I have no intention of leaving you behind, my

friends,' Raphael continued. 'My father may even be dead for all I know. The messenger told me that he had been searching for us for several weeks.'

'Your father may have yet recovered. Tis a pity the ship did not wait here for you as was promised.'

'The captain returned to England with a cargo. No doubt he intended to meet us here on time in the *Broken Vows* but the weather was against him.'

'Shall we ride in search of these other ships?'

'I shall speak to Captain Middleton and advise him of our intention.' Raphael dismounted, giving the reins of his horse to his squire. 'Wait here, Janquil. I shall not be long.'

Approaching the captain of the *Broken Vows*, Raphael told him of his intention to seek a berth elsewhere.

'I shall be ready to sail in two days, sir, once the mainmast is mended,' the captain said. 'If you do not return before then, I shall seek another cargo and sail for England.'

'Yes, you should do so. We shall return in good time if we fail to find berths elsewhere.'

Raphael turned away, intending to rejoin his friends. As he did so, he saw that the ladies had dismounted and were waiting to go aboard their ship. One of them was very beautiful with golden hair and a proud bearing; one was clearly a serving woman, but the other was less easy to place. She was very lovely but in a quieter way, her hair hanging down her back in a thick plait and the colour of burnished copper. Her eyes were green, her mouth soft and generous, and there was something about her that made him wonder if he'd seen her before. Her tunic was more modest than the proud lady's and yet she had the bearing and look of nobility. Perhaps she was a relation rather than a serving woman.

The knight's party was moving towards the ship as Raphael left the water's edge. Just as they were about to pass one another, the woman with red hair seemed to stumble. Instinctively, Raphael reached out his hand to steady her.

'I caught my heel.' Her cheeks were flushed as she looked down at her boot, the heel of which had wrenched from its socket and was hanging loose. 'Forgive me, sir.'

'It was nothing. That boot will need mending,' he commented.

'Yes, I should have worn my others…' She

glanced up, her eyes widening, as if shocked. For a moment she seemed to hesitate and he thought there was a look of appeal in her eyes, but then her gaze dropped. 'Excuse me, I must join my friends.'

'Yes, of course—as must I.'

She moved away towards the ship but Raphael stood where he was, staring after her as she boarded the ship.

She seemed to become aware of him staring at her and for a moment she turned towards him. Their eyes met and another delicate flush touched her cheeks but she did not immediately glance away. Raphael felt a stirring of interest; he crushed it immediately. She was not a whore to be taken to his bed and dismissed the next morning, and he would never allow himself to care again.

As memories of his dead wife stirred, his expression hardened and he averted his gaze. The woman was lovely but she could never be anything to him. The memory of that night when he'd found the family home burned to the ground and his wife's body lying in the yard was so strong and so sharp that he actually felt a stabbing pain in his chest.

Raphael realised that he had been staring at the English knight's party without really seeing them. The women were being taken belowdecks now. Raphael felt a sudden sense of loss. He did not even know her name—the woman with the plait—yet it could not matter. They would never meet again. As her turn came to go below, she looked back and he sensed that she was searching for him. For a brief moment a smile touched her mouth, almost as if she knew him. Once again he felt that she wanted to speak to him, perhaps to ask for help, then her companion spoke to her and she walked onto the ship and was lost to his view.

Raphael crushed the urge to go after her, sweep her up and carry her off with him. For a moment he had seen something in her that he'd believed long forgotten, the spirit and joy he'd felt when he had first set out for the Crusades. No, that was ridiculous. She was nothing to him and never could be. He had built up a barrier, shutting out the pain of grief and loss. To allow softer feelings in would be to relive the pain that had almost destroyed him.

As he remounted his horse, Raphael put the red-haired woman from his mind. She was lovely, but he would not seek beauty or sweetness again. If he married for a second time it would be purely to get himself an heir.

'What are you thinking of?' Angelina's sharp voice cut into Rosamunde's thoughts. 'I was speaking to you, cousin. Why did you not answer me?'

'Forgive me. I did not hear you, cousin. What was it you wished me to do for you?'

'I have a headache,' Angelina said. 'There must be something in my baggage to ease it. You are skilled with herbs—pray attend to it this instant.'

'Yes, cousin,' Rosamunde said. 'I am sorry that you are feeling unwell. I shall make a soothing drink for you at once.'

Leaving her cousin to harangue her maid, Rosamunde went to find the herbs and beg some water from the ship's quartermaster. She had been so lost in her thoughts that she had not heard Angelina speaking to her. The knight who had saved her from a tumble and then had stared at her—surely it could not be Raphael?

No, she was letting her imagination run away with her. The youth she'd remembered all these years had had such a merry smile, but this man looked harsh—and weighed down with sorrow.

She had been tempted to beg for his help but then, as she had seen him frown, had known she must be mistaken. He could not be the young knight she had met so many years before at her father's castle. And even if he was, he had not known her. True, he had stared at her, but even when he had touched her there had been no recognition in his eyes.

This knight was a stranger and she had not dared to approach him for help. She must simply wait for her chance to slip away to her father's house.

Chapter Two

'I am not sure I understand you, cousin.' Despite having overheard her cousin plotting with Sir Thomas, Rosamunde still found it difficult to believe that Angelina intended to go through with what she had just told her. 'You wish me to lie to Lord Mornay—to pretend to be you. Why would you expect me to do such a thing?'

'Because the ransom must be paid,' Angelina said, a flash of temper in her eyes. 'If I take it myself, Lord Mornay might decide he wants me as well as the money. He will accept it from you. You are not beautiful enough to arouse his interest and he is bound to let you go. Just give him the gold and then you may go home. I will give you fifty talents as your dowry, as I promised—though whether anyone will marry you for that sum I do not know.'

'What makes you think Lord Mornay wishes to wed you? Does he know you?'

'No, of course not. If he did I could not send you in my place,' Angelina replied. 'It was a condition of the ransom that I must take the gold myself— but Sir Thomas wants me to go to his home where we shall be married. After all, what can it matter to you? You have no prospect of marriage, even if I give you the money.'

'No, but he may discover the truth and then he might refuse to release Count Torrs. Do you not think you should do as Lord Mornay demands?'

'No, I shall not,' Angelina said sulkily. 'You must do this for me, Rosamunde. It is not so very much to ask considering what your father owes mine. If you oblige me, the debt will be cancelled. If you refuse, I shall ask for it to be repaid at once.'

Rosamunde felt coldness at her nape. Her eyes narrowed in suspicion. 'I did not know my father owed yours money.'

'Why else would he send you to me? You were to serve me until the debt was paid—but if you will not oblige me I shall send you home and demand payment at once.'

She was lying! Surely she was lying? Rosamunde could not believe that her father owed so much money to his brother-in-law and had not told her. If it were true, it would make her little better than a bondswoman.

'My father never spoke of his debt. You said I could see him when we pass my home. I beg you to allow me to speak with him before I give you my answer.'

'Are you accusing me of lying?' Angelina glared at her furiously.

'I am not accusing you of anything—but I must speak to my father before I give you my promise.'

'If he agrees there is a debt, will you do as I ask?'

'If I do, the debt will be paid?'

Rosamunde felt as if she were suffocating. She had meant to escape from her cousin and beg her father's protection, but if he owed his brother-in-law a great deal of money she was honour-bound to serve her cousin in whatever way she demanded. Indeed, she would be a bondservant and tied to Angelina until the other woman gave her leave to go. Serving her cousin as one of her ladies was one thing but to be bonded through a debt was very different.

'Yes, of course. Have I not said so?'

'Then I shall do what you want—providing my father admits there is a debt,' Rosamunde reiterated.

Angelina glanced at Sir Thomas. He inclined his head and she did the same.

'You may see your father—but remember that he is old and sick and his mind may play tricks on him. However, I have a deed that proves he owes my father more than he could ever pay.'

'May I see it?'

'Yes, if you wish.' Angelina turned to Sir Thomas. He handed her a small wooden coffer bound with iron. She lifted the lid and took out a roll of parchment, handing it to Rosamunde. 'There, look at the signature on the bottom—is that not your father's?'

Rosamunde looked and her heart sank. It was indeed her father's hand and the sum of money mentioned was five-hundred gold talents, far more than his land and keep were worth.

'Yes, this is my father's hand,' she said, her throat dry. 'It seems you have proof. However, I still wish to see my father.'

'Remember what I've told you. If you refuse me, I shall demand payment of the debt.'

Rosamunde returned the parchment. Her eyes pricked with tears she refused to shed. 'I shall visit my father and then I will give you my answer.'

'Your father lies on his bed sick to the heart,' Maire told her when she kissed her old nurse and asked for him. 'We've done our best to care for him, my lady, but he eats hardly anything and will not leave his bed.'

'I shall go up to his chamber and see him,' Rosamunde said. 'If he is truly ill, we must have the physician.'

'There's no money for such things. I bought a cure in the village from the wise woman but he refused to take it. 'Tis my belief that he wants to die.'

Rosamunde nodded, her throat tight with tears. It seemed that her father's financial situation had not improved while she had been away, but at least he still had a bed to lie on. If Angelina demanded the return of the loan, he would be forced to lie under the hedgerow. How long would he live then?

She saw the signs of neglect everywhere. The

servants might care for her father but no repairs had been done. The yard had not been swept and it looked as though no one had changed the rushes in weeks.

The room was dark and smelled of stale urine when she entered. Rosamunde felt angry. The servants had little enough to do; they could at least keep her father clean and his room smelling sweet.

'Who is it?' he asked as she approached the bed. 'I want nothing. Leave me be. How many times must I tell you to leave me in peace?'

'It is I, Father,' Rosamunde replied. 'Angelina has returned to England and she gave me permission to visit you while she rests at the inn this night.'

'Rosamunde?' His eyes opened and he looked at her. 'You should not be here. There is nothing left for you, child. I have wasted my fortune and there is nothing but debt. Make your life elsewhere and leave me to die.'

'I do not wish you to die, Father. Before I leave I shall see to your bed and have the room cleaned.'

Her father pushed himself up against the pillows, looking at her warily. 'If you've come to me for money I've none to give you. I can hardly feed the servants, let alone pay my taxes. Next time Prince John's collector comes, he will take what little we have left, but I shall not see it. I shall be in my grave.'

'Are you in pain, Father?' Rosamunde bent to plump up his pillows. He shook his head. 'Then you should try to get up and come down for your supper. It will be easier for the servants to clean if you are not here.'

'You want me to live but there's no hope left, child. All hope fled when she died.'

'Mother would be so angry with you!' Rosamunde exclaimed. 'The servants have neglected the house and the yard. She would not have liked that, Father.'

'I know it. She would also be angry that I sent you away to your cousin, daughter, but what else could I do? If you stay here you will end in poverty.'

'Could we not petition the King for a pension?'

'If Richard were home he might do something for us, but he will need money himself. His ransom has not yet been paid. I gave all I had, but I should have thought of you instead, Rosamunde.'

'Do not worry about me, Father. Perhaps I shall find someone who will marry me.'

'If I had a dowry for you it would give you a chance, but I have spent even that, child. Your mother would not let me while she lived, but when she died I spent it on building a tomb for her.'

'Do not look so sad, Father.' Rosamunde reached for his hand. 'Tell me, why did you borrow money from my uncle? Where did it go?'

'Where did all the money go? I wasted it on others instead of saving it for my child. Did I borrow from your uncle?' Her father wrinkled his brow. 'I cannot recall the debt, Rosamunde, but your mother's brother is a good man. If he says there is a debt, it must be so. He has helped me many times and I owe him more than I could ever repay. If he asks something of you, you must oblige him for my honour's sake.'

Rosamunde's heart sank. She'd thought for a moment he would deny the debt, but the truth was he was too old and sick to know. He had beggared himself by his generosity and now he was ill. At least she could make sure that he died in his own bed. Angelina had promised the debt would be paid if she took her place, and she'd also promised a gift of fifty gold talents. It was a large sum of money and would feed the household here for months, as well as pay her father's taxes.

'Well?' Angelina demanded when she walked into the inn bedchamber the next morning. 'You've seen your father—what did he say?'

'He does not recall the debt; he is too old and ill to know. But it does not matter if you are lying. You promised me fifty gold talents if I help you—will you keep your word?'

'Come to me after you've delivered the ransom and I will pay you.' Angelina's eyes gleamed suddenly. 'I shall give you my bond and seal it. It will be binding in law.'

'Very well, I shall do as you ask,' Rosamunde said. Her father had told her she must do all she could for her uncle for his honour and, though he could not have guessed what that entailed, Rosamunde felt duty-bound to obey him. Unless she took the ransom her uncle might languish in prison for ever. 'If Lord Mornay does not accept me as you, I shall forfeit all right to the money, but if he does I shall return to claim my dues.'

'Yes, of course. There is paper in my coffer.

Bring me a quill and ink and I shall write the bond for you,' Angelina said.

Her cousin sat down at a board. Rosamunde went to her coffer and brought her parchment, ink, a pen and sealing wax. She read the document. Angelina promised her fifty gold talents and the cancellation of her father's debt, once Count Torrs was released, and she sealed it with her own ring.

Rosamunde placed the parchment inside her tunic. 'If I am to pose as you, I should have servants. Is Margaret to come with me?'

'No, I need her myself. I will arrange for one of the inn servants to go with you.'

'I asked Maire to accompany me here, so I will take her with me. She is old and my father's other servants will care for him until we return.'

'What will you do afterwards?' Angelina asked, though for once she could not look her cousin in the face.

'I shall return to my father. I shall send Maire for my money and care for my father until he dies.'

'You should use the money to buy yourself a husband. Not many knights would take you for so little, but you might find a freeman who would wed you. It would set you up in a modest inn where you might earn your living.'

'I thank you for your advice, cousin, but my father needs someone to care for him.'

'Well, you must do as you please,' Angelina said a little uncomfortably. 'We shall send three men as your escort, but once you reach Lord Mornay's castle you and your nurse will go in alone.'

'But why? Surely they will wait and escort me home?'

'They will wait outside the castle for three days. After that, they will leave you to make your own way.'

'Why will they not come in with me?' Rosamunde frowned. 'What are you not telling me, Angelina?'

She sensed that her cousin was hiding something but could not tell what it might be.

'I am telling you how it must be. Lord Mornay demands that your escort leave once you are inside the castle. He will not admit armed men into his bailey.'

'I think there is more to this than you have told me,' Rosamunde said, suddenly suspicious. 'Will you not tell me the truth, cousin?'

'There is no more to tell. You should leave now. Lord Mornay expects you before nightfall.'

Rosamunde inclined her head and turned away. What had she missed that day when she'd overheard her cousin plotting with Sir Thomas to send Rosamunde in her stead? There was something more than the simple payment of a ransom—but what?

Rosamunde noticed the odd looks her escort gave her as they waited for her to approach them. She wondered what they were thinking, but did not ask. She was certain that Angelina had not told her the whole truth.

'Why are you going to this man?' Maire asked. 'I have heard of Lord Mornay. He is an evil, wicked man and people fear him.'

Rosamunde frowned at this; perhaps the old woman was simply exaggerating. 'I am to take the ransom for my uncle—I told you, Maire. When Count Torrs is free, my cousin will pay me fifty gold talents and my father's debt is cancelled. I shall come home and look after him—and the rest of you. Somehow I will earn a living for us all.'

'What could a girl like you do to earn money?' Maire looked scornful.

'I can sew and cook. Perhaps I can make dresses for the wives of noblemen. Even if I earn just enough to buy hens and a cow it will help. We could raise our own pigs and grow our own worts and soft fruits.'

'And what of the taxes? The prince's collectors took much of what we had the last time they came—armour, silver and pewter that would have fetched far more than your father owed them. If he had been stronger he could have forced them to take just what was due, but they knocked us aside and stole what they pleased.'

'If King Richard returns he will put a stop to his brother's unfair taxes,' Rosamunde said. 'It is not right that people should be treated so badly.'

'Aye, that's what everyone hopes, but it is not likely that the prince will pay his brother's ransom. Why should he when he has the power?'

'I am sure that the King has enough loyal supporters to raise the money. In time he will return.'

Rosamunde gave her hand to the groom and was helped to mount the horse she had been given for her journey. She decided that she would keep both Maire's pony and this horse. Angelina could deduct their worth from the fifty talents if she chose, but at least Rosamunde would have something. She did not trust her cousin at all, for there had been an odd, sly look in her eyes when she had given her the paper.

'I would help you if I could, lady.'

Rosamunde looked at the man who had spoken in surprise. An icy shiver ran down her spine despite the warmth of the day. It was late September and, though overcast, very warm. 'I do not understand you, Fitzherbert.'

'You will be in great danger, lady. The Lord Mornay is not a good man.'

It was what Maire had tried to tell her. 'Why do you say that?'

'He preys on his neighbours, takes them prisoner and holds them to ransom. Sometimes he steals their womenfolk and holds them until…' The man stopped, his cheeks red. 'It is wrong that Lady Angelina sends you in her place. In all honour, she should pay the price demanded, not you.'

Rosamunde felt chilled. What price exactly was she expected to pay? Something told her that Fitzherbert was not speaking only of the thousand gold talents strapped to the packhorse.

'What price is that, sir?' she asked.

'She has not told you? The last woman who took a ransom for her husband was disparaged and returned to her home after a month. She took her life by walking into the river, because her husband no longer respected her. He said he would rather have rotted in prison than have her lie with such a man.'

Rosamunde felt the heat sweep over her as she finally realised what Angelina had not told her— that Lord Mornay might force her to lie with him against her will. She hesitated. She could get down now, return to the inn and refuse to take the ransom for Angelina—but what then? Her father would be turned from his home when the prince's tax-collectors came for their money and there would be no fifty talents to restore their fortunes.

Surely Lord Mornay could not be as evil as rumour painted him? Besides, he would likely not think Rosamunde beautiful enough to bed. After all, Angelina was very lovely and Rosamunde knew she was not as beautiful as her cousin. Lord

Mornay might simply accept the ransom and let her go.

Yet what if he did not? She would be ruined, shamed before the world. Only, she had no hope of marriage, so what did it matter if she lost her innocence? She had no choice but to do as her cousin had bid her. Even if Angelina had lied about the debt, there was a debt of honour to be paid. Her uncle could not be left to languish in prison until he died. Perhaps when he was free he would know the truth—and he would force his daughter to pay Rosamunde the fifty gold talents she had promised her.

'I shall pray that this time he will be moved to mercy,' she told the groom. 'Mount up, sir. Time is wasting.'

'My father has been dead these past three weeks?' Raphael crossed himself as his steward finished telling him the news. 'God have mercy on his soul. If what you have told me is true, he will have need of it.'

'He changed much after you left, my lord, and became extremely bitter and angry. He quarrelled with neighbours and took them or their wives hostage for vast sums,' the steward revealed.

'So I have heard.' Raphael's mouth thinned. 'I do not like to hear these things, Mellors. My father was a stern man and forbade me to follow Richard to the Crusades—but before I left he was an honest man. I am sad to hear he changed so greatly in my absence.'

'Forgive me…' Mellors glanced over his shoulder. 'I risk my life to tell you, but it was the prince's influence. Your father became Prince John's lackey and it was on the prince's orders that he took Count Torrs hostage. The ransom he has demanded is exorbitant and I doubt it can be paid.'

'Is the count still a prisoner here?' Raphael asked, and frowned as the steward nodded. 'You will have him brought here to me instantly, please. Has the man been ill-treated?'

'He has been kept in a tower room rather than a dungeon, because your father knew he had powerful friends. Others have not fared so well.'

'I shall hear more of this another time. Release the count at once and then have wine and food brought to us. I must beg the count's pardon and hear his story before I give him his freedom,' Raphael said.

'You will not demand the ransom?' Mellors asked nervously.

'I have no wish to beggar any man,' Raphael said.

'The prince may be angry. He may demand his share of the ransom,' the other man pointed out.

'Prince John is not the King,' Raphael said. 'I have heard that Richard is still a prisoner in the Holy Land. Now that I am home, it is my intention to do what I can to have him freed.'

'I am heartily glad to hear it, my lord. We are all pleased to see you home again—and shall be happy when the King is back on England's throne—but you must be careful. Prince John does not suffer traitors to live in peace.'

'He is the traitor, Mellors. Leave me now and ask the count to give me the pleasure of his company at my table,' Raphael ordered.

'Yes, my lord.' Mellors bowed his head respectfully. 'Everything shall be as you order.'

Raphael watched as he walked from the room, then sat in his father's chair. It was heavy and carved from English oak, its arms smooth with wear. His grief for his father was muted by the knowledge that the man he knew had obviously died long ago. In his place a monster had come into being and he could not regret the passing of such a man. Lord Mornay had committed crimes against his neighbours and no doubt it would take some considerable time to mend fences.

The attack came suddenly towards dusk that evening. Rosamunde was deep in thought when she heard a cry from ahead of her and then saw a band of armed men rush out from the trees at them. They were on foot but armed with cudgels and swords, and there were enough of them to surround the small train that Angelina had sent with her.

Fitzherbert had been pulled from his horse and one of the robbers was threatening him with a sword. Money was being demanded and Rosamunde knew that at any moment they would steal the packhorse and ride off with everything—the money for Count Torrs's ransom and all her possessions.

She would have failed her cousin and her father would be forced to repay his debt. Without thinking, she took the reins of the packhorse and started to ride off, calling to Maire to follow. The robbers were immediately alert to what she was trying to do and two of them lunged at her, causing her horse to shy.

'Leave me alone,' she cried as she struggled to hold both her horse and the packhorse. 'How dare you attack me? I am the daughter of a nobleman and you will hang for this.'

'Not afore we've 'ad our way wiv yer,' one of the men said and laughed evilly as he grabbed her arm and tried to pull her from her horse.

Rosamunde screamed, realising the full extent of the danger she was in as she saw the naked lust in his eyes. These men would not be satisfied with her gold; they would rape her and leave her for dead. Angelina should have sent more armed men with her. The heavy load the packhorse bore had attracted the attention of these robbers and her escort was not strong enough to defend it.

The sudden cries and the sound of thudding hoof-beats drew her gaze in the direction of a party of men riding towards them. They charged, swords and lances at the ready, their leader giving a blood-curdling war cry that sent shivers through all that heard it. The robbers knew that they were beaten and immediately retreated, leaving Rosamunde's men to gather their dignity as best they could as the knight came up to them. Some of his men had followed the robbers into the woods to the side of the road and she could hear screams as the men-at-arms cut them down.

The knight who had come to their rescue was wearing chain mail under his tunic. The tunic was white and bore a red cross on the tabard, proclaiming him as a Crusader well-hardened in battle. It was hardly surprising that the robbers had fled; they had attacked two women and three men-at-arms and been confronted by a Crusader and at least nine men-at-arms in full battle-cry.

The knight's hair was covered by the hood of mail and a heaume, which hid his face from her. He drew his horse to a halt and saluted her with his sword.

'I trust you came to no harm, lady?'

'None. My thanks to you, sir. Had you not arrived in such good time I think we should have been robbed—and worse.'

'I dare say they would have killed you all, lady,' the knight said. 'You take risks riding with such a small escort in these parts. There are ruthless bands of robbers that take the law into their own hands.'

'I have heard that there is one such ruthless rob-ber—a powerful man whose castle is close by.'

'Do you speak of Lord Mornay?'

'Yes, sir. I am on my way to deliver something to him and if you are travelling in the same direc-tion I would crave your protection.'

The knight seemed to hesitate, then inclined his head. 'Your men will follow us, lady. It is to the castle of Mornay that we are bound.'

'You know Lord Mornay?'

Again the hesitation, then, 'Yes, I know him. Tell me, why do you visit this lord, since you fear him?'

'I have business that I may discuss only with Lord Mornay. Please do not ask for I may not tell you.'

'Very well, lady. Ride beside me. I shall escort you to the castle.'

'This is as far as we go,' Fitzherbert said as he drew his horse to a halt and looked at Rosa-munde. 'Our orders are to wait three days and then leave—but if you wish I will leave a man to watch for you.'

The party had halted outside the castle while the drawbridge was let down. The sound of chains rattling and the sight of high, forbidding walls sent a chill down Rosamunde's spine. A growing sense of foreboding had come over her as she rode beside the knight who had rescued them, and now her courage almost ebbed away.

'Would you wait at the village we passed an hour since?' Rosamunde asked Fitzherbert. 'We may need an escort when we return to my father's house.'

'I shall wait for two weeks,' he said. 'Send me word if you wish me to wait longer.'

'I thank you for your kindness,' Rosamunde said. 'We shall leave you now. Maire, ride close to me and lead the packhorse.'

'Forgive me,' Fitzherbert said as Maire tried to take the leading rein from him. 'I would come in with you, lady, if it were up to me—but I must obey my orders. However, I shall wait in the village, as I have said, and the others can return to Sir Thomas.'

Rosamunde looked at him steadily. 'Are you

sure you wish to disobey your master? He may be angry with you for not returning to your post.'

'I shall risk his wrath willingly in your service, my lady,' Fitzherbert replied. 'I have watched you since you first came to serve Lady Angelina and admired you. I am but a soldier with no hope of becoming a knight—but I would give my life for yours, lady.'

'Oh…' Rosamunde felt her cheeks grow warm. The man's look said more than any words and she felt her eyes sting. 'I do not wish you to die for me, sir—but I shall be grateful for your support. I—I do not know what awaits me, but if I need your help I shall send word to the village. Please do nothing that would draw Lord Mornay's wrath upon yourself. It will serve no purpose.'

'I shall merely observe and wait in the village, my lady.'

Rosamunde could not help but be comforted by the thought that he would be close if she needed him. Lord Mornay's stronghold was built of grey stone and its walls were stout, almost impregnable once the drawbridge was raised. A prisoner within those walls could not expect to be rescued.

How hopeless her uncle must feel as Lord Mornay's prisoner. Even had she been tempted to run away, Rosamunde could not have deserted him now. She had brought the ransom in her cousin's place and she must pray that it would be sufficient to secure her uncle's release.

The knight who had rescued her, and his men, had gone in ahead of her. He and his men were dismounting even as her horse clattered over the wooden drawbridge. The knight had taken off his heaume and was speaking to a thin man who wore the robes of a steward. The steward glanced at her and then leaned forward to say something no one else was meant to hear.

Rosamunde's throat felt tight and her heart was beating fast as someone came to help her down. She breathed deeply, because she had a terrible feeling that her escort was no other than Lord Mornay himself. He must have been angered when she'd accused him of being a ruthless robber, no better than the rogues from whom he had saved her. As she struggled to compose her thoughts, the steward came hurrying towards her.

'Lady Angelina? Am I right—you are the daughter of Count Torrs?' he asked, and bowed low as she nodded her assent. 'I am Mellors, steward here, and my lord has sent me to welcome you to the castle. He has business that keeps him from greeting you himself. I am to show you to your chamber. He will speak to you when he has time.'

'Lord Mornay knows that I have brought my father's ransom?'

'Yes, lady.' The steward gave her an odd glance before turning to lead the way inside. 'My lord knows why you are here, but for the moment he is too busy to see you.'

'You will please tell Lord Mornay that I wish to see him as soon as possible. I have no desire to remain here for longer than necessary.'

'It may be best if you wait until my lord is ready,' the steward replied. 'He has much on his mind at the moment.'

'You will please give him my message.' Rosamunde lifted her head in a haughty manner, imitating her cousin.

'It might be best to wait, my lady,' Maire whispered at her side. 'You do not wish to make him angry.'

She bit her lip but made no further request, a little shiver going through her as she mounted the stone steps to the room at the top of the west tower.

* * *

'You have not told the lady that her father has already been released?'

'You asked me to leave it to you, my lord.'

'Had she arrived a day sooner, she might have heard it from his own lips, but the count is already on his way to the Low Countries to meet in secret with others who seek Richard's freedom. Two of my friends have gone with him, to protect him and keep him safe until his mission is complete.'

'The lady seems impatient to leave, my lord.'

A wry smile touched Raphael's mouth. 'If she has heard stories of my father, it is hardly surprising. She may be in some danger, Mellors. If Prince John hears what I've done, he might seek to take her captive and gain his ransom that way. Besides, we discovered her at the mercy of a robber band, and there are many others in this country. Prince John's taxes have made the people desperate and they care little for his law. It may be best if the lady remains here under my protection until her father comes back to claim her.'

'Do you wish to see her?'

'Please ask the lady to join us at supper in the hall. I have more important tasks for the moment—

Prince John's messenger awaits an answer to his letter to my father. I must send him my answer before I attend to other business.'

'Yes, my lord.'

Mellors inclined his head and walked away. Raphael sat at his board and drew parchment, ink and a quill towards him. He frowned as he began to write. The prince must be informed that Lord William Mornay was dead and his son returned from the Holy Land. It would not do to antagonise the prince, for much might be gained by Raphael appearing to be a man after his father's heart. If the prince learned that Raphael had sent money with Count Torrs to help King Richard return to England and the throne, he might try to stop the gold reaching its destination. Better for Raphael to keep his silence and wait until the chance came to serve his king. If Prince John was determined to usurp his brother, he might plot to have him murdered when he set foot on English soil.

Besides, Raphael had recognised the woman he'd noticed at the quayside in France. She had not known him because of his heaume, but he knew her. He needed a little time to sort out his thoughts before he saw her again.

Chapter Three

Alone in the room at the top of the tower, Rosamunde looked down at the courtyard. She had been left waiting for two hours and her apprehension was growing. She had not been locked in her chamber but since there was no possibility of her leaving the castle without permission she supposed Lord Mornay did not feel the need to imprison her.

Why had he not sent for her? Did he hope to break her will by leaving her to reflect on her probable fate? She raised her head, feeling a surge of anger against the man whose face she had not yet seen. She would not show fear or let him break her resolve. Indeed, she would not wait here until she was sent for. Her father might be an impoverished knight, but she was of good blood, and Lord Mornay had no right to treat her like this.

Leaving the chamber, she ran down the stairs. In the hall, there were a few servants beginning to set up boards on trestles for the evening meal but no sign of the steward. Approaching one of the servants, she lifted her head proudly.

'I wish to see Lord Mornay. Please take me to him at once.' The man stared at her for a moment, seeming stunned. 'Do as I bid you, sirrah.' She assumed her cousin's haughty manner. 'Disobey me and I shall have you whipped.'

The man lifted his hand and pointed towards a door to the right of a rich tapestry hanging on the wall at the far end of the hall. Rosamunde nodded her head, feeling a little ashamed. She never spoke to servants in that manner, but she was supposed to be her cousin and she had to make the vile Lord Mornay believe her. He must have heard of Angelina's beauty and might be disappointed by Rosamunde's face. She must do nothing that might make him suspect she was not the lady Angelina.

Hesitating outside the door for a moment, she lifted the latch and entered without knocking. A man was sitting at a board on which were spread various books and papers. He had been writing and did not look up as he said, 'Yes, Mellors? What is it?'

'I wish to know why you have kept me waiting—and why you did not tell me who you were on our way here,' Rosamunde said before she lost her nerve. 'I am the daughter of a nobleman and I demand respect. Please allow me to pay my father's ransom and leave.'

'So anxious to leave? I wonder why?'

The man lifted his head and looked at her. Rosamunde was so shocked that she could hardly hold back her gasp of surprise. Surely he was the man she'd seen before they had left port in France? He had stared at her as she'd been about to go on board the ship and she'd thought that she recognised him, though she'd been uncertain. Now that she was closer, her doubts deepened. This man's eyes were devoid of warmth and his mouth hard. He could not possibly be the youth who had rescued her kitten from that vicious dog those years ago. Yes, there was a strong resemblance, but it was very likely only the colour of his hair and eyes.

'Why have you come here, lady?' His gaze narrowed. 'My steward asked that you remain in your chamber until you were sent for. I have important matters that keep me busy until then.'

'Why will you not let me pay the thousand gold talents and leave? It need only take a moment and my father may be released. We shall trouble you no further, sir.'

'Thousand? I believe you only brought five-hundred gold talents with you, even though you were asked for a thousand.'

'It is all I was given,' Rosamunde faltered, uneasy as she saw his mouth harden. No wonder Angelina had been desperate to send her cousin; she must have kept half of the money for herself. 'The remainder will be paid once my—father is released.'

'Indeed?' Eyes that had been as cold as mid-winter ice suddenly crackled with blue fire. 'Supposing I am not prepared to release him for only a fraction of the money demanded?'

'Then you are a wicked rogue and deserve to be thrashed,' Rosamunde burst out. It was foolish to lose her temper this way but she could not control her disappointment. He looked something like the youth she'd lost her heart to years earlier, but he was a cold, hard man. He could not possibly be Raphael—could he? 'If I were a man I would challenge you to combat and kill you.'

'You might try.' He stared at her for a moment and then laughed. 'You are a bold wench, Lady Angelina. What are you prepared to pay for your father's release—besides the gold?'

'Oh!' Rosamunde's heart raced. Fitzherbert had been right; this man would not be content with merely the ransom money. He wanted more—the surrender of her modesty. 'How *dare* you suggest such a thing, sir? I have heard what you did to other unfortunate women—of the poor lady that walked into the river because her husband no longer wanted her after you had disparaged her.'

The smile left his face, his lips turning white as he glared at her. 'Now you are too bold, lady. Return to your chamber until you are sent for or you might be sorry.'

'I am not a servant to…'

Rosamunde quailed as he took a step towards her. She wanted to run away but stood her ground, looking at him defiantly. For a moment he hesitated, then reached out and drew her against him, his right arm about her waist as he held her pressed tight to his body. She could feel his strength and power and her knees turned to water. For a moment her head whirled and she had a foolish desire to melt against him, to subdue her will to his.

'You deserve your punishment, wench,' he muttered and bent his head to take possession of her lips.

Rosamunde struggled wildly, but his arm was like a band of iron holding her tight. His mouth was hard, demanding, as if he sought to subdue her to his will, to show her who was the master here. As her head swam, she opened her mouth to protest but his tongue moved to block her words, touching hers. The feelings he aroused were strange and yet pleasant. She moaned, because the sensations sweeping over her were so bewildering, and then she pushed her hands against his chest as common sense returned.

He let her go abruptly and stepped back, a look of such anger on his face that she was terrified. Now she truly believed all the stories she had been told.

'Go back to your chamber or I might not be responsible for my actions.'

Rosamunde gave a yelp of fright, turned and ran

from the room. She fled through the hall and up the stairs and did not stop until she reached her chamber.

Raphael cursed as the door closed behind the woman. What on earth had made him react that way? Holding her close, his body had responded in a way he had not expected, arousing passions he'd believed dead. He'd known her at once as the woman he'd seen on the quayside in France. She had been dressed less richly then and he'd imagined she was a relative of the beautiful lady she'd accompanied on board ship. She was certainly haughty enough to be the daughter of a nobleman, though something was not quite as it seemed, for the boots she had worn that day in France had been old and worn through. He had a feeling that she was playing a part, pretending to be other than she was, but that did not excuse his behaviour. She was undoubtedly a lady and did not deserve to be treated like a harlot.

Her sudden arrival had startled him, because Messalina would never have dreamed of disobeying an order from either her father or Raphael. She had been modest and sweet—and she had been foully slain, her death still unavenged. The pain slashed through him once more, making him smash his fist against the stone wall of his chamber in a sudden burst of agony.

Why must he be haunted by the vision of her broken body night and day? She called out to him for justice and he could give her none. He was angry with himself for letting the lady Angelina beneath his guard. Her scent had inflamed his senses and her spirit had amused him, but then, when she had assumed that he was his father, something had snapped in his head.

God knew he was no saint! Raphael admitted freely that he'd done things of which he was ashamed. He'd killed men in battle and given no quarter. He'd stood by without comment when Richard had ordered the execution of the Muslim prisoners at Acre, which had led to a bloody retaliation by Saladin, and he'd hurt his wife... No matter how much he tried to forget it, the memory of her tears returned to haunt him.

'Please tell me, what is wrong, husband? What have I done to displease you?'

'You've done nothing. Do not be foolish, Messalina. I would not see you cry, but I cannot always

be here at your side. I am a man and a warrior. I must meet with my fellow Christian knights this evening.'

'They will persuade you to return home and you will leave me.'

'I would never leave you. I love you.'

'No, you desire me; it is not the same. If you loved me you would not go tonight. I fear...' Messalina had looked at him imploringly. *'I love you, Raphael. If you care for me at all, do not leave me this night.'*

He'd ignored her tears, resenting the soft arms that clung to him and her sweetness, which was sometimes cloying and made him feel as if he were being smothered. Messalina had constantly needed reassurance that she was loved and adored. Raphael had tried to show her his feelings in the way he understood, which was with kisses and presents, but she had wanted something more—something he had not been able to give. Was it a lack in him? He bitterly regretted that he'd left her that night despite her tears. If he'd been there he would have fought to the death to try and save her.

Thrusting the bitter memories from his mind, Raphael sat down at his board and tried to concentrate on the letter he had not yet finished. With an oath of disgust, he screwed it into a ball and threw it to the ground. Dipping his quill in the ink, he began again. He would not use guile or disguise. A simple message telling the prince of his father's death and his own return would be enough.

Why had his stomach turned at the thought of playing a double game? Could it have anything to do with the scorn in the lady Angelina's eyes when she'd accused him of ravishing another man's wife?

Raphael had never taken an unwilling woman.

'Damn her,' he muttered. He scrawled his signature then frowned as he saw he had used de Valmont, the name he'd chosen to take when he had been knighted by Richard. He was Lord Mornay now and Lady Angelina could not be expected to know that he was not his father. He should tell her the truth, explain that he had already set her father free and that she was at liberty to return to her home or stay here under his protection until Richard returned to the throne and her father could fetch her home.

Rosamunde glanced at herself in the handmirror of burnished silver; it had belonged to her mother and her father had insisted that she keep it, for otherwise it would be sold to pay his debts. The image was not clear but she knew that she looked as well as she could. A lock of her hair was plaited and curled about her head at the front, the rest hanging loose to the small of her back. She wore no cap or jewels for she had none, but she was dressed in a dark-green tunic of fine wool that Angelina had given her because her own were too shabby.

She had been sent for some time ago, and she was ready, yet still she delayed, reluctant to face Lord Mornay again. For a moment in his arms she had wanted to melt into his body, to let him do as he would with her, her lips begging for kisses. How could she be lost to all modesty? To enjoy the caress of a monster such as he was to be lost to all sense or decency.

She had expected an older man, a man steeped in vice and depravity. Her first impression of the handsome, virile man had been that he could not possibly be the evil monster Fitzherbert had warned her of. Yet his behaviour subsequently had seemed to confirm it. No true knight would subject a lady to such a dishonourable display of temper. For he had been angry. She had felt the passion and fire in him, and for a moment she'd feared that he would take what he wanted, but he'd drawn back, giving her a chance to escape.

Why, if he was all that people said of him, had he allowed her to escape him with her modesty intact?

Rosamunde was puzzled. Had she built an unreal picture of her uncle's enemy in her mind—or was there truly an evil monster beneath that handsome façade?

'You should go down, lady,' Maire told her. 'If you do not the lord may be angry.'

'He is already angry because I disobeyed him.'

'Take care, lady. You are his prisoner here. He can do whatever he wishes with you. If you do not wish to lose your virtue, you must make him see that you are chaste and devout.'

'I doubt that either chastity or devotion will win my freedom if he is determined to keep me here,' Rosamunde replied. 'Yet I must go down, for I am hungry, and if I disobey him he might starve me into submission.'

Leaving her chamber, Rosamunde began to walk down the spiral stairwell of worn stone. Her mouth felt dry and her steps were slow for she was apprehensive of her next meeting with Lord Mornay. She had disturbed him when he was busy but he might have more leisure to pay her attention this evening.

Lost in her thoughts, she did not hear the sound of soft-soled shoes as someone ascended the stairs, so when they met face to face midway she was suddenly breathless.

'My lord. I was about to attend you, as you commanded.'

He was so tall and strong, his shoulders broad, the muscles rippling beneath the thin wool tunic he wore over dark hose that evening. He had changed since she'd last seen him and smelled of soap that was slightly perfumed with a woody essence which made her senses reel. His hair looked darker at the roots but he wore it long and the sun-bleached ends just brushed the braided neck of his white tunic. Yet he was somehow gentler, more of a knight and less the savage now.

'Command? I sent you an invitation to dine with my people and me in the hall. You seem to imagine you are a prisoner, lady. What have I done to deserve your anger?' he asked.

'I… Nothing, except take my father captive and demand that I bring the ransom in person.'

He was standing so close to her, towering above her, so masculine and powerful. She caught her breath, her heart hammering against her ribs as if it were a caged bird seeking to escape the bars of its prison.

'Please believe that I mean you no harm,' he said. He held out his hand. 'Come, lady. We shall go down together. Later, after we have dined, I shall explain much that you do not know. Until then I must ask you to trust me.' He needed to be careful what he said and where he spoke to her. Apart from his steward Mellors, who had already proven his loyalty, he was not yet certain who amongst his inherited household staff he could trust.

Rosamunde took his hand and allowed him to lead her down the last few steps and through the great hall. The trestles and boards had all been set up now and were laid with wooden trenchers. At the high table there was a huge silver salt and either silver or pewter goblets stood at intervals down the board. Dishes of fruit, dates and nuts brought from overseas were set along the centre of the board for the guests to nibble at between courses, and the platters of pewter shone like dull silver.

She was conscious that all eyes were on her as she was led to a place of honour beside him. He waited until she was seated, then turned to the expectant gathering.

'As you see, my friends, we have a special guest this evening. I ask you to lift your cups to toast the lady Angelina.'

The men stood, lifting an assortment of horn, pewter or wooden drinking vessels according to their status. Having drunk her health, they sat down and the meal began. Fresh bread, soups, messes of meat and worts, neats' tongues, roasted boar and a great carp covered in rich sauce and onions were brought in succession to the table.

Rosamunde ate sparingly of the dishes presented to her. Neither her uncle nor her father had kept a table like this other than when entertaining important guests; she thought Lord Mornay must be rich. How much of his wealth had come from robbing his neighbours?

She sipped her wine and found it sweet, much more pleasant on the tongue than the rough vintage she was accustomed to. She tasted the pigeon in red wine and ate a little roasted capon followed by stewed plums and a junket of wine and curds.

'You hardly eat, lady. Is the food not to your taste?'

'I am not used to such rich fare, sir. I have eaten sufficient, thank you.'

'You must try a peach. I insist.' Lord Mornay reached for a succulent peach and began to peel it for her. He handed a slice to her on his knife. 'I had these brought from Normandy. I have inherited an estate there and if the fruit is picked before it is quite ripe it travels well enough to be pleasing at table.'

Rosamunde stared at him, because to send for fruit from his estate in Normandy was such an extravagant thing to do, and she could not imagine what it must have cost to bring the fruit to a ship and then across the channel. She tasted the slice he had cut for her and smiled.

'That is truly delicious. My uncle had peaches growing in his garden in Normandy but they were not as sweet as these.'

'Your uncle?' Raphael's eyes narrowed.

'Yes,' Rosamunde dropped her gaze because

she'd spoken without thinking. 'My uncle of Saxenburg—my father's brother.'

'Ah, yes, I see. I know little of your family, lady. Do you have brothers, sisters, cousins?'

She could not look at him as she replied, 'My uncle of Saxenburg has two sons. I have also a cousin on my mother's side; her name is Rosamunde Meldreth.'

'Then she must be the very beautiful lady I saw you with at the harbour in France.'

'Yes, my cousin is very beautiful.' Her heart was beating wildly and she dared not look at him.

'You are beautiful too,' he said. 'In a different way.'

'I do not think I am beautiful,' she contradicted him flatly.

'You should leave such judgments to others.'

Rosamunde could feel her cheeks burning. She reached for her wine and sipped it. Her hand was trembling and she had to hold the cup with both hands to steady it.

'Why do you tremble? Are you afraid of me?'

Rosamunde raised her eyes to his. 'I—I'm not sure. Should I fear you, Lord Mornay?'

'Will you not call me by my name? I am Raphael

to my friends. I travelled home with them but only
one remains; the others have gone on a mission
of importance. Sir Jonathan is here and you shall
meet him later.'

Raphael? Her heart jerked because it was the
name her hero had given her all those years ago.
Could it be him after all? No, the youth who had
so gallantly saved her kitten could not be the evil
man of whom she had been told.

Her mouth was dry as she said, 'You ask me to
use your given name but I do not know you, sir.
I am here as your hostage for my father but I beg
you will treat me with the honour due to a lady of
good virtue.'

'Supposing I told you that I had already set your
father free?' he murmured in a low voice that did
not carry.

Rosamunde's eyes flew to his face. 'Why would
you do that when the ransom has not been fully
paid? What is it you want of me, sir? I beg you,
tell me so that I may prepare myself.'

'You think I mean to disparage you and send
you back to your family in shame.' His gaze narrowed and his voice remained soft. 'I believe it is
time...'

What he meant to say was lost as a commotion was heard from the door and a struggle ensued as his men tried to stop someone entering. Raphael rose to his feet.

'Who demands entrance here?'

A tall man stepped forward, at least ten armed men at his back. 'I am Lord Danforth and here on Prince John's business to see Lord Mornay.'

'May your business not wait? Come, sir, bring your men and join us. You see that we are at table and there is a lady present.'

'My business is urgent,' Henry Danforth said. 'I have travelled at some speed to bring you the prince's commands, my lord.'

'Yet I would ask you to wait, sir. I dare say your errand is important, but I am the master here.'

'And I am your prince. Will you defy me, sir? I am come to call the traitor Count Torrs to account.' A sudden hush fell as a man stepped from amongst the cluster of men at Danforth's back, throwing back the cloak that had hidden his rich clothes and the jewels of state that proclaimed his rank as Prince John himself.

'The count is not a traitor. He is loyal to the King.'

The words left Rosamunde's lips before she realised, and brought a sharp look from Prince John.

'He is a traitor, lady, and you would do well to mind your manners in the presence of your prince.'

'Be quiet, lady,' Raphael reiterated urgently in a low-toned voice and left his place. 'You are welcome, sire.' He walked towards the man, who was a head shorter and seemed almost puny beside him. Making an elegant bow, he apologised. 'Had I known you were come in person, I should of course have acquiesced to your wishes immediately. Yet even so I would offer you food and wine.'

'In private, sir.'

'Yes, of course. I shall have food and wine brought to my solar.' He turned his head, 'Master steward, conduct His Highness to my solar and arrange for food and wine. His men can be accommodated here.' The steward came hurrying forward, bowing his head. 'I shall join you in a moment, Highness. I must speak with someone first.'

Raphael returned to his place at board amidst the sound of shuffling as the men closed up to allow the newcomers to find seats. One of the men sitting at the high table got up and offered his place to Lord Danforth, who took it with a word of thanks. Servants hurried to bring him a cup of pewter and a trencher of bread to which was added a mess of meat, worts and rich sauce.

Raphael looked at Rosamunde and his voice dropped to a whisper. 'I believe you should return to your chamber now, lady. Stay there and do not leave it unless I send for you.'

'My lord? I do not understand. What is happening here? Why has the prince come? Why does he call my father a traitor?'

Raphael's hand gripped her wrist. 'Do not ask questions. Go to your chamber and await my coming. Trust no one else if you value your honour and your life.'

Rosamunde's heart jerked. She inclined her head. There was something about the sudden arrival of Prince John and his escort that frightened her. Her fear of Lord Mornay had lessened as they had eaten their supper. His warning seemed to imply that she was in danger—a danger that came from somewhere beyond the walls of his castle.

Leaving the hall with her head held high, Rosamunde wondered what had brought Prince John here—and what Lord Mornay might have said to her had they not been interrupted.

Upstairs in her chamber, Maire was waiting to help her prepare for bed, but she dismissed her, sending her to her own blankets.

'I shall not retire just yet. I should not sleep if I did and…' She shook her head as Maire's brows rose in enquiry. 'Do not ask for I cannot answer you. I know only that something has happened and I may be in more danger than I was before.'

'May I ask what brings you here, Highness?' Raphael said once they were alone. 'I have prepared a letter informing you of my father's death and my return and was about to send it to the court in London.'

'I learned of your father's death as I travelled from Nottingham and thought it best to speak with you in person. You have here a dangerous enemy of the state—a man I require you to hand over to me immediately.'

'I do not believe I understand you, Highness. Of whom do you speak? There is no one in my service that would seek to harm England. We are loyal to the crown.'

'I speak of Count Torrs. Your father had him captured on my behalf, and a ransom was demanded from his family, but I have since learned that he plots with others to murder me and bring havoc to the land while my brother rots in prison.'

'Where did you learn such a thing, Highness?'

'From my friend the Shire Reeve of Nottingham. He has served me well on more than one occasion, though as yet he fails to bring the notorious outlaw Rob-in-Hood to heel. That rogue defies my laws and robs my tax collectors. I believe Count Torrs to be in league with outlaws and robbers.'

Raphael's mind worked swiftly. If the prince learned that he had set free a man he considered his enemy, he might send his army against them. If the King was to have friends when he returned, there must be someone prepared to rally support in secret. Robin of Loxley, a man Raphael had known slightly in the Holy Land, was now an outlaw and lived by his wits; alone he could not rally the noblemen of England to support their king, but perhaps Raphael might. First, he must convince the prince that he was a friend rather than an enemy.

'Then you have solved a mystery for me, sire.

On my arrival I discovered that some rogues had bluffed their way into the castle and rescued an important prisoner. I did not know then that he was held on your behalf.'

A look of anger flared in the prince's eyes.

'You tell me the count has escaped? This is outrageous. Your steward has been neglectful and you should punish him and others for this man's escape.'

'My steward was in a difficult position, Highness. He did not know when I would return—nor could he have known that my father held the prisoner on your behalf. He understood it was purely a matter of a ransom. Indeed, I am not certain of the count's crime or the nature of your agreement with my father,' Raphael said calmly.

'He would have kept half the ransom and the count would have been recaptured as he tried to reach a ship. Your father has contributed to my funds on more than one occasion and I have been grateful to him; because of this, I ignored the demands from his neighbours that he should be punished for his crimes against them,' Prince John replied.

Raphael inclined his head, because the underlying threat was clear. The prince could if he wished charge Raphael with some crime of his father's and the estate might be forfeit. John's treachery towards those that displeased him was well known, which was why Raphael had taken care to leave his fortune with the French goldsmith. His father's estate meant little to him, and he might return to Normandy in time, but if he had a power base in England he might help Richard regain his throne.

'I believe my father became a bitter man in his last years. It is my hope to make amends and live on good terms with my neighbours. If it cannot be done, I may decide to leave England and live abroad,' Raphael commented.

The prince's eyes narrowed. 'The lady at your board—is she the count's daughter?'

'What makes you ask that, sire?'

'Your father demanded that she bring the ransom in person for reasons of his own. If you have her, then keep her under close guard for we may yet gain something from this business.'

'Do you speak of a ransom?' Raphael enquired.

'It is expensive to hold court and keep the loyalty of fickle nobles,' the prince said. 'My purse has too many demands on it and I would take half the ransom, as your father agreed—but it might be that we could use the lady as bait to bring her father back. If he believes his daughter's life forfeit, he might return and offer his life for hers.'

Raphael's hands balled at his side and it was all he could do to keep them from the prince's throat.

'You would surely not murder an innocent lady, Highness? This is not the justice your barons expect in England.'

'If you wish to keep your own head you will obey me. If the lady has a ransom you will hand half to me—and she is to remain here as your prisoner,' Prince John demanded.

'I am sorry to disappoint you, Highness, but the lady is a kinswoman who has come to me for protection. As yet there has been no sign of the count's daughter, but I shall of course obey your orders if she does arrive with the ransom,' Raphael assured him smoothly.

The prince's eyes narrowed in suspicion but at that moment a succession of servants arrived with food and wine, which they offered to him.

'Taste them,' he said, glaring at the servant who had offered a dish of lampreys.

'You need not suspect poison in this house, sire,'

Raphael said and tasted a portion of each dish set before the prince himself. 'You may eat and drink without fear.'

'Very well,' the prince said and took a leg of capon, tearing into the soft flesh and speaking with his mouth full. 'My men and I will sleep here for one night. Your hall will do well enough for my men. I shall sleep here on the bench by the fire.'

'As you wish, Highness. If you will excuse me, I must speak to my steward and make the arrangements.'

The prince nodded but made no reply as he investigated a mess of meat and worts with his fingers.

Raphael went out. He summoned his steward and gave him certain orders, then took the stairs that led to the tower room where the lady Angelina was resting.

Rosamunde's heart jerked as she heard the knock at her door and then saw it open to admit the man she had half-expected.

'Sir,' she said, and rose to her feet. 'What news? What demands did the prince make?'

'He bid me keep you a captive here on pain of

death. You are to be hostage for your father's good behaviour. Unless he obeys the prince, your life will be forfeit.'

'No!' Her throat tightened. 'My father…the count…it cannot be. He would not surrender his honour for me.'

'Why? Surely any man of honour would surrender his person for his daughter's sake?'

Rosamunde's breath caught. She hesitated, but knew that she must confess the truth. 'I am not his daughter—I am Rosamunde Meldreth, merely Lady Angelina's cousin on her mother's side. Count Torrs would not give his life for me.'

'Are you telling me the truth?' Raphael's hand shot out and gripped her wrist. 'Do not lie to me or it will go ill with you, lady.'

Rosamunde almost cried out for his grip was firm on her flesh but she would not show fear. She raised her head to look defiantly into his eyes.

'My cousin did not wish to surrender herself to you. She knew of your reputation and so she sent me in her place.'

'Why did you come? Surely you could have refused her?' Raphael asked.

'My father owes hers money and she said he

could be imprisoned for debt. My father is ill and if I do as she asked the debt is cancelled.' Rosamunde's eyes pricked with tears. 'She only gave me half the ransom money and now I do not know what will happen.'

'You are safe enough for the moment. The prince does not know you came as the count's daughter. I have told him you are my kinswoman and for the moment he has accepted it. He came here looking for money. I shall give him a small donation to his coffers and hope that he will leave us in peace,' Raphael revealed.

'You lied to me!' she gasped.

'Because I believed you were lying to me, and I needed the truth if I am to help you. If the prince knew your identity he might still make you his prisoner,' he pointed out.

'Where is the prince?'

'Resting. He leaves in the morning.'

'Will you let him take my uncle with him when he leaves?' she asked breathlessly.

'I have already informed the prince Count Torrs escaped before you arrived,' Raphael said, deciding that it would be best to tell her as little as necessary. If, God forbid, she was ever held as the prince's prisoner she couldn't tell what she didn't know. 'You will not be required to pay the ransom.'

'Will you allow me to leave? One of my escorts is here in the village waiting for me,' she said.

'My men knew his intention and it was reported to me. Fitzherbert has been sent away. You will remain here under my protection for the moment,' Raphael told her.

'But if...' Rosamunde's knees trembled. 'Am I your prisoner?'

'We live in uncertain times, lady. You would not be safe if I let you leave here. I cannot be sure you have told me the whole truth but, even if you are Rosamunde and not the lady Angelina, you must remain here until I have time to escort you to your home.'

'Fitzherbert would have seen me home.' She gave him an accusing look. 'Why did you send him away?'

'For his safety and yours. If Prince John became suspicious and believed you were the count's daughter, he might take you with him. Here you will be my guest, though not at liberty to leave. The prince might yet cast you into a dungeon and, if the count did not surrender or pay the ransom demanded, leave you to rot.'

Rosamunde shivered. 'And you—what do you want of me, sir?'

'What makes you believe I want something of you?' he parried lightly.

'Why did you take my uncle captive and hold him for a ransom?'

'You ask too many questions, lady. I shall answer when I am ready. At the moment I have a royal guest to keep happy or we may all be in trouble.'

He gave her a look that made the back of her neck prickle.

Rosamunde stared after him as he turned and left her. She was still shivering but more from apprehension than from fear. He'd said she was under his protection and told her she would not be asked for the ransom—but he wanted something of her. Otherwise he would have provided her with an escort and sent her home.

Chapter Four

Raphael watched as the prince and his escort rode away the next morning. He had given him five-hundred silver talents, but he knew it was not enough to satisfy the greedy prince for long. He'd wanted its equivalent in gold and would no doubt return to demand more before long. If a tribute was not offered freely, the next thing would be a visit from the prince's tax collectors. Any noble who refused to pay might be subject to a royal decree and the confiscation of property, or even his estate. The poor of the land suffered far worse injustices, for the tax collectors had been known to strip a village of all its grain, pigs and any other item of value. It was hardly to be wondered at that the people cried out for help and, it was said, held the outlaw Loxley in high regard, often protecting him from the Shire Reeve of Nottingham.

'Did he suspect anything, my lord?'

His steward's question brought Raphael from his reverie. 'I think he may have been suspicious but he knows nothing for sure—besides, the lady is only cousin to the count's daughter. She was sent in her cousin's stead. However, that might not save her if she fell into the prince's hands. He might try to use her as a tool to bring the count to heel. She may not be his daughter, but I found the count a man of honour. He might feel obliged to surrender his person to Prince John if his daughter's companion were in danger of her life.'

'He should surely be on board a ship or have reached his destination by now?' Mellors asked.

'We must hope both he and the gold I sent are safely on their way to Richard. England has suffered too long at the hands of a tyrant and Richard is badly needed at home.'

'What will the King find if he returns? There are those that believe Prince John will make certain his brother is murdered as soon as his feet touch English soil.'

'We must make certain that does not happen. In a day or so I shall send out messengers and then, when I have answers, I may have to leave for meetings with men who wish to see Richard on the throne once more,' Raphael revealed.

'What of the lady, my lord? Is she to be kept a prisoner?' Mellors enquired.

'She has the freedom of the castle but may not leave unless I give the word. It is for her own sake that I keep her here. I believe her to be extremely vulnerable, as her father is unable or unwilling to care for her, and her cousin obviously cares nothing for her safety. Until I can find the time to escort her home, she must stay here,' Raphael said with a frown.

'I think she will not be content to be idle for long, my lord. She sent for me this morning and asked that she might be given some work,' Mellors told him.

'Is there no mending to be done?'

'Your father neglected such things. I believe there are whole chests that are filled with linen needing repair,' Mellors said with a smile.

'Then show her where they are to be found and let her see to it. You have done well in difficult circumstances, Mellors, but this house needs a woman's touch. Until such time as the lady Rosamunde leaves—or I find a bride—we may as well take advantage of her industry.'

'She will need women to help her, my lord. We have none here save her own servant, and an old crone who sits by the kitchen fire and mutters that she remembers the old times when your mother lived.'

'Is old Deborah still here? I thought her long dead.' Raphael smiled. 'Send for women from the village to attend Lady Rosamunde.' He saw the steward's expression. 'What? You think they will not come because of my father's reputation?' He frowned, then added, 'Tell them my father is dead and I am home—ask for their pardon and say I will swear that no harm shall come to any woman who attends the lady Rosamunde.'

'Very well, my lord.' Mellors smiled. 'I think the women will remember you. You are not as your father was and they will come.'

'We must hope that you are right.' Raphael turned towards the house. 'My father's crimes must be redressed. I shall need your help in costing what must be paid to those he harmed. Attend to your other work and then come to me in my solar.'

'The prince left it in some disarray, sir. It looks

as if he—or one of his men—searched for something. The servants are setting all to rights, but I think someone took a silver ewer.'

'The prince's men are all thieves and rogues,' Raphael said, his lips curling in a sneer of disgust. 'We must think ourselves lucky that for the moment he does not demand the surrender of my father's lands. As for his search of the solar, there was little to find. My father's gold has gone to buy Richard's freedom, and his ledgers are locked in my coffer.'

'It will be a happy day when the King returns to this country, my lord,' Mellors said fervently.

'Pray God it is soon. Please excuse me, I have work to do.'

'My lord asks for your help in the matter of some mending, lady,' Mellors said. 'We have sent to the village for women to help you, but you will have the charge of them.'

'I am very willing to set the work in motion,' Rosamunde said. 'Please show me where the chests of linen are stored and I will make a start myself.'

'There is a considerable amount. I do not think

a stitch has been set since the late Lady Mornay died.'

'I thought Lord Mornay had several wives.'

'I meant Lord Mornay's mother—the only true lady to set foot in this house until you came, lady.'

'Lord Mornay's mother?'

Rosamunde followed the steward through the hall to a storeroom at the back of the house. She frowned, for the steward's words did not make sense unless...

'How long has the present Lord Mornay been the lord of this castle?'

The steward pointed to three chests and then turned to look at her. 'His father became ill two months since, just after Count Torrs was taken captive. He ordered us to send word to his son. We had heard that Sir Raphael was on his way home from the Crusades but were not sure where to find him. We sent messages to Normandy, France, Italy and the Low Countries and at last he was found. Alas, his father died just three weeks before he returned.'

'The present lord did not order the capture of my uncle, then, did he?' Rosamunde stared at the steward. 'Why did he not tell me? Why was I allowed to believe he was the one who had done such heinous things?'

'It is not my place to explain my lord's actions, lady. The linen is in those chests. You will find threads in the smaller chests and mending in the larger two. If you will excuse me, I shall leave you to your work,' Mellors said.

'Yes, at least I may have something to occupy my time while his lordship keeps me prisoner here,' Rosamunde retorted bitterly.

'You are at liberty to go where you please within the castle, but please do not try to leave. The men will be forced to stop you,' the steward warned gently.

'I must speak to Lord Mornay. He must understand, my father needs me. I have to go home!' Rosamunde exclaimed in frustration.

'Forgive me, lady. I have my orders. My lord is busy; you disturb him at your peril.'

Rosamunde frowned as the man inclined his head and then walked away, leaving her to examine the contents of the chests. Opening the first, she discovered torn garments and bed linens in a disgusting condition; everything looked as if it needed laundering before being stored. Closing the lid of the first coffer, she opened the other and discovered that it contained a very different kind of work. Taking the first piece from the chest, she saw that it was a half-finished wall hanging; the work was delicate and beautiful and the silks needed for its completion were folded inside it.

She lifted the other tapestries and discovered that most of them had been started and then abandoned. Such work would be a pleasure to do and Rosamunde would gain great satisfaction in completing the almost-finished wall hanging. Sighing in regret, she replaced it in the coffer. She would return to retrieve it later, but first she must make a start on the garments from the first chest, since these were clearly what Lord Mornay had asked her to repair.

She plunged in and pulled out an armful of linens. Her first stop would be the outhouse where she could set up a washing tub, though why most of these items had not been consigned to the fire in the first place she had no idea. Even when washed and mended they would not be fit for the lord of the manor and ought to be given to the poor.

Raphael gave up on the muddle of his father's accounts and left his chamber, going through to the hall. Servants were busy setting up the trestles for the evening meal, but he had more than an hour before supper, and the thought of a stroll about the castle grounds appealed after too many hours spent poring over ledgers. As he walked through the hall into the courtyard he checked as an amazing sight met his startled eyes: everywhere he looked there were lines of rope with what looked like wet rags thrown across them.

'What is this mess?' he demanded of a servant carrying a wooden pail of water in the direction of one of the outbuildings.

'It is the lady, sir,' the servant replied. 'She has been washing linens the whole day and bid us set up these lines to dry it all. I am taking her water to rinse the last of the linens.'

'Then lead on and I shall follow,' Raphael said and swore under his breath. What had the foolish woman been doing? Most of what he'd seen looked fit only for burning.

As he entered the outhouse Rosamunde had commandeered for her marathon task, he saw her bending over a large wooden tub, her sleeves rolled up above her elbows and her arms plunged into water. She was intent on her scrubbing and did not look up immediately.

'What possessed you to do all this?' he demanded. 'My bailey looks like a washerwoman's yard. How are my men supposed to train and do their work with wet linen everywhere?'

'You asked me to mend these things,' Rosamunde said, and pushed a lock of hair back from her eyes. Her arms were red from the water and harsh soap used for laundering and she looked exhausted. 'I cannot mend linen in such a disgusting state. Everything had to be washed first.'

'Did Mellors not tell you women were to be brought from the village to help?' Raphael picked up a linen tunic that had large holes in it. 'What do you imagine I want with such rags? Have some sense, wench. I meant only to give you some mending or fine sewing. If I wanted all this linen sorted I would've set the servants to it.'

'Some of the garments need only a few stitches to make them useful again—though I must admit I thought others fit only for the fire.'

Raphael stared at her, seeing the frustration and tiredness, and then he laughed. 'Well, my lady, you wanted employment and it seems you found more than you bargained for.'

'It is all very well to laugh,' she said crossly. 'Your steward showed me the chests. I would have preferred to work on the tapestries I found, for they are beautiful, but I thought it was my duty to do as you wished.'

'Tapestries?' A mixture of emotions flitted across his face: remembered love, affection and sadness. 'My mother was a skilled needlewoman. I dare say she left work half-done when she fell ill.'

'The one I saw half-finished was very beautiful.'

'Would you like to finish it?' Raphael asked softly.

'Yes, very much.'

'Then leave such menial tasks to others. Tomorrow you will have women to attend you even if I have to kidnap them and bring them here myself,' he said wryly.

'You will do no such thing!' she said sharply. 'You should send me home with a small escort. My father needs me. I should be there to care for him.'

'I am sorry your father is not well. I will send someone to see how he fares and bring you word of him, but I cannot allow you to return home just yet.'

Rosamunde dried her arms on a cloth and let her

sleeves down with some relief. 'I do not see why I should be forced to remain here if I do not wish it. You said you did not require a ransom—why then will you not let me leave?'

'Because it would not be safe for you, Rosamunde. Your father cannot protect you and you unwisely angered the prince. He might decide that he would hold you to ransom instead of your cousin,' he pointed out.

'My father has nothing left. He beggared himself to help the King—and he gave all he had left towards Richard's ransom. He has nothing but the roof above his head and even that may be forfeit when the tax collectors discover he has nothing for them to steal,' Rosamunde told him sadly.

'Have they stolen from your father in the past?'

'The prince's tax collectors steal from anyone who cannot protect himself or his family.'

'Is that why you were forced to obey your cousin and bring the ransom here?' he wanted to know.

'My father cannot pay his debts. I had no choice.'

'What would you have done had I demanded the ultimate sacrifice of you?' he asked curiously.

'I—I do not know,' she whispered. He saw the colour drain from her face and cursed softly.

'I would not have you fear me, lady. I have no intention of demanding such a price of you or anyone else. Come; leave this foolishness and prepare to dine with me this evening. I think we should try to come to terms with the situation. It was not I who held your uncle to ransom. Nor did I bid you come here. I must keep you until such time as it may be safe for you to return to your home, but there is no need for us to be enemies.'

'What, then; would you be my friend?' she whispered.

Raphael hesitated. 'Tomorrow I shall take the hawks out. My father always kept a good aviary and that has not changed. Would you like to come with me?'

'Ride with you and watch the hawks fly? When I was a child it was a treat to be taken hawking. I remember stroking them and I thought that one day I should like a hawk of my own, but things changed. Yes, I think I should like to ride out with you, sir,' she answered, her eyes sparkling.

'I do not know if it is possible for a man and woman to be purely friends,' Raphael continued as they walked together. 'But I will be as a brother to you. You have my word that you are safe here.'

'Then I accept your word,' Rosamunde said and smiled. 'I cannot be certain but I think you visited my father's house once—when you were merely a squire and on your way to the Crusades.'

'That time seems far away,' he replied, his eyes narrowing as he looked at her. 'It may explain why I thought I had seen you before that day in Normandy.'

'You saved me from a vicious dog that was—'

'After your kitten?' Raphael smiled ruefully as a memory flashed into his mind. 'I had forgotten, just as I had forgotten my mother's tapestries until you reminded me. So much has happened since, and I am no longer the youth I was when we left England.'

'You must have seen so much—suffered.' Rosamunde hesitated. 'We sometimes heard stories. I believe many died, in battle and in other ways.'

'You heard what happened at Acre?'

'We heard that Saladin killed all the Christian prisoners.'

'Yes. I had friends in that prison.' Raphael's voice dropped to a harsh whisper. 'Richard made a terrible mistake when he executed those Muslim prisoners. It brought instant retaliation and broke the trust. Things changed after that for it placed a stain upon our honour. Saladin used to send us fresh fruit and he showed honour in his dealings with Richard, but after that everything changed. Had I allowed my friend Janquil to be taken, he too would have died in that prison. Richard would have done better to show mercy. Men are men and brothers beneath the skin.'

'Janquil?' Rosamunde frowned and then remembered a servant with dusky skin and dark eyes. 'He waits upon you at table, I think.'

'Janquil is my friend, though he serves me as a body servant. It is his choosing. I would have given him money and set him free but he chooses to serve me and I protect him,' he explained.

'He knows that his life would have been lost had you not saved him.'

'Perhaps.' Raphael shrugged his shoulders. 'I remember your father now. He entertained us lavishly and some of your men came with us to the Crusades. I am sorry that he has fallen upon hard times.'

'Father was always too generous. He gave more than he could afford. My mother scolded him but he never listened. He thought it was his duty to support the King and a holy cause,' she said.

'He was a good man. I think such men have suffered in Richard's absence. Prince John is greedy; he takes all a man has and still wants more. Until Richard is once more on the throne, the people will continue to suffer.'

'My uncle felt as you do and that is why he came to England to raise money for Richard's ransom. He will be sorry to have failed.' Rosamunde sighed.

'Can you be sure that he has failed?' Raphael raised his left eyebrow. 'Go up to your chamber, lady. Supper will be ready soon. Do not make me fetch you again this evening.'

'No, I shall hurry,' she said, a flush in her cheeks. 'It seems that I have misjudged you, sir. I beg you will forgive me.'

'We shall speak again another time,' he replied and turned away, going into the hall as she ran up the stone steps of the tower.

Rosamunde stared at herself in her hand mirror, wishing that she might see her face more clearly. Angelina was so very beautiful. Rosamunde wished that she might be as lovely. For the first time since her arrival at the castle, she had lost the feeling of apprehension that had hung over her after leaving her cousin.

Raphael might bear his father's title but she did not think him cruel or depraved. He seemed to be an honourable man, though stern and sometimes fierce. She could not doubt that his experiences in the Holy Land had changed him from the merry, laughing youth he'd been when they had first met, but when he laughed she could still see something of the brave squire that had saved her from the dog's fangs.

She had no time to dwell on such things for if she were late he might come to fetch her. Rosamunde had begun to feel relaxed and even content. The work she'd done that day had been hard, and much of it useless, since the rags would be thrown away and most of the other garments given to the poor of the village once she had mended them. However, she was used to work, and had found a sense of purpose. When she had the leisure to work on the embroidery, her life would be much as it might have been had her mother lived and her father not lost all his money.

Her mother had always been busy, directing the

servants, overseeing the making of preserves and salting meat for the winter. She had also made cures for many ailments and Rosamunde had her recipes which she prepared and used whenever someone came to her for help. If Raphael would permit her, she would like to be useful here in that capacity too. She had already noticed one or two servants with small afflictions that she was certain she could ease, if not cure.

Walking down the twisting stairs, she was thoughtful. The life of a chatelaine was busy and fulfilling. To live in the castle would be pleasant enough if she were not anxious for her father. At least here Angelina was not constantly looking over her shoulder and complaining about her work.

The men had not yet taken their places at table that night. She heard a buzz of laughter and, glancing round, saw that two of the servants were laughing together. Her gaze travelled round the room, noticing the smiles and air of well being. Raphael's men seemed content to serve their master.

He was waiting for her. As she approached him, he gave the nod and a horn was sounded. The men moved towards their places as he held out his hand.

'That colour becomes you well, lady,' he said. 'You should wear green more often.'

'My cousin gave me this gown when I came here. I could not have afforded to buy it, because the cloth is too costly,' she remarked.

'She wished to fool my father into believing you were her,' Raphael said and did not smile. 'I think your cousin did you no favours, lady.'

'At first she was kind but then she seemed to resent me—I do not know why,' she admitted frankly.

'Perhaps she realised that your beauty outshone hers.'

'No, how can you say it? You have seen Angelina; you know she is very beautiful!' Rosamunde exclaimed with a little laugh.

'She has a certain appeal,' he replied seriously. 'However, I think your beauty runs deeper.'

'You think my character is more steadfast,' Rosamunde said. 'I will admit that my cousin is a little spoiled by her father, but she is lovely none the less.'

'I would not deny it.'

He led her to her seat, waited for her to be seated and then took his place beside her. Immediately, the servants began to bring a succession of rich dishes to the table. Seeing that a sucking pig had been served to them, Rosamunde accepted a slice of the sweet dish, holding it daintily with her fingers to eat and then dipping them in the little bowl of water supplied by a page.

'You hunt with the hawks tomorrow, and we had venison yesterday, so you hunt deer and boar with your men sometimes—but what of your larder, sir? Do you salt meat for the winter?'

'We must certainly make preparations before then. Perhaps when the women come from the village, you might teach them what to do—in case you are not here when the time comes.'

'Yes, of course, if you wish it. However, I must see my father before the autumn is done. He may not last the winter. I fear he was quite ill when I visited him on my way here.'

'I am sorry for that, lady. I promised you before that I shall send someone to see he has all he needs. You have my word on it,' he vowed.

'Thank you.'

Rosamunde ate a dish of quinces and curds. Her companion seemed to have lapsed into thoughtful silence and she left him to his contemplation, looking about her with interest. She thought that some of the walls had been freshly cleaned and the hangings changed. Raphael's father had neglected his hall, but now that the son was home the servants were inspired to work harder.

She sighed, thinking of her father's hall. She ought to be there, caring for him and making sure that the servants did their work properly.

'That was a deep sigh. A silver penny for your thoughts, lady.' Raphael smiled.

'I was wondering how my father fared. It is nothing to concern you, my lord. I do not wish to weep and cause you trouble. I know you have concerns enough,' she said.

'It is true that I have much to occupy me, but I have time enough to listen to your worries.'

She shook her head and turned away as Raphael's personal body-servant offered her a dish of almond cakes sweetened with honey and dates.

'These are delicious. I tried one last night and much enjoyed them!' she exclaimed, smiling at the man in pleasure.

'These were prepared for my lord's lady,' Janquil said, his expression inscrutable. 'It was noticed that the dish pleased you.'

'Oh. I'm not...' Rosamunde floundered and stopped, her cheeks warming at the remark about her being 'my lord's lady'. 'You are Janquil, are you not?'

'Yes, lady. I serve my lord and I shall serve you with my life.'

There was such intensity in his tone that she was startled. Did he imagine that she was in danger?

He placed the dish in front of her and Rosamunde took another cake, nibbling it with pleasure. One of the men had risen from table. He was dressed in Raphael's colours of blue, silver and black and he held a viol, which he began to strum. Instantly, a hush fell as he strolled towards their table, his rich voice seeming to fill the hall. His song was of love and the deeds of brave men and their ladies. Approaching the high table, he finished his song, bowed to Rosamunde and smiled.

'My song is for you, lady. 'Tis many a day since we have had such beauty to enrich our lives. You are welcome amongst us.'

'Thank you.' Rosamunde smiled, feeling warmth spread throughout her body. 'I thank you, sir. May I know your name?'

'I am Jonathan de Vere, knight of the Crusades

and loyal servant of the King. Raphael and I served together at Acre and returned to England with other friends.'

'It was remiss of me not to introduce you before this,' Raphael said. 'Lady Rosamunde is to accompany us when we ride out with the hawks tomorrow, Jonathan. You shall have your opportunity to talk further with her then.'

Sir Jonathan inclined his head, smiled and struck another note on his viol. He began to sing again, this time a ditty sung by men before a fight, which was taken up across the benches by a hundred voices.

'Our friend is charming, but heed his flattery at your peril. He breaks hearts, so I've heard,' came a quiet voice she did not recognise. Rosamunde looked at the knight sitting to her right. It was the first time he had spoken to her and she had hardly been aware of him.

'Sir Jonathan seems honest enough. I do not think I've heard your name, sir,' she mentioned pointedly.

'I am Sir Edmund Roth and I served Raphael's father for some years. You were fortunate that the old lord died. You would not have been treated so leniently had Lord William lived.' He leered at her in a way that sent shivers down her spine.

'You know why I came here?' she whispered.

'It is common knowledge amongst those of us that served Lord William. You would not be the first lady to lose your honour in this hall. We had fine sport in the old days—but Lord William's son is a very different man.'

Something in his manner made Rosamunde's nape prickle. He was a strange man, threatening somehow. She was not certain that she trusted Sir Edmund and disliked the way he looked at her.

'Tell me, sir, have you sworn allegiance to the new lord?' she asked.

'We all did on his return. Why do you ask?'

'It was but an idle question. I wondered if you were content in his service. I dare say he has made changes,' she commented lightly.

'Aye, and more to come.' Sir Edmund lapsed into a brooding silence and sipped his wine.

Rosamunde had a feeling that he was playing a waiting game, reserving judgment. Lord William Mornay had been utterly ruthless, quarrelling with his neighbours and imposing his will on others. But perhaps his way had suited some men more than others: men who saw profit for themselves in preying on the vulnerable. It was inevitable that when a lord made war on his neighbours some of the spoils would also fall to the men who served him.

'If you have finished your meal you should go up, Rosamunde.' Raphael's words cut across her thoughts. 'After your labours of the day you must be tired, and I would have you rise early. We set out as soon as the sun is up.'

'Then with your permission I shall leave you,' she said. 'Good night, my lord. I wish you pleasant dreams.'

'And you, lady.'

He inclined his head. Rosamunde rose to her feet and walked away. She had an uncomfortable feeling that she was being watched by some hostile eyes. Raphael had returned to his father's hall as the rightful lord, but she sensed that not all those who had taken service with him were pleased to see him home.

Had some of them imagined him dead, believing that they might continue in the old way and divide the spoils between them? On her way here she had been attacked by a band of rogues, and she knew that the barons quarrelled amongst themselves, often taking land and property from their neighbours by right of force.

Did Raphael have enemies within his stronghold—and did he know that all was not quite as tranquil as it seemed?

Chapter Five

Rosamunde's heart was racing with excitement as she went down to the courtyard the following morning where the men had gathered ready for the day's sport. She saw that Sir Jonathan, Sir Edmund Roth and three other knights were to ride with them, besides three armed soldiers. The keeper of the hawks had gone on ahead to the flat sweep of grassland close to woods where the sport was to take place. He had conveyed the various hawks in a small cart, keeping them hooded so that they did not become over-excited. When Rosamunde and the party of knights arrived, he bowed low to Raphael and asked which bird he required.

'Give me Jessamine,' he said. When the keeper brought the female peregrine, he took the hood from her head holding his arm up so that Rosamunde could see her. 'She is the best of my father's hawks. I would wager on her skill above any other.'

'I think my Romana will give your hawk a run for her money,' Sir Edmund said, bending down to take his bird from the keeper. 'What will you wager against your hawk taking more than mine?'

'Fifty silver crowns,' Raphael said. 'If you care to wager so much.'

'I'll wager as much again on your bird, Raphael,' Sir Jonathan said quietly, leaning towards Rosamunde so as not to be overheard. ''Tis not the bird so much as the handler. Roth is a clumsy fool and treats his hawks ill. Watch and see if I am not right.'

Rosamunde smiled but made no answer. The other knights were wagering for and against the two hawks, two of them favouring Raphael's bird, the other saying loudly that he was sure Sir Edmund's Romana would win.

The servants were opening a wooden crate and two pigeons were let loose. Immediately the knights let their hawks fly. Jessamine was the first to strike and bring down her prey, but Romana seized the second. The hawks were recalled and given tiny slivers of meat to reward them for their work, and then, after a few minutes' respite, another crate was opened and more pigeons were let free. The hawks went into the hunt and once again the birds were caught swiftly, first by Jessamine and then by Sir Edmund's bird.

'They are impossible to split but the target is too easy,' Sir Jonathan said. 'For a true test you should try them on something smaller. Let the sparrows free.'

Other voices were raised in agreement and the servants opened a small cage letting half a dozen small birds fly free. The knights sent the hawks up and a merry chase began as they swooped and dived, trying to catch the smaller prey as it sped towards the wood in an effort to reach safety before the hawks could strike.

Jessamine swooped seconds before her prey reached a thick canopy where it might have found sanctuary, but Romana dived and missed, the sparrow narrowly escaping certain death as it disappeared into dense undergrowth.

Raphael's bird brought her prey back to him and was rewarded by a treat. Sir Edmund's hawk received a scowl and its hood was replaced without the customary reward.

'Wretched bird,' he muttered, then recollected and nodded his head to Raphael. 'I must give you best, sir, on this occasion.'

Raphael smiled but made no comment. He sent his bird up again and watched it hover. No birds were let free for it to hunt and yet its keen eyes spotted a small bird feeding in the grass; it swooped, seizing the unwary songbird.

'Enough for today, my lovely,' Raphael murmured. 'Come to me, my sweet lady. You have done your work.'

When Jessamine returned to his arm, he gave her to the keeper and selected another hawk. Turning to Rosamunde, he offered her the bird. She took it on her hand, waiting for the signal before letting her hawk fly. The other knights were also taking turns to fly various birds and the time passed swiftly.

When the hawks were all returned to the keeper, Raphael dismounted and invited Rosamunde to do the same. He took her to admire the birds and stroke them before the keeper took them back to their home in the aviary.

'Have you enjoyed watching the hawks, Rosamunde?' Raphael asked.

'They are magnificent, my lord—especially Jessamine.'

'Yes, she is my favourite too, but Sir Edmund's bird would be as good if he took more care of her. I think I shall try to buy her from him if he will sell.'

Rosamunde hesitated. Sir Edmund had not taken his defeat kindly and might resent Raphael's offer, for it surely meant that he felt the bird could do better with another handler.

'Is that wise, my lord?' she ventured.

'What are you implying?'

His narrowed gaze made her uncomfortable. It was too difficult to explain, because she had only her natural instinct to go on. She could offer no proof that the knight was not completely to be trusted.

'I am not sure,' she said. 'Yet sometimes it is better not to offend.'

'You think my offer would offend Sir Edmund?' he asked curiously.

'Perhaps. I do not know, sir. I am merely a woman and I dare say your judgment is superior.'

'Do you mock me, Rosamunde?'

'No, my lord. It is merely that…I do not quite trust Sir Edmund,' she explained in a rush.

He frowned, then inclined his head. 'Would you care to tell me why?'

'I cannot, sir. It is a feeling. Instinct only. I may be wronging him.'

'A woman's intuition?' Raphael's expression gave nothing away but she sensed a stillness in him. 'I should advise you to be careful not to let Sir Edmund see that you dislike him.'

'My feelings do not enter into this, sir. I simply wondered if he was truly loyal to you, but I see that I have spoken out of turn,' she said uncomfortably.

'You must never be afraid to speak your mind to me, lady, but with others you would do well to take care,' Raphael reiterated but did not smile. 'I believe we should return to the castle.'

Rosamunde felt that he had withdrawn from her. As they walked back to the horses, she regretted that she had spoken so plainly. She ought to have remembered that she was a woman and a hostage. Men preferred quiet, gentle women who knew their place and did not voice their opinions. Even Rosamunde's father had accused the wife he loved of nagging when she told him a truth he did not wish to hear.

'Do not look so,' Raphael murmured as he helped her into the saddle. 'I shall heed your words but I need your discretion.'

Looking into his eyes, she saw a warning and nodded. He was not denying her, merely reserving judgment. She smiled, feeling oddly shy of a sudden.

'You have it, my lord.'

Raphael smiled and her heart jerked. How handsome he was, and, when he smiled, she could see a likeness to the youth she'd been so drawn to all those years ago. His experiences had changed him, but in that moment she'd seen something that made a sweet warmth flow through her body.

On her return to her own chamber, three women from the village awaited Rosamunde. Two of them were of much her own age, and when they curtsied to her in an awkward, shy manner, she knew they were inexperienced and had never worked for anyone but their parents. The third woman was older and neat in her appearance. She inclined her head but did not curtsey.

'My lady,' she said. 'I have been asked to return to the castle to help you with sewing and other tasks. Before I married I was Lady Mornay's serving woman but when she died I left to marry. These are my daughters, Beth and Lilia. We are willing to work for you and do all that you require.'

'Thank you.' Rosamunde smiled at her. 'Your name is…?'

'I am Elspeth, my lady.'

'I am pleased to have you here,' Rosamunde said. 'There is some mending you might begin on today. Most of the garments are fit only to give away to the poor, but we may as well make them serviceable. After that we may work on some tapestry, if you feel up to the task?'

'I helped Lady Mornay sometimes and I believe my work is considered adequate, my lady. My daughters may do the mending—but is there nothing more you wish us to do? What of your clothes and person?' Elspeth asked.

'I have Maire but there will be plenty for you to do. Tomorrow in the morning we shall gather herbs, berries, sloes and any other fruits that we may find. I think there is a lack of preserves and simple cures. When the time comes we shall also salt meat for the winter, and make inventories of the good linen and silver,' Rosamunde instructed.

Elspeth nodded and smiled. 'We did all these things when Lady Mornay was well. The castle was a different place then.'

'Yes, I believe things have not been as they ought in the past few years,' Rosamunde commented neutrally.

Elspeth glanced over her shoulder. 'The old lord was a bitter, unhappy man, my lady, but…' Her voice dropped to a whisper. 'There are some still here that were worse than their lord.'

'Can you tell me of whom you speak?' Rosamunde asked, somewhat alarmed.

'I dare not, my lady. If it were learned that I had told you of these men, I would be punished. I mean only to warn you to take care. You are safe enough while Sir Raphael is here but if he should go away…'

'Yes, I understand you,' Rosamunde said. 'I believe I may know at least one person I should be wary of but there may be others.'

'There is one here that boasted he would be lord when the old lord died, but others sent in secret for Sir Raphael to return. If you care for him, you should warn him to watch his back.'

'I believe he may be more aware than either of us knows,' Rosamunde said. 'Now, I will show you the mending so that your daughters may begin on the clothes for the poor, and you may help me with a tapestry. It was begun by the late Lady Mornay, I believe, but never finished.'

'My lady was working on something when she became ill. After her death it was packed away with other silks and materials she had bought for future use.'

'I found them yesterday but until now had no time to begin.' Rosamunde smiled at her. 'I was looking forward to making a start but it will be even more pleasant now that I have someone to share my task.'

'It will be pleasant indeed to work with you, my lady. Since my man died it has been hard to keep a roof over our heads and food on the table. Now that we can live and work here, our lives will be better,' Elspeth admitted.

'And the castle will be better for some female laughter,' Rosamunde said. 'I think it has been a place of men for far too long.'

* * *

Raphael frowned over a ledger that had puzzled him before. Entries had been made in a hand that was neither his father's nor the steward's. A clever attempt to cover the theft of five-hundred gold talents had been made, but the figures had bothered him and now he saw how it had been worked. A total had been changed and an incorrect balance carried forward, but the ink used had not been made to the exact shade and, as it dried, the alteration was clear. When a new tally was made the discrepancy became plain.

He had no doubt that someone within the castle had stolen money from his father at least once. As yet he had not been able to trace other instances of false accounting but he suspected there might be more. It hardly mattered; a thief was a thief. What more had been taken—and what other secrets might he uncover?

There were at least three of his father's former servants that he thought sly and unreliable, and one or perhaps two knights that would bear watching. Rosamunde had tried to warn him of one of them. He had spoken harshly to her for he did not wish Sir Edmund to guess that he was being watched.

Rosamunde did not trust the knight and Raphael also suspected that the man was a secret enemy. On the night of his return home, he'd found a note written on a scrap of parchment hidden amongst the bedcovers in his chamber, warning him to be wary. Two names and the names of the knights' servants had been inscribed in a hand that was difficult to decipher, the letters badly formed.

Raphael had no idea who had left him the message and at first had been inclined to dismiss it. The knights in question had been amongst the first to offer their allegiance and he would be wrong to listen to malicious spite against them. Yet there was something about Sir Edmund that chilled him. The other named knight, Sir Ian, was a foolish little runt who followed in his friend's shadow, sly but probably harmless alone. However, he was Sir Edmund's willing slave and might do anything to please him.

Raphael had so far held his silence but the men had not escaped his notice and certain things had been observed. It was strange that Rosamunde had seen immediately that Sir Edmund was not entirely to be trusted. Her woman's instinct had served her well. Raphael had warned her to keep silent because an enemy was best kept close where he could be controlled if necessary. If Sir Edmund and his cronies left the castle they might make trouble amongst the lawless bands that roamed the countryside.

Raphael had wondered at the attack on Rosamunde as she had journeyed here. It was true that she had but three escorts and yet he could not help wondering if it was mere chance that had brought her so close to disaster. Sir Edmund knew of the demands to her uncle and he'd also known that Count Torrs had been given his freedom. Had he seen a chance to take the woman and the ransom for himself?

Had Raphael not chanced to ride that way with his men she might never have reached the castle. She could simply have disappeared, the money stolen and… A shiver went down his spine as he thought of Rosamunde's probable fate. He clenched his hands, a surge of anger making him curse as he realised that he might never have seen her face to face, never have heard her voice. It would have been a loss to him, though he might never have known of it.

He had for years forgotten the incident at her

father's castle. Yet somewhere at the back of his mind, the picture of a young girl's terrified face, and her smile when he'd rescued her and her kitten from the dog, had lingered, tucked away with other memories of childhood. When he thought of sunlit days in the meadows with his mother, the picture of a young girl clutching a kitten to her breast might flit through his mind.

He had remembered the child with amusement, but the girl had become a woman, and a very beautiful, special woman. Her beauty appealed to his sensual nature, but there was also something in her nature that he found attractive. She thought of herself as a hostage, and in a way she was, because he could not let her return to her home until he was certain it was safe. She was under his protection and he could not allow her freedom when it might mean her death. Prince John might suspect that he'd lied and he might send men to take her hostage for real.

The thought of her confined to one of the prince's prisons horrified Raphael. No; she was vulnerable and far too lovely to surrender to the mercy of a man known for his selfish cruelty. Much better that she remain under Raphael's protection!

He had enjoyed observing her as she had watched the hawks fly. Her excitement and pleasure had reflected in her face and the fresh air had brought roses to her cheeks. For the first time in many months, Raphael had felt the shadows lift from his heart.

'My lord.' Raphael's thoughts were suspended as his steward entered.

'Yes, Mellors?'

'There is a messenger come from Baron Sigmund of the Dark Towers. He says his master is on his way to visit you and will arrive before nightfall.'

'Sigmund of the Dark Towers?' Raphael frowned for the name struck terror into most of his neighbours. The baron was the leader of many of the lawless bands who robbed and murdered unwary travellers. 'Tell me, was my father in the habit of entertaining such a rogue?'

'Your father would have none of him, my lord. As bitter as he had become, his quarrels were personal or at the prince's bidding. Baron Sigmund is a veritable devil and even those who serve him fear him,' Mellors said.

'We should close our gates,' Raphael said. 'Tell the men to be alert for signs of an attack. If Sigmund comes in peace we shall admit him and five of his men, but no more. If he has brought an army we shall resist him.'

'Yes, my lord. I shall alert the men.'

'I shall come with you. I do not know if we could withstand a long siege, but we shall not give in easily.'

Rosamunde glanced up from her sewing as Maire entered. It was obvious that the elderly woman was anxious and she rose to greet her.

'Come, sit by the fire, my friend. What is it that upsets you?' Rosamunde said gently.

'Have you not heard the commotion outside?' Maire asked and her hands trembled as she held them to the flames. 'They have closed the gates and the men are ready to defend the castle from attack.'

'Who would attack us here?'

'I heard someone say it was Baron Sigmund of the Dark Towers.'

Elspeth gasped. 'He is a terrible man. I have heard that no man or woman is safe from him and his soldiers. If he breaks down our defences we shall all be killed and the women ravished.'

'Lord Mornay will not allow that to happen,'

Rosamunde said confidently. She went to the narrow window and looked down at the scene in the courtyard. It was a hive of activity with men scurrying here and there. 'We are preparing to meet an attack if it is made, but I think it unlikely. Why should this baron attack us now?'

'He needs no reason. Besides, I think there was unfinished business between the old lord and Baron Sigmund. I have heard it said they quarrelled over a woman but I do not know the details,' Elspeth said.

'I think I shall go down and discover what is happening,' Rosamunde said. She turned to glance at Elspeth and her daughters, who were intent on their work. 'Come with me, Elspeth. I have no experience of a siege, for my father lived at peace with his neighbours, but there must be something we can do to help.'

'Yes, my lady. It happened only once when I was with Lady Mornay. I remember that we helped to pass buckets of boiling oil up to the ramparts on the walls, and of course we nursed the wounded— but there may be other things we could do,' Elspeth replied.

'Your daughters and Maire will stay here for

the moment, but we shall send for them if they are needed.'

Rosamunde went quickly from the room, Elspeth following behind. They ran down to the hall and discovered that servants were everywhere. Pikes, crossbows and spears had been brought up from the armoury and were being taken out to the men on the battlements; a giant of a man was carrying a basket of rocks on his head and another under each arm. They would be hurled down on the invaders, who would be subjected to all manner of missiles, including burning pitch.

Seeing Raphael talking to two of his knights, Rosamunde went up to him.

'Forgive me for disturbing you,' she said. 'But my women and I are ready to serve in any way we can. Give us your commands, my lord.'

'I should have come to you when it was needful. We take necessary precautions but it may be that Baron Sigmund comes in peace,' Raphael explained. 'His reputation does him no credit, but if he comes to parley I shall give him fair hearing.'

'I pray that he comes in peace, sir. We shall await your commands, but I will keep you no longer from your business,' she said.

He hesitated, then reached out to touch her cheek. 'Do not fear, Rosamunde. If the worst comes to pass, the castle can stand a long siege. I promise nothing will happen to you while I live.'

'I was not afraid for myself, sir. I merely wished to do something useful,' she told him.

'Since the kitchen servants are needed for other tasks, your women might help prepare food and drink for the men.'

'Thank you. We shall be glad to be of service to you,' she said honestly.

Rosamunde returned to Elspeth. 'For the moment we can best serve by preparing food for the men. Fetch your daughters and Maire. I shall go to the kitchens and discover what needs to be done.'

'Yes, my lady.' Elspeth smiled at her. 'My daughters are both good cooks. The men will eat well this evening.'

Elspeth sent Lilia and Beth off with a bucket of good hot broth, a ladle and cups. Maire had a basket of rolls fresh from the oven; the bread was coarse and brown but it was substantial and it would fill the stomachs of the men on the ramparts. There was another bucket of broth waiting and a second basket filled with chunks of bread.

'We shall take this to the men at the west side ourselves,' she said to Elspeth. 'Once the food is distributed we shall eat ourselves and then we shall warm ale and take that to the men later.'

'We shall need to keep them supplied with drinks, for it will be a long night,' Elspeth said. 'If an attack comes it will surely not be before morning.'

Pleased with the results of their endeavours, the two women went out into the courtyards. The night air was cool after the heat of the kitchen and an unnatural silence seemed to hang over the castle, as if the men were holding their breaths. Somewhere in the darkness a bird's strange cry echoed.

When they reached the west wall, Rosamunde began the ascent of some steep steps leading up to the battlements. One of the men saw her and came down to meet her halfway, taking the heavy bucket from her.

'This will be welcome, lady, but 'tis heavy for you.'

'I managed well enough,' she said, and turned

to take the basket of bread from Elspeth. 'Go back and see if the others have returned. The men will want more food and wine soon.'

She followed the soldier up to the battlements. The moon had just that instant sailed out from behind the clouds and it was possible to see for miles around. At the moment there was no sign of anyone.

'Will the attack come from this direction?' she wanted to know.

'The ascent is steep here,' the soldier said and dipped the ladle into the bucket, pouring it into the men's cups as they presented them. Rosamunde offered the basket and they each took a chunk of bread and thanked her. 'If I meant to attack I would come from over there. The woods offer cover and then 'tis but a short charge to the castle, though it would still give us time to take up the drawbridge if we had not already done so. So perhaps the best way is to come from behind us, even though it is steep.'

'Perhaps they will not come tonight.'

'I pray you are right, my lady,' the soldier said and lifted his cup to drink. 'This is very good, far tastier than we sometimes have.'

'Elspeth's daughters prepared it.'

The soldier nodded but continued to eat and drink in silence. The men had all taken their share of bread and soup. Rosamunde picked up the empty bucket and began to descend the stone steps that led back down to the outer bailey. She had reached the bottom when she heard a shout from above. Looking up, she saw the men had crowded to one spot on the battlements and were looking out towards the woods. From the cries and excited gesturing, she guessed that some kind of activity had been noticed.

A shiver ran down her spine. Being under siege would not be pleasant for any of them. She'd checked the stores at the back of the kitchen and knew there was sufficient food to feed them all for two to three weeks, but after that they would run short of many foods. Meat would need to be rationed and so would flour, for it was only September and the stores had not yet been ordered for the winter. Of preserves there were almost none. Raphael had brought fresh peaches and other luxuries from Normandy, but nothing had been pickled or dried for winter use, and that meant if a siege went on for too long they would starve.

Returning to the kitchen, Rosamunde found the

women warming ale. More bread was being prepared for the morning and some oats had been put to soak to make porridge.

'What is happening?' Elspeth asked. 'We thought we heard shouting.'

'I think there is some activity, but for the moment I know as little as you. We must wait until someone sends to tell us what is needed,' Rosamunde replied.

'What shall we do if the enemy breaks through the defences?' Lilia asked and looked frightened.

'It will not happen,' Rosamunde assured her. 'Lord Mornay is an experienced soldier. He knows how to defend the castle.'

She smiled at the other girl confidently, but inside she too was suddenly anxious. Supposing the baron's forces were too strong? They might all be killed. She might never see her father or her home again.

She pushed the thought to one side. Raphael would never let that happen. She did not know why but she had learned to trust him implicitly.

Raphael went to the ramparts to look down. A large group of armed men had gathered beneath the walls. He judged Baron Sigmund had brought perhaps twenty of his men with him, which was enough to make a statement but not sufficient to lay siege to the castle.

'It seems he comes in peace,' Mellors said cautiously.

'Perhaps. This may be just the advance. We shall go carefully. Send a man out under a white flag to ask his business,' Raphael ordered.

Even as he spoke there was a fanfare of trumpets. When it ended a knight rode up to the gates bearing a white flag.

'My lord Baron Sigmund begs entrance. He would speak with Sir Raphael, now Lord Mornay. He comes in peace.'

'If we let twenty men inside they could wreak havoc,' Mellors said. 'Give me your terms, my lord, and I shall go down.'

'The drawbridge stays up,' Raphael decided quickly. 'Go out through the side gate on foot. The path is narrow across the moat and only one man may pass at a time. Baron Sigmund and five of his knights may pass, and I shall guarantee their safety, but no more.'

'Yes, my lord.'

'God protect you. Know that if you are foully slain we shall avenge you,' Raphael said solemnly.

'I have no son or wife to mourn me. I do not fear to die, my lord,' Mellors said bravely.

'Yet you shall not if we can prevent it. A dozen bows will be trained on them. If I sense treachery we shall fire and you must retreat swiftly,' Raphael urged.

'It shall be as you order, my lord.'

'Go then, for I would know what Sigmund wants here.'

Raphael watched as his steward went back down the steps that led to the ramparts. The men and horses jostled impatiently outside but there was no attempt to bring up engines of war or attack the walls.

After a few minutes, he saw his steward emerge from the small side gate and go across the narrow walkway to the assembled soldiers. He was carrying a white flag and it seemed that his words were listened to and heard. The talking went on for longer than Raphael liked, and he sensed that there was some anger amongst the men below, but then an agreement was reached and six of them dismounted and followed Mellors back across the narrow ridge of rock into the castle.

Raphael left his position and went steadily down

to the courtyard, where he waited alone to greet the incoming party. He knew that at least a dozen bows had turned in his direction and would fire if any of the newcomers attempted to attack him.

'This is a fine welcome,' a deep voice boomed at him out of the darkness and a large, thickset man stepped forward. 'I sent word of my coming and yet you close your gates against me.'

'These are parlous times, sir,' Raphael replied and walked towards him. Now he could see the bushy red beard and flowing locks that he'd been told of and knew it was Sigmund himself. 'Yet if you come in peace you are welcome, sir.'

'Your father and I quarrelled,' Baron Sigmund said. 'Now you are lord in his place and I would have peace between us. I came to offer my friendship despite our differences. Your father was for Prince John and I stand for the King.'

'I have just returned from the Crusades and have no desire to quarrel with any man. If His Majesty returns to claim his throne I shall welcome him, but I take no sides until then,' Raphael said cautiously. After all, the baron could be Prince John's man and hiding it to try and flush Raphael's true loyalties out.

'You have a wise tongue for one so young,' the baron said, gaze narrowed and wary. 'Come, will you take my hand and accept my friendship?'

'Friendship is something that must be earned,' Raphael replied. 'However, I am not your enemy, sir. My father quarrelled with his neighbours and I would live in peace with them all. If you truly wish to end your quarrel with the Mornay estate, I shall not refuse you.'

He strode towards the man, offering his hand. Baron Sigmund took it, clasping hard with both hands.

'Come, sir,' Raphael said. 'May I offer you some wine and a bed for the night? You are welcome to stay with us this night, and those men you have brought to protect you, but the others must remain outside. I shall ask if there is bread and ale for them, and for you I dare say a more tasty supper may be prepared.'

'My escort will sleep on the floor of your hall and I need only a blanket by your fire. I am a rough man, and much of what they say of me is true, but I am honest. I shall not break the truce between us, but be warned: if you betray me, I shall take my revenge,' the other man said gruffly.

'I am a man of my word,' Raphael said, looking him straight in the eye. 'Your men may rest easily here. We have no quarrel with you or them.'

'Then I shall sup with you and we shall discuss the future. Your father and I crossed swords and quarrelled because we both wanted the same woman. In future, it would be best to set boundaries and take our share of the spoils,' the baron declared.

'I have no wish to prey on others. I came home to live in peace, sir. My father may have taken prisoners for ransom but it is not my way,' Raphael replied, courteously but firmly.

'Then we shall not argue over the spoils,' Baron Sigmund said and laughed. 'Yet I would warn you to watch your back. If others believe you to be weak, they will seek to take what is yours. In this world only the strongest survive.'

'I am not ignorant of the world, sir. I know that ruthless men take what they please and care not for the pain they inflict. Yet *I* would warn *you*, and any others who may think me weak, that I protect what is mine—and that includes my women *and* my servants,' Raphael said grimly.

Sigmund's eyes narrowed, then he gave a harsh

laugh. 'You are no fool, Sir Raphael. I believe we shall deal well together.'

'We shall take some wine together while supper is prepared,' Raphael said. 'Come, sir, we shall talk privately in my chamber.'

'He has invited the baron to take supper with him?' Rosamunde stared at the steward in dismay. 'Does my lord not know of the man's reputation?'

'Baron Sigmund is a ruthless enemy and he rules much of the countryside around here. My lord must walk a tightrope, at least until the King returns to bring order and justice to England. Then perhaps the baron will be brought to heel—but until then we must tread carefully. The baron did not come to fight this time, but it might be different another day,' Mellors explained.

'I think Sir Raphael risks being tainted by association,' Rosamunde said snippily. 'We shall prepare supper, as you ask, but pray tell my lord that I shall not sup with him this evening.'

'I believe Lord Mornay intends to dine in private but I shall convey the message to him at a convenient time,' Mellors replied respectfully.

Rosamunde inclined her head. She fetched a

capon that had been plucked and cleansed earlier from the larder and threw it onto the board, taking up a small axe to chop it into quarters and toss it into a pan with butter, herbs and onions.

'At least we are not being threatened by a siege this night,' Elspeth said as she prepared some worts and added them to a mess of stew that had been simmering for the past hour or more. 'Be careful, lady, or that pan will burn.'

'It would serve them both right,' Rosamunde said crossly as she tossed the chicken and moved it to a part of the grid where the flame was not as hot. A part of her was relieved that the tension of the evening had melted away and there would be no bloodshed, but she was disappointed that Raphael had invited a man like Baron Sigmund to dine in private with him. She had thought him different but now it seemed he was much like his father. Surely he would not join the lawless bands that became rich from preying on others less strong than themselves?

Chapter Six

'You should be wary of Sir Raphael, mistress,' Maire said the following morning. They were alone in Rosamunde's chamber for she had sent the other women to break their fast. 'If he dines in private with a rogue such as Baron Sigmund, you should not trust him.'

'We do not yet know his reasons,' Rosamunde said, though Maire's thoughts were not unlike her own. 'Mayhap he would make a friend of the baron rather than bring an army upon us.'

'I warn you for you own good, my lady,' her maid said. 'If you begin to like this man too much, he will break your heart. I have seen the signs before and I would not see you caught in his trap.'

'You need not fear for me,' Rosamunde said brusquely. 'I mean to ask him later if he will permit me to gather herbs and berries in the woods with my ladies. Indeed, I shall go in search of Lord Mornay now and do just that.'

Ignoring Maire's shake of the head, she left her chamber and ran lightly down the stairs to the hall. There she stopped abruptly, catching her breath, for she saw Raphael in conversation with a large man with flowing red hair. The man had seen her over Raphael's shoulder, his gaze narrowing as it moved over her. His intense stare brought heat to her cheeks and, instead of approaching Raphael as she'd intended, she turned away and went out to the courtyard.

'Are you ready to go foraging?' Elspeth asked. She and her daughters had brought baskets and were clearly prepared for the morning's work.

Rosamunde had honestly intended to ask permission before leaving the castle but a sudden surge of rebellion had overtaken her. If she were truly a hostage, she would be locked in her chamber. There was no reason why she should ask Lord Mornay's leave to go foraging for herbs and berries.

She looked at Lilia, who was much her height. 'Please give me your cloak, Lilia. You will remain here and continue with the mending, so you will not need it.'

Lilia looked surprised but removed her cloak and handed it to her. Rosamunde slipped it around her shoulders, bringing the hood up to cover her head.

'Let us go now,' she said. 'Some things are best gathered while the dew is still upon them.'

Glancing back, she saw that Raphael and Baron Sigmund had emerged from the hall and were standing together in the courtyard. Neither of them looked at the women as they left the inner bailey. As they walked through the outer bailey, to the small side gate used by tradesmen and the previous night to broker a parley, Rosamunde's heart was thudding. She could not help wondering if they would be ordered to stop and prevented from leaving the castle. However, only one of the men patrolling the walls gave them a second glance, and he merely smiled and waved at Beth.

'Ferdie is my sweetheart,' the other girl confessed and blushed as Rosamunde looked at her. 'One day, when he has saved enough money to buy a house and land for the pig, we shall marry.'

'You should not hold your hopes too high,' Elspeth warned her daughter. 'Ferdie needs more than a pig and a cottage before you can marry. He needs a strip of land where he can grow wheat or rye so that you have corn to make your bread for the winter. While your father lived we always had bread, but after he died and the strip passed to his cousin life was very hard. Had Lord Mornay not sent for us, we might have starved this winter.'

'Perhaps Ferdie could hire some land from Lord Mornay,' Rosamunde said. 'If Ferdie is a freeman he has the right to work the land for himself.'

'The old lord stuck to the feudal system and demanded service two days a week,' Elspeth said. 'I did not know that it was possible to hire land for coin. How do you know this, my lady?'

'I know because my father had tenants who farmed land that belonged to him. He allowed them to pay him in silver pence, but then he had to sell most of the land and the tenants lost their rights, for the next lord would not let them pay in coin.'

'Then it is no different,' Elspeth said. 'He would still be dependent on the will of the lord.'

'Perhaps. There might be another way,' Rosamunde said and then smiled and shook her head.

'I cannot make promises yet. Now, tell me, please, where should we look to find the best herbs, berries and wildflowers?'

'Who was the beauty?' Baron Sigmund asked Raphael as Rosamunde walked away. 'I had not heard that you were married.'

'I once had a wife,' Raphael replied, his lips white and his mouth set in a thin line. 'The lady you saw was my—guest. She is under my protection until I can see her safely to her home.'

'I remember you warned me that you protect your women.' Sigmund grinned at him. 'I need a wife, for my last died in childbed. Will you give her to me? I like red-haired women. They are more spirited than their fair cousins.'

'The lady is my guest, as I told you—but not mine to give in marriage to anyone, even had I a mind to part with her. I may ask her to be my wife if things go well between us.'

Why had he added that last sentence? Marriage had not been in Raphael's mind until this moment. Yet if Sigmund thought it was true, she should be safe from his attentions.

'So that's the way the wind blows.' Sigmund

chuckled. 'I wish you joy of her, my friend. Yet, if you change your mind, I will reward you handsomely for her. Now I must take my leave for I have other business.'

'We are agreed on a truce between us, then, for Richard's sake?' Raphael asked.

'Aye, my lord, we are. I live by my own rules, but Richard is our rightful king and Prince John a tyrant. He will suck us all dry with his taxes. The sooner Richard is home, the better,' the baron declared.

'More money is needed for his ransom. It is my intention to approach lords who might be of like mind. I thank you for your advice, sir,' Raphael said.

'I am glad of this meeting. Now, if you will excuse me, I shall leave you,' the baron replied.

The two men walked out into the courtyard. The drawbridge was let down on Raphael's signal and horses were brought for the baron and his men. He watched as the column of armed men moved away and frowned as he recalled the baron's request to be given Rosamunde. The idea of her wed to a man like that appalled him. She had said her father was poor, and therefore such a marriage might be approved for her, but the very idea of it turned Raphael's stomach. She was too beautiful and fine for such a coarse brute. If Raphael had her guardianship, he would never let her go to a man like that!

Raphael turned back towards the castle. He was thoughtful as he entered the hall. Baron Sigmund had assured him that he was for Richard, which Raphael believed was true, and they had agreed not to interfere with one another. It would be an uneasy truce at best but was better than open warfare. Even on the Crusades the proud barons had quarrelled and fought amongst themselves. At home quarrels frequently resulted in fighting over land or women.

He had an uneasy feeling that they had not seen the last of Baron Sigmund. He had not liked the gleam in his eyes when he had spoken of liking red-haired women because they had more spirit; Raphael could just imagine what that meant! He would never let Rosamunde go to such a brute— never. She would no doubt be safer wed—but to such a man? Impossible.

It was a pity that the baron had seen Rosamunde at all. Raphael had hoped that he would be on his

way before she left her chamber that morning. He
supposed he had been remiss in not sending word
that she was to remain in her chamber. He had not
wanted to restrict her freedom, but now he regretted the lapse. He'd seen Sigmund's intense interest
and knew that, despite his fair words before he
left, the baron would not hesitate to take her for
himself if the chance came his way.

He ought to warn her that she must not leave
the castle alone. Raphael had told her once before
that she was free within the confines of the castle,
but he'd also intended to allow her some freedom
outside, providing she was accompanied by at least
three of his guards. Now, he thought it best that
she stay safe within the castle walls until he was
certain the baron had moved on.

Running up the curving stone stair to her chamber at the top of the tower, he knocked. After a
moment the door was opened and Maire looked
at him from suspicious eyes.

'I would speak with your mistress.'

'My lady is not here.'

'Pray tell me where I may find her. Is she in the
kitchen or the stillroom?' he asked.

'I do not know. She wished to speak with you,' the woman said.

'Then I must look for her.' Raphael turned away, then a fresh voice called to him.

'My lord…' He swung round and saw one of the village women. 'I know where my lady has gone.'

His gaze narrowed. 'You are?'

'Lilia, my lord.' She bobbed a curtsey. 'My lady asked me to give her my cloak when we were in the courtyard. She, Beth and my mother have gone to the woods to gather herbs and berries.'

'Gone to the woods?'

Raphael swore beneath his breath. Had the foolish woman *no* idea what danger she might be in with hostile knights in the vicinity? Baron Sigmund might have pledged his friendship, and within his walls she was safe enough, but a woman wandering alone without an escort was fair prey for a man such as the baron.

'How long since they left?' he barked, but did not wait for her answer. It was only a short time since the baron had asked about her. She must have seen that Raphael was busy with their visitor and taken advantage to slip away wearing a serving woman's cloak.

She had deliberately set out to deceive him! Raphael felt a surge of fury. How *dare* she disobey him when he had warned her it was not safe to leave the castle without him or his men?

He ran down the stairs and out into the courtyard, yelling loudly for his horse and for an escort. She could not have gone far, but Baron Sigmund and his men might have passed her as they left. She and her women might be in mortal danger— might even have been abducted.

As the men mounted up and followed him across the drawbridge, Raphael's heart was racing. Had she meant to go foraging or was she trying to run away from him? If anything happened to her he would never forgive himself.

The women found a patch of edible fungi soon after entering the woods. Elspeth had harvested them the previous year and they were growing again near the edge of the woods, a profusion of large white mushrooms, and also some rare and delicate caps.

'These are wonderful,' Rosamunde said and held some delicate fungi to her nose to smell them.

'These are really delicious when cooked. They have so many uses and are my favourites.'

'In spring you can find violets here. We harvest them for they grow in profusion. Their perfume is wonderful for scenting clothes and balms for the body,' Elspeth said. 'But they are also good for sweetmeats and cleansing the breath—though I think lavender and roses have as many uses, if not more, for I make wine and cake with lavender and syrup from rose hips.'

'Yes, indeed, they all have their uses. I suppose it is that violets come earlier and are a herald of the summer. I fear we must wait for next spring for we shall not find violets this late in the year. We must not take all the fungi but leave some for others,' Rosamunde replied.

Seeing a clump of wild garlic growing a little further into the wood, Rosamunde wandered on and knelt down to examine them. There were many kinds of plants that could be used for fla-vouring food and in simple cures, but one had to be careful that, if any poisonous specimens were picked for use in particular lotions, they were not confused with those for cooking. She was look-ing at a clump of fungi that she was uncertain of as she spoke. 'I believe this is something I have not seen before. Is it edible? What do you think, Elspeth?'

'My lady—horsemen.' Elspeth rose to her feet and looked towards the sound. She beckoned Beth to her and they both retreated to stand with Rosamunde.

'You do not think Baron Sigmund…?'

Elspeth drew a trembling breath as a small group of horsemen burst through the trees. Their leader caught sight of the women and held up his hand to halt his men.

'We have found them safe,' he said, and dismounted and walked towards Rosamunde. She looked into Raphael's eyes and shivered, seeing the fierce anger that simmered beneath the surface. 'So, my lady, you were merely foraging. I thought perhaps you sought to run from me.'

'Why should I do that?' Rosamunde asked, her throat tight as she sensed his fury. Why was he so angry with her? 'I noticed the lack of certain herbs when cooking supper last night and thought my women and I might supply the need. If we are to make preserves for the winter we shall need berries and fruits that grow wild here as well as anything you can provide, sir.'

'You did not think to inform me of your intention—or perhaps ask my leave?' he forced out through tightly gritted teeth.

'You were busy with your visitor. I understood you wished to be private with him and thought it best not to intrude,' she explained.

'He saw you and remarked on your beauty. Do you think it was wise to expose yourself to his gaze, Rosamunde?' he pressed.

'I did not know I was supposed to hide myself away,' she said with a defiant toss of her head.

'Your common sense should have told you what kind of man he was. Had it been he and his men that found you, what do you suppose would have happened then?' Raphael growled.

Rosamunde looked him in the eye. 'I might have supposed that he would behave honourably since you chose to entertain him in private, as a *friend*.'

'Had it not occurred to you that I might have wished to keep him from seeing *you*? I do not trust Baron Sigmund but neither do I want him as my enemy.' His eyes narrowed shrewdly. 'Is that why you sneaked away—to punish me?'

'I intended to ask, but then…' Rosamunde shook her head. It was unfair of him to be angry with her. She took a deep breath. 'If I am a prisoner then you should not treat me as an honoured guest one day and then lose your temper because I go walking with my women on the next. How am I supposed to know what I am?'

'You *are* my guest,' Raphael assured her and some of the anger left his face. He looked uncertain now. 'Forgive me for losing my temper. I was worried when I learned you had left the castle—especially as Baron Sigmund and his men may still be in the vicinity. Women wandering alone without sufficient protection are always at the mercy of such rogues.'

Rosamunde accepted the truth of his words. 'Yes, I ought to have thought of that for my women's sake, if not my own. Had it been he instead of you, we might have been in difficulty.'

'You would almost certainly have been abducted,' he told her.

'Surely a friend would not abduct a woman under your protection?' she gasped, looking shocked.

'A true friend would not, but I trust no man that hath not proved himself. I was forced to entertain him but that does not mean I trust him. I never take any man at face value,' Raphael stated bluntly.

'Or woman either?' Rosamunde raised her eyes to look into his. 'I admit that I ought to have told you my intentions for courtesy's sake, if no more, but will you admit that my position here is not clear?'

'Come, we shall not quarrel further,' Raphael said and turned to his men. 'Two of you remain, the others may return to the castle. I shall stay and help my lady gather what she needs.'

Rosamunde was surprised. 'Surely you have other more important matters to attend?'

'Much of what needed to be done is in hand,' Raphael said. 'Although there are some within the castle that I am uncertain of, most are loyal. I may need to leave you for a few days shortly. Until then I would spend some time with you, Rosamunde. I would learn who you truly are and what you think. Now, tell me what you seek.'

'I was wondering what uses this hath,' she said, showing him the strangely shaped fungi. 'I am not sure whether it is poisonous or good to eat.'

'I think that is edible,' Raphael told her. 'I believe my mother used to add them to soups and a mess of rabbit and turnips to add flavour.'

'Yes, my lady,' Elspeth said. 'It has a pinkish underside and is safe to eat, but there is a similar cap with a black underside that would make you very ill if you ate it.'

'We call that one the death cap,' Rosamunde said and added the fungi she'd picked to her basket. 'I was hoping we might find blackberries but I think it may be too late.'

'I know my mother sometimes found late berries around here,' Raphael said and looked about him. 'We are not far from a pleasant clearing. If there are any, it is there that we shall find them.'

'I shall leave you to pick fungi here,' Rosamunde said to Elspeth. 'We shall explore a little further and see if there are any blackberries to be found. Follow us when you are ready.'

With her basket on her right arm, Rosamunde took Raphael's arm with her left and smiled up at him.

'Tell me, my lord, did you often come foraging with your mother?'

'Not often enough,' he replied. 'I was mostly set to learning my Latin verbs or training with my father's men, but sometimes I escaped. We always came a-maying together and in the autumn we would gather nuts and blackberries. I remember a fine liqueur she made from elderberries and we also gathered sloes for preserves and wine.'

'And then you became a squire and went on crusade?'

'After my mother died things changed. I did not exactly quarrel with my father, but we hardly spoke to one another. I believe now that he was grieving for her, but I did not understand him and thought that I alone felt the pain of her loss,' Raphael admitted.

'Perhaps it was because he lost you both that he became so bitter,' she suggested.

'Yes, perhaps—but a man must conquer his bitterness. Pain and grief does not give one the right to inflict suffering on others,' he said sadly.

Rosamunde saw something in his eyes then that made her wonder. She did not pursue the subject but pointed to a clump of plants.

'Horseradish, my lord. Take your knife and see if you can pull up a root or two. It will sharpen the palate and is delicious with roasted beef, and also in cream with fresh fish.'

Raphael bent, took his knife from its sheath and dug into the earth, bringing her two large roots.

'Thank you.' She smiled at him, their hands brushing as he passed it to her.

'You are very beautiful, lady.' He leaned his head down, his lips brushing hers softly. 'I had almost forgot how pleasant it was to pass time this way.'

Rosamunde cast her eyes down. His kiss was very different from the last he'd given her—soft, even tender, instead of punishing. It made her heart leap but she tried to hide her feelings for she must not let him see how his kiss affected her. Although he did his best to make her feel she was his guest, she knew that she was in truth a hostage and at the mercy of his whims.

'You spoke of leaving—may I ask why, my lord?' she asked.

'I must speak with other lords of like mind,' he told her. 'My business is important, or I would keep my word and take you to your home, but I shall not forget you.'

'You must do as you think fit, sir. A man has his work and a woman hers. I am content to wait, as long as my father wants for nothing.'

'I shall dispatch someone very soon to make sure he has all he wants. I apologise that I have not already done this; I have been exceedingly busy,' Raphael said ruefully.

'May I make a suggestion?'

'Yes, of course.'

'You have a man in your service—his name is Ferdie and he is promised to Beth, one of my women,' she said.

Raphael's eyebrows arched. 'You wish me to send them—why?'

'Because my father still has a little land but it is neglected. I will grant Ferdie the right to work the land for himself and his family. In return he will see that my father has food and his wife will tend my father on his sickbed.'

'And if your father should die?'

'Then they may continue in possession of the land on payment of a fair rent,' she announced.

'Will you set your hand to such a document?' he asked.

'Yes, if your scribe will draw it for us—and you will bear witness to the bargain.'

'Do you not think your husband might perhaps wish to claim the land?' he pressed.

'I do not expect to marry. I have no dowry worth the notice of a knight, and would rather remain unwed than take the yeoman my cousin would have me wed,' she said honestly.

'You give away what little you have very easily,' he murmured.

'I had plans to raise a few pigs, and perhaps take in sewing, but I could not plough the land nor afford to pay others. The rent I require will be little enough—merely some corn to make bread and perhaps a few coins, whatever is fair. My cousin promised me fifty gold talents if I brought the ransom to you in her place. I think she might have refused to pay me when the time came, but since you are not intending to keep the ransom money she sent I may keep what I am owed and return the rest to her.'

'Why should you not keep all of it?'

'That would be dishonest, sir. I am no thief.'

'No, I see that, my lady.' Raphael looked thoughtful. 'When I escort you home we shall call on your cousin and return what is owed. If she demands the fifty talents back, I shall protect you from her anger.'

'You are generous, sir. While you are away I

should like to begin stocking your shelves with preserves. Would you have your steward send to market for anything that we need?' she asked.

'Of course. You have only to ask. I am grateful for the work you do. I believe my home is in sore need of a woman's touch.'

'Your wife will supply it when you marry,' she said quietly.

'*If* I marry. I am not certain that I shall—or not for some years. In time I should perhaps think of an heir, but it is not urgent just yet for I am in good health,' he said, suddenly looking sombre once more.

Rosamunde glanced away. She wondered why he had no plans to marry but would not ask. It was not her business to press for details that were clearly private.

Her gaze moved away, and suddenly she saw the little cluster of fruit. She gave a glad cry and ran to the bush where a patch of plump blackberries was growing; she stretched up in delight, picking a lush berry. She popped it into her mouth and sighed with pleasure.

'There is nothing like the first blackberry of the year,' she said as he bent one knee and knelt beside her. 'You must taste the treat, my lord.' She pulled a ripe fruit and held it to him, placing it on his tongue as he obediently opened his mouth. 'Crush it against the roof of your mouth and let the flavour flood out before you swallow.'

He smiled and followed her advice, nodding agreement. 'There is nothing to compare with the special sharp and yet sweet flavour of these, unless it is a wild strawberry.'

'We must pick them very carefully. Added to other fruits, these will make a wonderful conserve. My ladies and I will make quince and plum jams, also blackberry and apple conserve—and if we can find them we shall make pickled walnuts and almond paste for the feast at Christ's Mass.'

'I am not certain that we have walnuts or almonds here—but there should be hazelnuts at the edge of the clearing,' he offered.

'I think there is a clump of bushes over there.' Rosamunde pointed and they moved towards the far side of the clearing to harvest the small nuts.

Raphael helped pick the fruit, then, when their baskets were filled to the brim, they smiled and sat on a fallen tree, enjoying the pale sun that filtered through the canopy. The sound of voices and laughter heralded the arrival of the two serving women and the men-at-arms.

More fruit and berries were found at the edge of the clearing. For some minutes laughter and chattering voices echoed through the clearing. Sun was shining through the trees, the air crisp and sweet with the scents of autumn.

Looking about her at the smiling faces, Rosamunde was aware of a feeling of happiness that had been lacking from her life for many a year. The thought crossed her mind that it would be pleasant to live this way, enjoying the pleasures of a simple life with people she cared for.

'A silver penny for your thoughts?'

Raphael's teasing voice close to her ear sent a tingle running down her spine. She shook her head, because her thoughts had been foolish and must remain her own. They were merely fancy, a whimsical dream on an unseasonably warm day.

'Oh, they are worth far more,' she replied teasingly, and laughed softly. 'I thank you for a lovely morning, my lord. It is time we returned to the castle, for the sooner the fruits of our labour are put to work the better.'

'I must leave soon if I am to persuade others to contribute to the ransom for Richard.' Raphael toyed with the stem of his wine cup as he looked at

Sir Jonathan across the table in his private chamber. He had been considering how best to protect Rosamunde whilst he was gone. His friend was the best man he knew to care for both the lady and his castle. 'Will you remain here to see that the men do not neglect their training—and watch over the lady Rosamunde?'

'Of course. I have no family awaiting my return and shall stay to celebrate with you this Christ's Mass. One day I must buy land and a house and marry, but for the moment I am content to serve you. I shall keep the men to their work—but what of the lady? Do you not fear that she will try to leave when you are gone?' his friend asked.

'She has given her word not to leave whilst I am absent. I believe she understands that she is vulnerable without my protection. Give her as much freedom as possible, but she is not to leave the castle grounds without at least three men to guard her,' Raphael warned.

'Do you fear an abduction?'

'I think Prince John might take her prisoner if he could—and Baron Sigmund respects no woman and would use her for his own pleasure. She ought in all conscience to be wed. 'Tis the only safe estate for a woman as fair as she,' Raphael mused.

'And what does the lady mean to you?' his friend asked pointedly.

'She is under my protection, nothing more. Why do you ask?' he said defensively.

'I thought you might have plans to wed her,' the other man murmured.

'My wife has been dead hardly a year. It is too soon to think of such things. I hinted to Baron Sigmund that I might wed Rosamunde to show him that he had no hope of her, but I had not truly thought of it.'

Even as he spoke, Raphael knew that he was not telling the whole truth. The idea had been forming at the back of his mind ever since that morning, but it was foolish. She would do better with Sir Jonathan. After all, Raphael had found Messalina's love restricting. He had chafed at the bonds she'd put on him, and no doubt it would be the same with Rosamunde. The lady deserved more than he could give her.

'Yet I sense something between you,' Jonathan continued. 'The men suspect you intend marriage, and I think it pleases them, because if you marry an Englishwoman you will settle here.'

'Perhaps.' Raphael sipped his wine and looked

into his cup, a brooding expression in his eyes. It would be best to speak out now rather than let a breach grow between himself and his friend. He brought his gaze up to meet Jonathan's. 'I suspect you have an interest here, my friend?'

'I shall not deny I find the lady enchanting. We have spoken only rarely, but she seems true of purpose and steadfast. I think she would make a good wife for any man.'

Raphael hesitated. 'If you care for her, I shall not stand in your way, should she wish to wed you.'

'Alas, I do not think the lady has noticed me,' Jonathan said ruefully. 'But I would not see her hurt, Raphael. If you cannot offer her anything, you should not give her false hope.'

'Have I done so?' he asked, alarmed.

'You alone can answer that, my friend. I meant no insult, but she is innocent and lovely, and I think hath little family to support her.'

'Perhaps *you* should offer her marriage.' Raphael's gaze narrowed, needing to hear Jonathan's answer.

'As yet I hardly know the lady, but if I thought she would be happy as my wife I should not be averse to the idea,' his friend said placidly.

'I wish you good fortune,' Raphael muttered and drained his cup. He did not understand his own reaction to Jonathan's interest in Rosamunde. She would be safe and content as his friend's wife; after all, he had no plans to wed himself. Yet there was a small voice at the back of his mind that protested she must not marry anyone but Raphael. No; that was foolish and selfish. He knew that he had cared for Messalina as much as he could probably care for any woman, yet he'd tugged at the bonds of marriage, resenting her clinging ways. He was being unfair to both Jonathan and Rosamunde to be unhappy at the possibility of a relationship between them. 'Do whatever you think best, my friend, but keep her safe. Now, I must make my final inspection before we sup. Do you care to come with me?'

'I must beg you to excuse me. I shall see you at supper.' With that, Jonathan put down his cup and left the room.

Raphael lingered for a moment. His thoughts were deep and he was frowning as he left to make a tour of the castle grounds to make certain the men on duty were at their posts. Baron Sigmund had agreed to a truce and left, but he was not the only rogue baron to cast greedy eyes on his neighbour's lands. No man could afford to be careless or let down his guard in these uncertain times. Prince John's rule had nurtured such men, for he taxed unfairly and used force to take what he desired. It was perhaps natural that the barons should follow his example. England needed strong governance and a king to lead by example. Richard the Lionheart was not perfect, but he would bring justice back to a land that sorely needed it.

There was little reason for Raphael to linger here when there was work to be done. He was not sure why he was so reluctant to leave.

He had given Sir Jonathan leave to court the lady Rosamunde if he chose, but found that the idea of her as his friend's wife did not sit at all well with him. Why? He had believed his heart incapable of true love, but something about Rosamunde had touched him from the first moment he had seen her. He'd kissed her twice now and he knew that he desired her. In the wood he had been tempted to lead her to a secluded spot and make love to her, but she was a lady, not a whore. Jonathan was right; Raphael would indeed be a rogue to break her heart.

What kind of a man was he? Nothing could wash away the stain of his guilt; his wife's blood was on his hands because he had not been there to protect her. He believed now that she had sensed impending doom and had begged him to stay with her in the belief he would protect her. Raphael had refused and his dreams were now tortured. He had abandoned Messalina and, because he had not been with her, she had died.

He sighed heavily. He did not deserve to know happiness again. Rosamunde should not think of him. Sir Jonathan was a good man and he would make her happy. Far better she married him than remain a tempting morsel for someone like Baron Sigmund to snap up. When Raphael left the castle on the King's business, Rosamunde and Jonathan might come to know each other better and the problem would be solved.

Ruthlessly, he pushed all warmer feelings to one side. Love made a man weak. He would not permit himself to care for a woman again.

Rosamunde glanced at her companion. Raphael had been silent throughout the meal, as different from the man who had shown her where to find the blackberries as it was possible to be. What had changed? Why had he withdrawn from her?

'We made a rich jelly with the blackberries,' she told him as he looked at her. 'It will be added to sauces and puddings. The fungi were added to the pottage this evening, my lord. Did you notice the enhanced flavour of the gravy?'

Raphael frowned. 'You are an excellent chatelaine, lady. I think you will make someone a good wife.'

'I told you I had no expectation of marriage, my lord,' she said shortly, somewhat taken aback.

'You should not underestimate yourself, Rosamunde. I dare say more than one of my knights would look favourably on you if you encouraged them,' he continued.

'I should not dream of doing so, sir. I have no dowry to offer and I shall be no man's doxy!' she exclaimed.

'I meant marriage. Sir Wilfred lost his wife six months since and looks for a mother for his three children. Sir Thomas is a little old for you, but he needs a gentle lady to nurse him through his last years and has monies enough not to care for your dowry. And, of course, there is our minstrel, my friend Sir Jonathan. He would be a fine match for any lady,' Raphael persevered.

'I think you jest with me,' Rosamunde said in a reproachful tone. 'None of these gentlemen have shown me any particular attention, nor should I welcome it. You know my situation, sir. I must care for my father whilst he lives.'

'And afterwards?'

'I shall think of that when the time comes.'

'It may be too late. You should consider marriage to a man who would care for your father and protect you both. You should look about you more, lady. You might be surprised. At least one of the gentlemen I mentioned might offer marriage if you smiled at him,' he hinted.

Rosamunde shook her head firmly. She could not meet his gaze, because she felt that he was warning her she must not look to him for marriage. Why should he feel that necessary? Had she inadvertently given him a sign that she encouraged his attentions? She lifted her head proudly.

'If you permitted me I should leave tomorrow for my home. I do not see why a small escort cannot be provided, my lord. There is no need for you to trouble yourself,' she said.

'I was commanded to hold you here, lady. Would you have me disobey the prince?' he asked quietly.

Her startled gaze flew to his. 'Then I am a prisoner after all?'

'Nay, lady.' Raphael smiled. 'I but tease you. I must leave in another day or so. I take an escort with me and could not spare men to take you home now.'

Rosamunde felt tears sting her eyes but she refused to let them fall. 'I would not be a trouble to you, sir. Had you not dismissed Fitzherbert, he might have seen me safely home.'

'One man could not protect you.' Raphael's look was intense. 'Your beauty makes you a valuable prize. Some would seek to hold you for ransom, others to use you for their own ends. You are safer here until I decide what should become of you.'

Her head went up and she shot him a fiery glare. 'Who gave *you* the right to decide my future?'

'You delivered yourself to me as a hostage for your uncle's release,' Raphael said simply. 'It was of your own choosing.'

'Now I choose to leave,' Rosamunde said and would have risen. She knew that tears were close and she wanted to weep in private. His hand moved to clasp her wrist, restraining her. She felt his strength and looked into his eyes. 'Pray let me go to my chamber.'

'Not until you give your word that you will not be foolish enough to try and run away,' he stated flatly.

'I have already told you that I shall do nothing foolish. Besides, I do not think I should get far on foot—and I would not be permitted to take my horses and leave, would I?' she scowled.

Raphael smiled as her beautiful green eyes flashed with temper. 'I have made you angry, but I must have your word before I leave here to conduct my business. You are under my protection and I would not have harm come to you.'

'It can matter little to you what happens to me,' she snapped.

'There you are wrong. I already have one sweet lady's death on my conscience. I would not have yours too.' He released her wrist. 'Go, then, for I cannot prevent you if you wish to leave. Yet I would ask you to wait here until after Christ's Mass. In the New Year I may have time to take you to your father.'

'Very well, my lord. I shall wait for you to take

me home. I gave my word to my father before and I do not break a promise lightly.'

With a toss of her head, Rosamunde walked away from him. She was foolish to care for him but he had made his feelings plain enough; he did not return her regard. She was under his protection but he valued his honour more than her.

She was not sure why that should hurt so much. She realised she had always loved the youth who had saved her kitten, but this man was a very different person indeed. It should not matter to her what he felt for her—yet it did.

Chapter Seven

Three days later Rosamunde decided that she would make an inventory of the linen, pewter and silver. Now that the mending was done, and for the moment they had used all the fruit and herbs they had, Lilia was idle for much of the time; she was sulking because Beth had been married to Ferdie before they'd both left for Rosamunde's home.

'It is not fair,' she grumbled to her mother within Rosamunde's hearing. 'Beth was a year younger than me. I should have been the first to wed.'

'Your sister has been fortunate. Had it not been for the lady Rosamunde, she would've had to wait many years. Stop your complaining, daughter. Do your work well, and then perhaps a match may be made for you,' Elspeth advised her.

'I could not spare you just yet,' Rosamunde told the disgruntled girl tactfully. 'Soon we shall have more leisure and then I shall ask you to help sew the wall hangings. Perhaps we can find some material to make new gowns for both you and your mother.'

Lilia looked more cheerful at that thought and the three women spent the morning checking chests of linen, the coffers and cupboards where silver and pewter used for the table were stored. They counted all the platters, cups, ewers, goblets, porringers and dishes, Rosamunde making a note of the lists in a ledger she had begged from Mellors.

It was when they came to take account of the silver and other valuables in the hall that Rosamunde noticed a small silver urn was missing from a niche in the wall where it normally stood. She made a note, remembering that it had been there two nights previously, and when she took her lists to Mellors she mentioned it to him.

'Are you sure the urn is not there?' he asked and frowned, glancing through the lists. 'These will be useful, my lady. I cannot be certain, but I believe more than one item of value has gone missing of late.'

'You think there is a thief in the castle?' she asked with concern.

'I suspected it before but no accounting has been done for years. Sometimes things are mislaid and then reappear, but I shall mention my suspicions to my lord,' the steward promised.

'The urn was definitely there two nights ago for I stopped to admire the work; it was beautifully chased around the rim,' she said.

Mellors examined the lists again and frowned once more. 'In the coffer where the silver is kept—you saw no sign of a chalice with garnets and turquoise set into the silver?'

'No, I am certain it was not there.' Rosamunde saw that he looked worried. 'Who would steal from Lord Mornay?'

'I do not know, my lady, but I shall make him aware of what is happening here.'

'If you wish it, my ladies and I could make an inventory of the armoury,' she offered.

'I think I shall set men I trust to do that, my lady. Now you have begun, I think it wise to check everything in the castle. The old lord was lax and did not care as he ought. Things are different now and I would not have my master cheated.'

'Then we shall leave the armoury to you, sir. May I give you a list for the market? If you bring me sugar and fruit I can have the women make preserves to last you throughout the winter. I shall not be here then, but if preparations have been made you will have much of what you need,' she said.

'Soon we shall be into winter and it will be time to kill some of the cattle for salting. The huntsmen will bring in wild boar to salt. I would be grateful if you could oversee it, my lady. Last year little was done and we had to rely on domestic pigs that were needed for rearing this spring. It meant we had to buy replacements this year and had to be satisfied with inferior stock,' the steward explained.

'I shall see that sufficient is put aside for your needs, sir, but I do not know when my lord may have time to take me home. He spoke of the New Year, so I believe I shall spend Christ's Mass here with you,' she told him.

'When Lady Mornay was alive we had a big feast at the castle and the leavings were distributed to the poor of the village, together with a silver penny,' Mellors said.

'That is a good custom,' she said with approval. 'If my lord permits, we shall do so again this year.'

'My lord may not be here, lady, but it could still be done if you were to stand in his place,' he advised.

'I should be happy to do so,' Rosamunde said. 'He spoke of leaving three days ago on business but as yet…' She sighed. 'I dare say estate business hath kept him here.'

'Yes, mayhap. Thank you for the lists, my lady. They are useful.' He bowed and then left.

Rosamunde had been working all day and decided that she would take a turn in the fresh air before going up to change into a clean gown for the evening. Each night she had expected to hear Raphael say that he was leaving the next morning but still he delayed—why? She could not flatter herself that it was for her sake, so why did he not leave as he'd intended? Was he concerned about something?

She wandered through the inner bailey, hearing the hammer of iron on steel as the armourer sweated at his furnace. There were small workshops everywhere, craftsmen busy at their trade. The cooper was fitting iron bands to specially weathered casks that would be used for storing the ale the brewer had fermenting in vats. Here in the castle they were self-sufficient in many things, though she knew that Raphael had had fruit brought in from Normandy, and also wine and dates from the markets in London. Most of the fish they ate came from their own stewponds, and the geese, ducks, capon, beef and pork were supplied by the lord's own farms. As yet there were no sheep on the sloping fields that lay to one side of the castle, which meant that they could not make their own cloth unless wool was brought in.

Rosamunde thought that if she lived here she would wish to have sheep grazing the rich grass so that they could make their own homespun. Of course, Raphael bought in silks, brocades and fine materials from the merchants who frequented the various fairs or had shops in the larger towns, but for the most part the people wore homespun; it was expensive to buy cloth when they could spin and weave their own.

Lost in contemplation, she had wandered towards one of the outhouses that should have been used for storing fleeces when she heard the voices.

'I saw them making an inventory,' one voice

said. 'If Mellors makes an inventory of the armoury, he will discover that swords and pikes have gone missing. He will not stop looking until he discovers the culprits. I think we should take what we can tonight and leave.'

'Since Sir Raphael came home he has kept the key to the strongbox on his person. I thought he might lay it down in an unguarded moment but as yet there has been no chance to steal anything of real value. That urn was hardly worth the bother. Perhaps you are right; Sigmund would offer us work more to our taste. We shall take what we can and leave this night.'

'If we could get that key we could take the jewels Sir Raphael has hidden.'

'If he were dead we could take everything of worth.'

'*Dead?* You would *kill* him?'

'I owe him no allegiance. If we leave he will know who has been stealing from him and I think he would make a bad enemy. Dead, he will trouble no one—and we'll take the woman too. Sigmund would pay well for her.'

'I know Sir Raphael thinks she belongs to him. He said as much to Sigmund.'

'Then it will serve him right if we snatch her from beneath his nose.'

The last words were said as two men, Sir Edmund and his shadow Sir Ian, walked round from behind the outhouse. Rosamunde gasped, because she knew they had been talking about abducting her. The two men were planning to murder Raphael, rob him and abduct her. In the instant she saw them, they saw her and Sir Edmund swore, realising that she had heard them.

She gave a little cry of alarm, turned and ran. Raphael must be warned at once. She heard Sir Edmund shout and knew that he was pursuing her. She had wandered some distance from the hall and most of the craftsmen had disappeared, probably in search of their evening meal. Could she reach help before the knights caught her? As her foot twisted in a rut in the ground she stumbled, and in the next moment Sir Edmund was upon her. His large hand went over her mouth, his other arm about her waist as he lifted her from her feet.

Rosamunde struggled and tried to scream but the normally busy courtyard was empty and there was no one to notice as she was carried back to the outhouse where the men had met earlier and thrust inside. Literally thrown to the floor, she landed with a bump and lay with her eyes closed, listening to the men arguing over her.

'You took a risk. Supposing someone saw you?' Sir Ian said.

'Stop worrying; everyone has gone in for supper. Give me that rope. We'll bind her hands and feet and gag her. No one comes here these days. Besides, we shall leave as soon as we have finished our work here,' Sir Edmund replied persuasively.

'He will look for her,' Sir Ian objected. 'When she does not join us for supper he will send for her and search the castle. We should leave now; take what we have and go before the castle is alerted.'

'Damn the wench,' Sir Edmund spat, seeing the truth of his confederate's words. 'If it had not been for her interference we should have been away with his gold and jewels before anyone knew what had happened.'

Rosamunde lay with her eyes shut, hardly daring to move while they argued over what to do with her. She was in great danger but her fear was more for Raphael than herself. She felt someone kick her feet.

'Open your eyes, harlot,' Sir Edmund demanded,

scowling at her. 'You brought this on yourself, spying on us and meddling in our business.'

'I was merely out for a walk,' Rosamunde protested. 'You will not get away with this. Master Mellors knows there is a thief in the castle. If I do not appear for supper, Lord Mornay will search the castle, and when he finds you, you will wish you had never been born.'

'Be quiet, woman. You will change your tune before we've done with you. Stand up and put your arms behind your back or I'll beat you to within an inch of your life,' Sir Edmund snarled.

Reluctantly, Rosamunde stood, putting her hands behind her back. Sir Edmund made short work of tying her hands and gagging her. She was then made to sit down and her ankles were bound. Raising her head, she glared at him defiantly over her gag.

'You're a proud wench but I'll humble you,' he vowed then glanced at Sir Ian. 'Get the horses ready. If Mornay has the castle searched, it may work to our advantage. In the midst of the panic we can leave by the side gate.'

'Why not take what we have and leave now? Forget the woman,' Sir Ian begged.

'Leave her behind to tell all she knows? He would hunt us down if it took a lifetime!' Sir Edmund exclaimed, shaking his head.

'Kill her, then. The dead cannot speak.'

'No, she's worth good money,' Sir Edmund mused, looking at her speculatively. 'If he sends to look for her, I'll say I saw her leaving the castle. When they all ride out in search of her, we'll take her and leave.'

Rosamunde watched as the two men walked away, leaving her alone in the outhouse. What light there was came through a crack in the wooden walls but it was fading fast. No one would come here, for the building had not been used in years. She struggled furiously with the bonds that bound her wrists. If she could free herself there was still time to warn Raphael of their plans. Sir Edmund had done his work too well; the bonds held and she felt a wave of anger and despair sweep over her. Raphael had warned her of the dangers outside the castle but no one had thought the worst danger of all would come from within…

'Where is the lady Rosamunde?' Raphael asked of Elspeth. He had come in search of her himself when she did not join them at supper. 'Mellors tells me you have all been working hard on my behalf. Is your lady too weary to dine in the hall?'

'No, my lord. I believe she went for a walk. I saw her leave the hall and walked towards the area where the craftsmen ply their trades.'

'It is dark now. Surely she would not stay there so late? She must be hungry,' he said.

'Do you think something may have happened to her?'

'Why do you ask? What do you know, woman?' he barked, impolite in his sudden anxiety for Rosamunde.

'It is only… I have noticed the way a certain knight looks at her, my lord. In the past he was known as a vicious bully and it is because he remains here that many of the village people will not offer their labour here in the castle,' Elspeth said hesitantly.

'Of whom do you speak?'

Elspeth's gaze dropped. 'Forgive me—it is of Sir Edmund Roth I speak, my lord. I know it is not my place but I must warn you that he is not to be trusted. More than one village girl has been raped and beaten by that monster.'

'Why did you not tell me this when you first came?' he asked.

'I thought you might have me beaten or send Sir Edmund to punish my family.'

'Is that what my father would have done?' Raphael said a little bitterly, deeply unhappy at this further evidence of the previous Lord Mornay's iniquities.

'Forgive me. There were many injustices carried out in his name, though I cannot say he gave those particular orders,' Elspeth replied.

Raphael inclined his head. 'I thank you for your honesty. Sir Edmund and his friends shall be questioned—but first I must find Rosamunde.'

'Lilia and I will help to look for her,' Elspeth said. 'She spoke of being hungry. I do not think she would have missed her supper.'

'We shall make a search of the castle and outbuildings,' Raphael announced heatedly. 'If she has come to harm, the culprit will pay with his life.'

Turning, Raphael ran down the twisting stair. He could not think that Rosamunde had run away for she'd given her word that she would remain here until he could take her home. Perhaps she had been talking and had forgotten the time—yet he had a cold feeling at his nape, instinct telling him that something was wrong.

If anything had happened to her he did not know what he would do. She had somehow become important to him; he owed her his protection for his honour's sake, but there was more to his feelings than simply honour. He had no time to explore just how he felt, for Rosamunde must be found, but the sense of panic seeping through him told him that he could no longer afford to ignore her future.

He entered the hall, searching for his steward. Mellors might have some idea where she was, and if not a search must be made of the grounds.

'If you look for the lady, sir, I may be able to help you.' Raphael swung round, staring into the face of the knight he had now been warned of three times: by Rosamunde, her serving woman and the mysterious message awaiting him in his chamber the first night of his homecoming. He ignored those warnings at his peril.

'What do you know of her?' he barked at Sir Edmund, his suspicions now thoroughly aroused. 'Have you seen her this evening?'

'It must have been an hour ago, perhaps more. I saw her leaving by the side gate. She was carrying a bundle and seemed anxious not to be seen,' Sir Edmund replied smoothly.

'Why did you not send word to me at once?' Raphael snapped.

'I did not realise at first that it was Rosamunde. I thought perhaps the woman Elspeth was paying a visit to her home in the village, perhaps taking goods that did not belong to her. It was my intention to confront her when she returned, for I had heard of a missing item of silver,' the man said glibly.

'Indeed? If you thought her the culprit, why did you not go after her? I think you lie, sir.' Raphael saw the expression of alarm in the knight's eyes and knew he was right. Raising his voice, he cried out, 'Sir Jonathan—knights to your lord; we have a traitor amongst us.'

'Damn you,' Sir Edmund muttered. 'You and that interfering wench.' He drew a dagger from beneath his tunic and rushed at Raphael. 'You should have died in the Holy Land, as your father believed would happen. He was easily led and we grew rich on the spoils we took in his name. Now you would have us live as paupers.'

Raphael seized his wrist as Sir Edmund attempted to plunge the thin blade into his heart. They tussled for a while, Sir Edmund swearing, his face red with temper as he sought to murder the lord to whom he had so recently sworn allegiance. However, he was a bully who had lived on the fat of the land for years, forcing others to do his bidding and neglecting to train, while Raphael had spent months of hard fighting and continued to train every day. His grip of iron intensified and an oath of pain left the knight's lips as the dagger suddenly went spinning away. Then Raphael's fist connected with his chin and he staggered back into the arms of two burly men-at-arms. Roth's arms were taken and held, though he continued to struggle and spit defiance at his lord.

'You will not find her. Sir Ian has taken what we've stolen and she is…'

'Safe, my lord,' Elspeth's voice called from behind them. 'She is found. Sir Ian feared what had been done and has left the castle in a hurry. When I saw him saddling his horse, I asked where she was and held on to his bridle with all my strength until he told me where to find her. In desperation to be gone before the men discovered his treachery, he cried out that Sir Edmund had bound and gagged her and left her in one of the outhouses. I sent servants to look but it was I that found her.'

Raphael spun round to look at Elspeth, his eyes frantic. 'Where is she now? Is she harmed? And what of Sir Ian?'

'Sir Ian rode off after he told me where to find my lady. I thought it more important to free her than waste time having him apprehended. My lady is well enough and in her chamber changing her gown. She bade me say that she intends to dine in the hall,' Elspeth said with a smile. 'She begs you will go to her at once, for she has much to tell you.'

'I shall deal with you later,' Raphael growled to the prisoner, then glanced at his men. 'Make sure he is confined securely and see he does not escape. There is more to this business and I intend to discover the whole truth.'

Raphael walked swiftly from the hall, taking the steps two at a time as he ran up the twisting stair. He knocked at the door of Rosamunde's chamber. Lilia opened it, moving back to allow him entrance. Rosamunde was seated, having her hair brushed by the old woman Maire, but she dismissed both women as soon she saw him and took the brush herself.

'Forgive me for summoning you, my lord,' she said calmly as she finished brushing her hair. 'I wanted to speak with you in private. I heard something you should know concerning Sir Edmund and Sir Ian: they have been robbing you ever since your father took ill, and this night they plan to steal the key to your strongbox and murder you. It seems they prefer the old ways, and Sir Edmund in particular has been feathering his nest by terrorising your people.'

'How did you learn this?' Raphael demanded, his mouth set grimly.

'Most was from their own lips. I went out to take the air and wandered in the direction of the old wool-shed where I overheard their nefarious plans for you and me. Prior to that, some things I have noticed for myself—and Elspeth also told me that one of your knights has ill-treated village girls. Sir Ian is a coward and spiteful, but obeys

Sir Edmund in everything. It was not hard to piece the puzzle together.'

'Why did you not come to me at once?' he asked hotly.

'I would have done so but they saw me.' She laid down her brush and rose to her feet, turning to meet him. 'Sir Edmund realised that I had overheard them and ran after me. I tried to reach the hall but stumbled and was captured. He dragged me to the outhouse and bound me with ropes. My fate was to be given or sold to Baron Sigmund.'

'Damn them,' Raphael said under his breath and moved towards her. He reached out to touch her cheek, his fingers trembling as he traced the curve of her face, and then ran his thumb over her mouth. 'Roth shall be severely punished, and that knave Sir Ian too, when we catch him. Tell me, has he harmed you in any way? If so, I shall tear him limb from limb on the rack.'

'No, I beg you!' Rosamunde cried. 'I am unharmed apart from being somewhat shaken. Roth is a thief and he would have murdered you, but let him stand his trial and be punished accordingly. I would have no man tortured for my sake.'

'You are as wise and generous as you are beautiful,' Raphael murmured, and moved closer. He bent his head to kiss her, lips gentle and seeking as he explored her sweetness. A shudder went through him and he held her tighter, feeling the sweep of surging desire as she melted into his body. In that moment he finally understood that he could not stand by and watch her wed another man.

'I thought that I could never feel more than fleeting lust for a woman after Messalina died…' A little moan left his lips. 'God forgive me—I want you, Rosamunde. I thought it would be better to let you go, to give you a chance of happiness with a knight who could love you as you should be loved. But you belong to me and I cannot let you go.'

'I belong to no one but myself,' she said tartly, suddenly remembering what Sir Edmund had said. 'Why did you tell Baron Sigmund that you might wed me?'

'It was an impulse, said in order to protect you,' he said.

'Said without my consent,' she retorted, a flash of pure anger in her vivid green eyes. 'Why should I wish to be married to a man who cannot love me?'

'If we wed I would protect and care for you—
and make sure that your father is protected from
his enemies. I care for you as deeply as I am able,
Rosamunde. Do you not think it might be a good
match?' Raphael said persuasively.

'Perhaps. Why can you not love me?' she asked,
gazing up at him. 'And who is Messalina? You
say you want me but...' Her words were hushed
as he took her lips with a fierce passion that had
her swooning against him, her body heated with
desire and trembling, begging, for something she
did not fully understand.

'Messalina was my wife. I cared for her and
ended up betraying her,' Raphael said harshly,
finally drawing away from her with difficulty.
'Because of my neglect she now lies in her grave
and cries out for revenge I cannot give her. How
can I seek happiness in the arms of an innocent
woman when I am guilty of such a sin?'

'I am certain you did not betray her willingly,'
Rosamunde said softly, her eyes never leaving his,
for she felt his agony and her heart went out to
him, even as she flinched from the knowledge
that he had been married already. Despite that, she
wanted to comfort him for his hurt, and wanted

to be with him, to see him every day. 'Whatever happened was not of your doing.'

'You are too generous. But I will admit the sin was of omission. Messalina begged me to stay with her that night. I left her because I wanted to talk and drink with my friends. While I was gone a renegade band attacked her home and killed her and her father—and all but one of their servants.'

'You blame yourself for her death?' Rosamunde asked incredulously.

'I am surely guilty.' Raphael sighed.

'You are guilty of neglect but not of murder,' she said vehemently. 'Have those that committed the crime never been punished?'

'My friends and I sought them, but it was not possible to find the men who murdered and...' He shook his head. 'If I could avenge her, perhaps I should find some peace.'

'You must learn to forgive yourself,' Rosamunde said gently, and smiled. 'Yes, you were somewhat at fault, because you ought to have listened to her concerns—but the rest does not lie at your door.'

'You think she would forgive me?' Raphael asked hopefully.

'If she truly loved you, she would forgive you.

I am sure of it. She would not want you to grieve for ever, my lord,' she said.

'I wish I could believe that.' He held out his hand to her. 'Your hair looks pretty left loose. Shall we dine, lady? The men will have finished long before we join them, for I left orders they should not wait.'

'I am truly hungry,' Rosamunde said, her hand trembling as she allowed him to take it. 'We should show the men that I have not been abducted.'

'They already know it,' he said with a smile. 'I do not know what I am to do with you, lady. You might be safer wed, for your beauty makes you vulnerable. Sir Edmund is not the only man who may seek to take advantage of you.'

'I told you I have no thought of marriage. I have no dowry and cannot expect to wed,' she said firmly.

Raphael was silent for a moment. He knew that he must speak now or lose her. He could *not* lose her! He turned his head to look into her eyes. 'I should be proud to wed you, Rosamunde. I cannot promise to love you as you would have me love you. I may not always be kind—life has made me harsh and sometimes cruel—but I would swear to protect you with my life.'

'When I asked you why you could not love me, it was but an idle question, my lord.' Rosamunde's heart raced wildly. 'My lord, I did not mean to ask—I would not have you feel obliged to offer marriage to me. Also, what you said to Baron Sigmund about wedding me means nothing, for I know it was said only to protect me.'

Raphael smiled oddly. 'Do you imagine I would ask if I did not truly want you?'

'No.' Her breath came in a little gasp. 'No, I think we both knew what we wanted from that first night when you kissed me to punish me...'

'It was not meant to be a punishment,' Raphael denied. 'I was angry with myself for wanting something I thought beyond me. I am not worthy of another chance at marriage, but I would have you to wife, Rosamunde...if you will have me?'

'I... Yes,' she breathed softly, knowing she would never care for another man the way she did for Raphael. 'Give me a little time to accustom myself to the idea—but, yes, when you return from your business I will wed you.'

'Then it is sealed,' he said and raised her hand to

kiss it. 'My dear, I would give you time to accustom yourself to the idea of wedding me if I could, but I think we should announce it in the hall this night—and we shall swear our troth *before* I leave. That way my knights will swear to protect you with their lives and keep you safe until I return. Any man who dares to lay a finger on you will know the consequences.'

'My lord—' she smiled at him '—most of your men are loyal. Now the traitors are unmasked, surely you need not fear for me? Are you indeed certain you wish to wed me?'

'It is the only way I can keep you safe,' he said. 'As my betrothed wife I put my seal on you. Any man who tries to take you from me will know they become my mortal enemy.'

Rosamunde glanced away. Her heart was racing. She had agreed to wed him and she sensed, felt, the passion in him. He wanted her, but he had made it clear that he could never love her. He had obviously loved his wife greatly, but she was in her grave. He was only marrying Rosamunde to protect her. He considered it his duty to care for her and she knew he would keep her safe—but she wanted more from her marriage than that.

Her throat was tight, because she knew that she loved Raphael with all her heart. She had loved the youth that had rescued her kitten and now she understood how much she loved this fierce, stern man.

When she'd thought she would be given to Baron Sigmund and might never see Raphael again, she had realised how much she had come to love him. He did not love her in return, but he wanted her. It would be a marriage much as many others, for advantage and protection. Rosamunde knew that she wanted much more from him, but he had told her his terms plainly. She could only pray that he would find happiness in her arms. Perhaps then he might forgive himself for what happened to his wife—and one day he might come to love Rosamunde as he had Messalina. She could only pray that it would be so, because otherwise her heart might break.

'Forgive me,' Raphael said to his friend later. 'When I gave you permission to court her if you would, I did not understand then that my feelings for her were engaged. I am not worthy of her but the lady hath consented to become my betrothed and when I return we shall be wed.'

'I knew she would not look at me,' Jonathan said with a wry smile. 'I sincerely wish you joy, Raphael, but do not hurt her or you lose my friend-ship.'

'That would give me grief,' Raphael said and grimaced ruefully. 'I think it will pain you to stay here now. I shall be loath to have you leave us, but if you wish to go—'

'After you are wed I shall leave, but for the moment you still need my help,' Jonathan inter-rupted. 'You cannot yet be certain that your fa-ther's knights are all now loyal to you. Two sought to murder and rob you; there may be others who wish you ill. I know you have work on Richard's behalf. While you are gone I will make sure the castle and your lady are secure, then I shall see you wed and bid you farewell.'

'I thank you for your friendship.' Raphael frowned. 'I am not certain what to do about Sir Edmund. Some of what was taken has been re-covered, though Sir Ian must have taken a few of the more valuable items with him.'

'The punishment for what he did is death,' Sir

Jonathan said bluntly. 'What he did to the lady Rosamunde demands that he hang. Your knights expect it and it is the law.'

'Yes, I believe he must be punished. Yet he should have his trial. He may languish in the dungeons and repent his sins; we will deal with him when I return,' Raphael decided.

'In my opinion you should make an example of him now,' Jonathan urged. 'A show of strength is what is needed, Raphael. If you shirk your duty now, the men may think you weak.'

'Very well, bring the men together. He shall be judged by his peers and the sentence carried out immediately.'

'You have made the right decision,' Jonathan said, relieved. 'He would have shown no mercy to you or the lady and therefore he deserves none himself.'

Raphael poured himself a glass of wine and sipped it thoughtfully. He had hoped to show clemency to Sir Edmund. On the occasion of a wedding it was sometimes possible to mitigate a punishment, perhaps exchange a hanging for banishment, but his friend was right. After what Roth had done to Rosamunde, he deserved no less. While Raphael had little stomach for such punishments, Jonathan was also correct in pointing out that his position here was still very uncertain. Raphael could not afford to show weakness or mercy to a man that had betrayed him so foully in more than one way. Had it been simply a matter of theft he might have brushed the crime aside and banished Sir Edmund, but he had laid hands on Rosamunde. He had intended her serious harm and had plotted to murder his lord. For those crimes, Raphael had no choice but to hang him.

'You look beautiful,' Elspeth said as she helped to fasten the necklace of large pearls and garnets about Rosamunde's throat. 'Your betrothal will bring a smile to the men's faces.'

'After the feasting my lord will leave us,' Rosamunde said and sighed, for she knew she would miss him. 'He says that he will return for the feast of Christ's Mass if he can, but he is uncertain how long his mission will take. However, we shall have the wedding to look forward to when he returns.'

She was ready at last, dressed in the best gown she had and wearing the necklace that Raphael had sent up as a betrothal gift; her hair was left loose on her shoulders and held by a band of twisted velvet. Elspeth, Lilia and Maire followed behind as she went down to the hall where the betrothal ceremony was to be held that morning.

'Are you sure you wish for this?' Maire asked her as they saw the assembled men waiting to witness the ceremony. 'You know so little of this man. Supposing he has deceived you? You think him generous and honest, but I do not trust him.'

'You must learn to trust, as I do,' Rosamunde said softly to the old woman and smiled as she saw Raphael standing with Sir Jonathan beside him. 'I care for him and he will protect us—and my father.'

'Be sure of your heart, Rosamunde. Once you are his wife he will own you. You can never be free of him,' Maire warned.

She smiled at her old nurse. 'Today is merely a betrothal, but I long for the day when I am his wife.'

'I can say no more,' Maire said. 'But remember that I warned you.'

Rosamunde did not heed her warning. She walked towards Raphael, her head high and a smile on her lips. He did not love her, but he wanted her and he would care for her and her father. It was more than many young women could expect when they were married. Many were given in loveless unions in exchange for land. Rosamunde had nothing to offer but herself, and she had vowed that she would be everything her husband wanted in his wife. She would care for his home and his people, and she would bear his children. What more she gave would be up to him.

She was trembling inside but gave no sign of it as she took her place at Raphael's side. The priest asked her if she was willing to give her promise to marry and she said that she was. Raphael was asked the same question; he answered in a strong, clear voice and then took her hand, slipping a heavy gold band onto her finger.

'With this ring I plight my troth. I shall wed thee in all honour and protect thee with my life,' he vowed.

Rosamunde tingled with anticipation as he bent his head and kissed her to the accompaniment of roars of approval from the men.

'May I wish you future happiness,' Sir Jonathan said, taking her hand to kiss it. There was an oddly wistful expression in his eyes but she hardly noticed; all her being was focused on Raphael. 'My

lord is entrusting you to my care while he is gone
and I swear to protect you with my life.'

'Thank you, sir.' Rosamunde smiled, her cheeks
a little warm. 'I pray I shall have no need of your
protection, but I thank you just the same.'

'Come, we shall eat and drink with the men,
and then I must leave you,' Raphael said. 'I have
delayed too long already, but now you will be safe
until I return. My friend Jonathan will take good
care of you, as will all my men. You are their lady
now and they honour you.'

Rosamunde made no reply. Her heart was thudding in her chest because the look in his eyes
seemed to promise so much. She wished that this
was her wedding day rather than just a betrothal—
and she wished that her husband would be with
her that night rather than leaving, but she knew
that he must go. His work was important to him
and she would never seek to bind him to her when
he wished to be free.

As the men found places at table, Rosamunde
saw a small party of men-at-arms enter the hall.
One of them went up to Sir Jonathan and whispered something to him.

'Take your place as usual, Rosamunde,' Raphael

said. 'There is something I must see to; it will not take a moment.'

Rosamunde did as she was asked. She saw that Raphael spent a moment or two in conversation with his friend before coming to her. His expression was grim and she wondered what had made him angry.

'Is something the matter, my lord?' she enquired.

'Nothing that need concern you, Rosamunde. It was necessary business—unpleasant but unavoidable.'

Rosamunde did not press for details, but as her gaze travelled about the hall she sensed that a strange atmosphere ensued, almost as if the happy, carefree attitude that had prevailed had been overshadowed. Something had happened that made the men uneasy and she wondered what it could be.

A toast was proposed to her health and the men rose to raise their cups but the cheer was forced and muted. A cold finger trailed down her spine as she saw something new in the faces of the servants: fear.

Why were the servants afraid? She had seen nothing but pleasure in the return of their lord from the Holy Land before this. Now it seemed as if they felt that a dark shadow hung over them, as if they waited for something to happen. What had happened to change things in an instant?

'Something is wrong,' she said and touched Raphael's arm. 'This should be a joyous occasion but the men and the servants—they are uneasy.'

Raphael frowned. 'I did not wish you to know. As you say, this should be a joyous occasion, but Sir Edmund had to be punished. I had to make an example.'

Rosamunde stared at him, feeling suddenly chilled. 'You punished him…how?' she whispered.

'He was tried by his peers and received the lawful punishment,' he said evasively.

'Tell me, please.' Her nails curled into the palms of her hands.

Raphael's lips were tightly compressed as he met her gaze. 'He was condemned to hang and the punishment has been carried out.'

'No!' Rosamunde gasped, shocked and distressed. 'Surely you could have just banished him for life? Hanging is so cruel.'

Raphael's gaze hardened. 'Do not speak of what you do not understand, lady. Sir Edmund was a thief and much worse. Have you no idea of what he planned for you? While he lived, your life would have been in constant danger. His punishment was a warning to others. I protect what is mine.'

Rosamunde felt the gorge rise in her throat. She was simply Raphael's property, like his silver and gold. Her pleasure in the occasion was entirely lost; she could neither eat nor drink for the food would taste of ashes.

'Excuse me, my lord,' she said and rose from the table. 'I—I have a headache and must go to my chamber.'

She walked swiftly from the hall and, when she had left it, ran up to her chamber. Her chest felt tight and she wanted to weep for something precious that had been taken from her. How could he do such a thing on this day of all days? Had it meant anything to him at all, he would have shown leniency to Sir Edmund.

'Rosamunde!' The door of her chamber was thrown back and Raphael entered. He was frowning fiercely, his mouth set in a grim line. 'Why did you leave like that? The men will think it strange that you take no part in the feasting.'

'Tell them I am unwell.' She turned away from

him, fighting her tears. Her chest felt tight and she could scarce breathe for her distress. 'I cannot eat. It would make me vomit.'

'You are angry because of what has happened. Believe me, it was not by my desire this was done. I am recently returned from the Crusades, Rosamunde. Sir Edmund robbed me; he planned to kill me and abduct you. He *had* to be punished severely. If I had only banished him, it would have looked as if I were weak. In my position I have to be strong so that my men understand they must keep my law,' Raphael explained, one hand held out to her as though entreating her to understand.

'Your *father* was a strong man—would you have the people fear you as they feared him? Surely it takes more courage to show mercy than to lash out in revenge?' Rosamunde said pointedly.

Raphael recoiled as if she had struck him, a nerve flickering at his temple. 'My father did things of which I am ashamed. I have neither ravished an innocent woman nor killed a man in anger. Sir Edmund received a fair trial and the judgment of his peers.'

'You kept me here when I wished to return to

my father.' She slung the accusation back at him, her head high, manner haughty.

'For your own sake,' he ground out, his hands now clenched by his sides. 'Surely what happened here showed you the danger you stand in, Rosamunde? You had no one to protect you. Now you are my betrothed and the men know what will happen to them if they try to take you from me. It is the only way to keep you safe.'

'You did that horrible thing for *my* sake?' She put her hands to her face in distress. 'I would not have had it so. Had you asked me, I would have shown clemency.'

'You are but a woman and have a woman's weakness,' he said harshly. 'Come down and join in the feasting. Let my men see that you are pleased to be my betrothed.'

'I cannot smile when I feel so shamed,' she refused hotly. 'You are as bad as the man you condemned to a cruel death. I thought you different, above such petty vengeance—but you arc not the man I thought you.'

Raphael was silent for a moment, then said, 'Very well, I shall tell the men you are unwell.

I am leaving in an hour; it may be many weeks before I return. When I do, I shall take you home.'

'But we are betrothed…' she breathed shakily.

'I dare say a way may be found to break the vows we took,' he said coolly. 'You will remain here until I return and then we shall see what can be done to set us both free from an unwelcome bond.'

With that, he turned and left her. Rosamunde stared after him in despair and then sank to her knees as the tears began to fall.

'No,' she whispered, heartbroken, as she covered her face with her hands. 'I did not mean that—I do not wish to break the vows we took.'

How easily he had agreed to part from her. She was right to think that she was not important to him. He would have wed her had she been meek and acquiesced to his will, but now he would send her away.

It was her own fault for defying him. She had quarrelled with him once too often and he no longer found her desirable. He wanted to break his betrothal vows.

They had meant nothing to him.

Chapter Eight

Raphael did not look back as he rode out of the castle with six of his most trusted men at his back. He was angry because Rosamunde had questioned his actions in the matter of Sir Edmund. Damn the woman, had she no idea of what kind of a villain he'd been? Faced by a jury of his peers, Roth had confessed to the crimes he'd committed—not only those she knew of but also many others committed in the late Lord Mornay's name. He was a thief, rapist and murderer, and had remained unrepentant even when he was taken to be hanged. He had died with a curse on his lips.

The whole incident had left a bad taste in Raphael's mouth. He knew that he had done what was expected of him and no more than was justice under the laws of England. Sir Edmund had thoroughly deserved to be punished. Even had he never tried to abduct Rosamunde, he would still have been given a severe penalty, but she had chosen to feel his death as a stain on her own conscience and there was nothing Raphael could say or do that would ease her burden. God knows, he had felt sick to his stomach as he'd given the order to execute a fellow knight. It was something he would have avoided had it been at all possible, but in this case there were no mitigating circumstances, nothing to excuse the behaviour of a knight whose crimes would sicken any decent man.

He'd had no choice. Raphael forced the shadow from his mind. He was a just man and punished transgressions as lightly as possible, but there were times when there was no alternative. Rosamunde had showed her disgust of him plainly. If she had felt more for him than a passing fancy he had surely killed it. He should have sent her straight back to her cousin with the ransom and forgotten her.

Caring made a man weak. Raphael knew that the struggle for England was only just beginning. Prince John would not give up the power he had abused lightly and, if he could, would see his brother dead rather than restored to the throne.

Raphael had heard of men who felt as he did, that every effort must be made to bring Richard back before it was too late. He could not be swayed from his task by the reproachful look in *her* beautiful eyes.

Raphael had left the castle. Rosamunde's throat tightened as Maire brought her the news. Until the last moment she'd hoped that he might return and take her in his arms. It was her fault they'd parted on bad terms. She knew that she'd said terrible things to him; she had regretted them almost as soon as they had left her lips. Raphael was *not* like his father and she knew it. It had just been such a shock to her that he could order the execution on a day that was meant to be joyous. Also, the fact that Sir Edmund had been hanged because of what he'd done to her made her feel guilty, as if in some way she'd caused his death.

After a restless night, Rosamunde rose and went down to the courtyard. She saw that some of the men were already training; the craftsmen were at their benches intent on their work, and the servants were carrying water and baskets of food up to the men on the ramparts. It seemed that life went on as usual now that Raphael was gone, except that her heart felt as if it had been torn apart.

'My lady, I hope you are feeling better this morning?'

Rosamunde turned to see Sir Jonathan watching her. He looked concerned, as if he understood her distress.

'Good morning, sir. Thank you, I feel a little better. I wanted some air,' she told him.

'Perhaps we could ride together later? We might take the hawks out if it would give you pleasure. Raphael charged me to take good care of you, lady. If there is aught you need, you have only to ask,' he said.

'You are very kind, sir. I think I should like to go foraging with my ladies, if you will arrange an escort. I would see what more the woods and hedgerows have to offer for the stillroom. I have noticed that some of the men have small ailments that I might cure. Once I have the recipes made, I will hear their complaints in the hall.'

Rosamunde knew that she needed to keep busy. Raphael might be away for some weeks and unless she could find some occupation she would not be able to bear it. She must do what she could to fill the shelves with preserves, make cures for simple ailments and see that sufficient meat was salted for the winter. It was the kind of work that would have filled her time had she been at home with her father—so why did the future suddenly seem empty and bleak?

She could not hide from herself. Her heart had been given to Raphael for some time now, perhaps from the very first night when he had kissed her and her body had gone weak with longing. Of course, she had loved him when she had been but a child, and her memory of him had remained bright. He had been a chivalrous youth then. Now he was a battle-hardened man and in her heart she knew he'd had no choice but to administer the punishment to Sir Edmund that his men had demanded.

Why had she been foolish enough to quarrel with him? She had let him go believing that she cared nothing for him when all the time her heart was breaking for love of him. Looking up, she saw an expression of understanding in Sir Jonathan's eyes.

'I shall arrange a foraging trip for you,' he said, his gaze narrowed, thoughtful. 'You should not blame Raphael for what was done, my lady. Sir Edmund confessed to his many heinous crimes but he did not repent at all; rather he bragged of them and went defiantly to meet his maker.'

'I know that the punishment meted out to him was just,' Rosamunde admitted. 'But that a man should die because of me…' She shuddered. 'I would not have had it happen so.'

'It was wrong of Sir Edmund to try to abduct you and to rob his lord, but he also tried to stab Raphael to death—and he admitted to other crimes of murder and theft against the people. Raphael had no choice but to punish him according to the law,' Jonathan revealed.

'Yes, I see that now,' Rosamunde said. She smothered a little sob. 'I accused my lord of terrible things. Do you think he will forgive me?'

'In time the hurt will ease,' Jonathan said. 'Raphael has suffered much. The death of his wife haunted him for months, because he blamed himself for leaving her the night she was killed. When you came here those who love him felt that perhaps he would learn to be happy again. We still hope for it, lady.'

'He was very angry when he left here,' she whispered.

'Yes, he was angry. Your accusations wounded him. Do not imagine it was easy for him to give the order for Sir Edmund's execution. He is a fair man, and merciful whenever it is possible.'

'I should have understood that,' Rosamunde said. She hesitated, then asked, 'Do you know how long he intends to be away?'

'I believe he travels to the north to speak with important men. I cannot tell you how long his business will take, lady. I would say several weeks at least. It is November now and I shall be surprised if he returns much before Christ's Mass— though I am certain he will return to spend that joyous festival with us if he can.'

Rosamunde swallowed hard. It seemed she must wait at least seven weeks or more before she saw Raphael again. For a moment she considered asking Sir Jonathan to take her home, but then she realised that if she left now she might never see the man she loved again—and that was more than she could bear. She must wait in patience for his return and in the meantime she would work hard to fill her days.

'Thank you. I must not keep you from your work. I shall instruct my ladies that we go foraging. If you will arrange the escort for after we have broken our fast I should be grateful,' Rosamunde said and then walked away, her eyes stinging with tears which she refused to allow to fall.

'Why have you come to me?' Baron Sigmund's gaze narrowed as he looked at the knight who had arrived alone and looked as if he had not slept in days. 'Why have you deserted Lord Mornay?'

'It was Sir Edmund's idea that we should offer our swords to you, my lord. He tired of the new Lord Mornay's dictates and wanted the old ways again. The new lord is not popular with his men and they think him a tyrant. We spoke against him and he ordered our arrest. We decided to leave his service, and Sir Edmund planned to bring you a gift that would please you, but I fear that his plans went awry. I waited in the woods to meet him as we agreed, but he did not come. I fear he was discovered and may be imprisoned or dead,' Sir Ian said.

'Sir Edmund is dead?' Baron Sigmund frowned. 'What did he do to arouse Mornay's wrath? And what was the gift he planned to bring me?'

'His only crime was to speak out against unfairness, my lord. I believe he meant to bring you the lady Rosamunde. She was being held against her will and would have left willingly,' the knight lied.

The baron's eyes gleamed. 'Now, that would have been a gift worth having. What makes you think Edmund is dead?'

'I ventured near to the castle under cover of darkness and—' Sir Ian swallowed hard '—I heard a detachment of men talking of his trial as they patrolled the ramparts. They were jesting, laughing and taking bets against the outcome and his punishment.'

'Sir Edmund is my kinsman,' Sigmund said. 'He was the eldest son of my mother's brother and his second wife. I offered him a place here but he was feathering his nest well in the old Lord Mornay's service. If he is dead it means a blood feud between our two families. Sir Raphael gave his bond and I gave mine—but if my cousin has been foully slain that is all at an end.'

'I dare not re-enter the castle to discover the outcome, for I might have been taken too. I thought it best to come to you, my lord,' Sir Ian said.

'You did well, Sir Ian. You may enter my service if you will. But learn this now: I do not suffer traitors gladly. If I discover you have lied to me, I shall show you no mercy.'

Sir Ian bowed low, hiding his look of satisfaction. He had not even stopped to look back as he made his escape, let alone return to the castle, but he thought his lies lent colour to his story. The baron might not have taken him in if he'd known that he had deserted his kinsman, leaving Sir Edmund to sink or swim alone. Nor would the baron offer him service here if he knew that Sir Ian had stolen precious items from his overlord. His tale was nothing but lies, but there was no one here to disprove them. If Sir Edmund escaped and came here, they would stick to their story, but if he were dead Baron Sigmund would take his revenge on Sir Raphael. That suited him very well. He knew all the secrets of Mornay's castle and for certain considerations would share them with the baron.

Rosamunde spent the next few days working in the stillroom, making cures for simple ailments that she'd learned from her mother. There were lotions to cleanse festering wounds, balms to ease soreness and itching—which was a common complaint—and mixtures to help sickness and fever or a sore throat.

After the preparations were complete, she told Mellors that she was ready to treat any man in the castle who had an ailment that bothered him. For most of one day she and her women dispensed cures to the men-at-arms and the servants, many of whom had nasty rashes and blistered skin.

She talked to Elspeth afterwards, and they decided that the rashes might be caused by flea bites. The next day an inspection was made of all the bedding in the castle. Mattresses were dragged out and burned, linen and blankets taken to vats to be washed by servants and new straw provided for fresh pallets.

'I think it is years since the bedding was changed,' Mellors said. 'Some of the men may have found new bedding for themselves, but most did not bother.'

'In future the men are ordered to cleanse themselves all over at least once a week,' Rosamunde announced. 'And the linen will be washed once a week in summer and once a month in winter. The mattresses will be renewed every year in the spring. It should help to ease the discomfort suffered by so many of the men.'

'You have turned the household upside down,' Mellors told her with a nod of approval. 'Many of the men come from poor families and do not realise that keeping themselves and their clothes clean can bring benefits to their health. They are born in the villages and are used to sharing their homes with their pigs and goats.'

'In the winter it is often the only way to keep warm for many families,' Rosamunde agreed. 'We should lead by example, Mellors. If the men notice a lessening in their discomfort, they may decide it is worth a little extra trouble.'

'You are certainly an example to others,' the steward told her admiringly. 'You have scarcely stopped working since you came here.'

'It is my pleasure to be busy,' Rosamunde replied. 'We shall begin to salt meat for the winter months now. It will give us employment for a few days and keep us from going short of food when the huntsman cannot find game and the ground is frozen.'

She did not add that the only way she could get through the days was to work. Yet the days were only a part of her problem. Her nights were spent tossing and turning in her bed, tortured by the memory of what had passed between them the last time she had spoken to Raphael. She had been in distress and her words were harsh. She had hurt him with her accusations and her coldness towards him. Since then she had never ceased to wish that she could take back the angry words. Each day seemed longer than a week and she counted them dearly, longing for his return.

What would he say to her when he eventually returned? Would he still wish to break the vows they had taken?

Sometimes when she lay in bed she feared that she would never see Raphael again. Where was he? What was he doing, and did he ever think of her?

Why could he not put the wench from his mind and be done with it? Raphael swore as he paced the floor of his chamber. The night seemed long and, as ever when he was alone, his thoughts had turned to Rosamunde. He was staying with a lord loyal to the King and had been assured of his assistance. Baron Essien was the descendent of a Saxon thane, but his family had intermarried with the lords of Normandy and he had become rich and powerful in this part of the country.

'I shall bring a dozen lords and their followers with me when the time comes,' he had promised. 'As soon as Richard returns we shall rise for him, and Prince John's tyrants will be arrested and thrown out of office.'

'I have heard of an outlaw in these parts,' Raphael had said. 'He is called Rob-in-Hood by some, because he lives in the forest of Sherwood and wears the chaperone and clothes of the peasants and serfs. But some say he is in truth Robin, Earl of Loxley. If this is true, he is a man I once knew. He served Richard well and I cannot believe he has become a thief and murderer, as the prince would have him.'

'I cannot say either way,' Baron Essien had said and frowned. 'I have heard that such a man exists and that he robs anyone foolish enough to venture into the forest. It is not the first time tales of this nature have spread amongst the common folk, but who can tell if there is truly such a man in Sherwood Forest?'

'It was in my mind to travel that way as I return home,' Raphael had mentioned casually.

'I would think that foolish,' the baron had said. 'But it is your choice. You may lose your gold and your armour, for I've heard that this man uses many tricks to prey on the unwary.'

'Yet, if he is indeed the Earl of Loxley, he might help us when the time comes. Richard will need all the support he can muster, for otherwise the prince may prevail. He has his own men in positions of power throughout England and Richard will have only a small escort when he arrives,' Raphael had pointed out.

'Men will rally to him from all parts of the land. We are all heartily sick of Prince John's tyranny,' the baron had replied.

Raphael ceased his restless pacing. He had rallied support in the areas he considered the prince's stronghold and the words he'd heard from various lords had been reassuring. If most kept their word, the King would be welcomed on his return—yet still there was a chance that Richard might be murdered before his lords could rally to him. If this

outlaw existed, and was merely a thief and a murderer, as the prince had named him, Raphael might
never see his home again. But it would be worth
the risk to speak with him. If he were indeed the
man Raphael hoped, then only good could come of
it. He would venture alone into the forest, sending
his men on ahead of him by another route.

Would *she* miss him if anything happened to
him? A wry smile touched his mouth. She had a
fiery temper when roused, but then so did he. They
had exchanged harsh words before he'd left—but
she was his betrothed, and this separation had
shown Raphael that he could not contemplate a
future without her.

He had no intention of giving her up to another
man. If she wished to break the vows she had
given, she must take the opportunity to run away
while he was absent. Yet even then he knew he
would go after her and bring her back. For good
or evil, Rosamunde had taken root in his heart,
and he did not intend to lose her.

'Is it wise to ride alone into the forest, my lord?'
Janquil asked, looking at him with dark, anxious
eyes. 'Let me come with you, to protect your back.'

'You must go with the others,' Raphael told him. 'If I do not keep the appointment with you that we have agreed on, you must presume the worst and go on to my castle. Swear to me that if that happens you will protect my lady.'

'I swear that I will give my life for hers if need be,' Janquil vowed.

'Then I am content,' Raphael said and placed a hand on his shoulder. 'Do not look so downcast, my friend. I am certain nothing will happen to me.'

'The lady would break her heart if you were killed, my lord.'

'Would she? I wonder.' Raphael shook his head. 'If what I've heard is true, there is nothing to fear. Go with the others now and do not give up hope, for truly I bear a charmed life.'

Janquil bowed his head, turned his horse and rode to join the other men. At the crossroads they parted. Raphael was to ride alone into the heart of a forest some thought haunted, and others said was inhabited by a band of outlaws.

Weak sunlight was filtering through the canopy. Raphael saw a woodlark high above trilling its song and heard noises in the undergrowth as small animals went about their business. All seemed peaceful and quiet, no sign of either evil spirits or outlaws. He was beginning to think that the tales were all a myth when a missile thudded into a tree trunk just to the side of him. As he gentled his startled horse, he heard bloodcurdling cries and then he was surrounded by men, several of whom held bows, the arrows trained on him.

'I come in peace,' he said. 'If you are Robin Hood's men, I would have words with him.'

'Bring him down,' one of the men said and the other men flung themselves at his horse, hands grabbing him and hauling him to the ground where he lay for a moment looking up at them.

'This is foolish,' Raphael said. 'I come in peace to speak with your leader on a matter of importance.'

'Tie him and take his horse and gold,' the man who appeared to be their leader said. 'We'll leave him here for his friends to find.'

'No, let's take him with us. Blindfold him. Robin may wish to speak with him,' another said.

'Nay, 'tis a trick to find our camp. We'll take what he has and leave him here,' the leader replied.

'No! I have no friends nearby and if you bind me

I shall die here.' Raphael struggled, throwing off three of the men that were attempting to hold him. He hit out with his fists but then a crushing blow from behind sent him senseless to the ground.

'We should go to look for my lord,' Janquil said as the men debated what to do. The appointed time had passed and Raphael had not come to meet with them. 'If we ride on now, he may be injured or dying and alone in the forest. We should look for him.'

'His orders were to wait here one day only and then ride on to Mornay,' Sir James reiterated. 'Raphael would be angry if he returned to the castle and we were still out searching for him. He may have other plans.'

'Aye, we should obey his orders,' one of the others said. 'Our duty now is to the castle and the lady Rosamunde. Sir Jonathan will decide if a search party should return to look for him.'

'It may be too late then,' Janquil warned. 'I think my lord is in danger. I shall go alone if you will not come with me.'

'Lord Mornay ordered you to serve his lady,' Sir

James growled. 'You gave your word—will you break it now?'

Janquil stared at him. Torn between his loyalty to his lord and the promise he had given, his anguish was plain to see. 'What of my lord?' he finally wailed.

'Raphael can look after himself. We should obey his orders or he will be most angry. If he is dead, it will be harder to defend the castle. His enemies will strike quickly and try to take it from us. This is why my lord wished us to return. Without him, the castle needs a leader and will be vulnerable. We must expect attacks,' Sir James explained.

'We go on,' the men said in a murmur of agreement.

Janquil saw they would not be swayed. Alone, he would be of little use to Raphael. He was not a fighting man and his skills were to blend into the background, watch and wait. He had promised Raphael that he would protect the lady and it might be that he could be of more use to his lord at the castle.

Reluctantly, he rode at the back of the small train, feeling as if his heart were being torn from his body. Instinct told him that his lord was in terrible danger but alone there was little he could do but pray to his god that his master would return safely.

Rosamunde tasted the wine they had made from elderflowers and smiled as Elspeth poured it into flasks. As the days and weeks had passed, she had come to like and trust the woman's judgment, knowing that she had found a true friend. Life here was good. If only Raphael would return.

'It has a pleasant flavour. The herb you added has given it more taste. I should not have thought of it,' Rosamunde remarked.

'It was a recipe Lady Mornay loved. I helped her many times to prepare various wines. In a few weeks this will have matured and be stronger, but it is refreshing on the tongue when first made,' Elspeth said.

'Do you know if Lady Mornay had a journal of her recipes? I should very much like to have it, for I am certain it could teach me much.'

'I do not know, my lady. Perhaps it might be amongst my lady's things. You should ask Mellors.'

'Yes, I shall, for I should like to see it. Indeed,

I should have liked to know my lord's mother,' Rosamunde murmured.

'She was a lovely…' Elspeth's words died away as the door of the stillroom opened and Lilia came rushing in. 'Be careful you do not knock something over. Whatever is the matter, daughter?'

'The men are returned,' Lilia said. She looked at Rosamunde, distress in her eyes. 'Lord Mornay is not with them. I heard them say that he may be dead—killed by outlaws in Sherwood Forest.'

'Killed?' Rosamunde swayed, her heart catching with pain. 'How can this be? Where are the men? I must speak with them immediately.'

'In the hall, my lady,' Lilia said and looked frightened. 'Forgive me. I thought you would wish to know.'

'The foolish girl, to come prattling to you,' Elspeth said and frowned at her daughter. 'You should rest, my lady. Mellors can bring the news when he knows more.'

'No, I must hear it from the men immediately,' Rosamunde said. She ran from the room where the preserves and cures were made and stored, and through a long, covered walkway to the great hall. The sound of uproar met her ears even before she entered as men cried out and pressed for details. As she entered the sound died away to a whisper and then absolute silence as the men turned to look at her

'Who brings the news?' she asked clearly and two of the men stepped forward. 'Where is my lord? If he was killed, who else was hurt?'

'None, my lady,' one of them answered her. 'He rode alone into the forest to meet with outlaws. We were to have met at an appointed time but he did not come to the meeting. His instructions were to return home to guard you and the castle if he did not come.'

'Did no one go to look for him?' she asked, raising incredulous eyebrows.

'We obeyed his orders, lady.'

'How could you leave him to die alone?' she cried accusingly. 'We must send a detachment to look for him.'

'I fear it may be too late,' Mellors said. He looked to Sir Jonathan for instructions. 'What say you, my lord?'

'I think we must send volunteers to look for him,' Jonathan said. 'I would go myself, but Raphael charged me particularly with the care of his castle and his lady. Step forward, five men who are willing to return and search for their lord.'

Several men including Janquil stepped forward. Sir Jonathan called out the names of the chosen five. 'Not you, Janquil. We need fighting men for this task. You may play your part if Raphael is wounded or ill.'

'How long will it take to return and look for him?' Rosamunde asked, her eyes dark with anxiety.

''Tis but two days' journey, my lady, but the men may need several days to make a search. Had I been with him, I should not have left without making that search—but the men obeyed their orders and I cannot punish them for doing their duty,' Jonathan said.

'I too would not have them punished,' she said, tears stinging her eyes. 'It was my lord's choice to go alone into the forest. He risked his own life but wished to protect the others.'

'It was ever the same when we were fighting in the Holy Land,' Jonathan said. 'He saved my life and that of others more than once.'

'So we must stay here as he bid us until we know

whether…' Rosamunde could not continue and, turning, fled from the hall.

She ran up the twisting stairs to her room, securing the latch from inside as the tears fell. She had hoped that he might return in time to spend Christ's Mass with them, for it was but a week away, but now she was not certain that he would ever return. He must. He must, for she could not bear it if they never met again. Surely fate could not be so cruel? She had parted from Raphael in anger and now he might be dead or dying of his wounds.

If she were never to see him again, she did not think she would wish to live.

'You must have courage, lady,' Janquil said. He had found her wandering alone in the cloisters by the chapel and come up to her silently. 'I feel my lord is alive. He is a brave warrior. Even if he died he would not wish you to weep too long.'

'You love him too,' Rosamunde said. 'I know you must be blaming yourself for not going back to search for him.'

'The men would not disobey his orders and alone there was little I could do. His last words to me were to watch over you, my lady. I have done as he asked, but like you I grieve.'

'Yes.' Rosamunde lifted her head, forcing a smile. *Let him return for Christ's Mass. Please, God, let him return to me.* 'These past three days have been almost unbearable. I do not know...' She broke off as she saw Elspeth running towards them and her heart stood still. 'There is news. Pray God he is alive.' Hurrying to meet the other woman, Rosamunde's throat was tight with fear. 'What have you heard?'

'All is well, my lady,' Elspeth said and now Rosamunde could see that she was laughing. 'It is wonderful news—my lord hath returned and he brings company. A friend from the Holy Land.'

Rosamunde was overwhelmed by such a wave of relief that she felt weak. Tears rushed to her eyes and she turned and fled towards the hall. Entering, she saw that the huge room was filled with men and the noise of their cheering and laughter made her hesitate. She saw Raphael in the midst of them but suddenly felt unsure, so she turned away and ran up the stairs to her own room. There she sank down on the edge of her bed, silent tears trickling down her cheeks.

Raphael was home but would he wish to see her? Or would he send her back to her father's house? She had said such terrible things to him. She could not blame him if he did not wish to see her again.

'Where is my lady?' Raphael asked of his steward once the men had dispersed to their various tasks. 'I would introduce her to my friend, the Earl of Loxley.'

'I would think she might be in her chamber, my lord. Would you have me send for her?'

'No, I shall go myself. Make sure that our guests have all they want, Mellors. We must dine well this night for it is a celebration!' Raphael laughed.

'We all thought you dead, my lord. The men will indeed wish to celebrate,' Mellors said.

'It was unfortunate that the men brought such news, but I was taken captive, and it was a day or so before my friend returned to the camp and told his men to set me free,' he explained.

'We must thank God that he did, my lord.'

Raphael nodded. He had indeed taken a great risk but his instincts had proven right and all was well. 'Excuse me, Loxley,' he said to his old comrade. 'I must speak with the lady Rosamunde. I shall see you later.'

Raphael left the hall, put his foot on the bottom stair and then ran lightly up the deep stone steps of the tower. Why had Rosamunde not come to the hall to greet him? Was she still angry? Had she hoped that he would not return?

Pausing outside her door, he knocked. A voice that was hardly more than a whisper bid him enter. He did so and saw her standing there, head up, proud and beautiful. Yet he sensed her uncertainty and saw the signs of tears on her face. His heart caught and he felt something; a deep need to comfort and protect swept through him.

'Forgive me,' he said. 'I said such terrible things to you before I left. Believe me, I have regretted that we parted in anger.'

'It was *my* fault, not yours,' Rosamunde answered and took an uncertain step towards him. She was trembling, her heart racing as she met his searching gaze. 'I know that you were right regarding Sir Edmund's punishment. You did what you had to do—and you are not unjust or cruel. I said harsh things to you and I beg you to forgive me.'

'There is nothing to forgive, sweet lady. What you said struck me to the heart, because I would have shown mercy if it were possible. Even though he would have murdered us both without hesitation, it pained me to have Sir Edmund hanged. It should not have happened on such a day; our betrothal was meant to be a joyous occasion,' Raphael said regretfully. 'It was my only option as I was leaving that day on my business.'

'You will forgive me?' Rosamunde moved closer, looking up at him, tears hovering on her lashes. 'When I thought you might not return...' She choked and could not continue. 'You will not send me away?'

'No tears, Rosamunde,' Raphael said and stroked her cheek with his fingers. 'I am sorry that you were made anxious by news that should never have reached you, but it could not be helped. I was missing and the men feared the worst.'

'They should not have left you. Janquil begged them to return and look for you, but they said they must obey their orders,' she said crossly.

He smiled. 'They did as I wished them to do. Had they come in search of me, they might all have been killed. Half of Loxley's men were for leaving me tied up in the woods. They thought I was an enemy, in league with men who have sworn to hang Robin. Had a band of armed men come tramping through the forest, I think they would have killed us all. Loxley tells me it is because the Shire Reeve of Nottingham has tried all manner of tricks to trap him—and the last two men to be captured by his men were tortured and executed before he could aid them.'

'The men said you were captured by outlaws.'

'Rob-in-Hood and his men *are* outlaws, but the Earl of Loxley is loyal to the King. He breaks the law in order to protect the poor from the outrages of Prince John's tax collectors. I sought him out because we are of like mind in this—Richard must be brought home so that this tyrant and his henchmen no longer oppress the people. Their plight is terrible. The tax collectors often take all they have and they are left to starve. The King must return soon or England will be in flames. This situation cannot be allowed to continue,' Raphael said passionately.

'Yes, it is what all loyal Englishmen and women must wish for,' Rosamunde said. 'Have you brought the earl to visit with you?'

'He and two of his men escorted me here. We took longer because we called on other men of influence Robin knows whom we hoped would join us.'

'You do not need to explain your actions to me. I am simply glad that you are safe home again,' she murmured.

'Is that truly how you feel? You do not hate me?' he asked eagerly.

'I could never hate you,' Rosamunde replied, her cheeks slightly flushed now.

She wanted to tell him that her feelings for him were much stronger than mere liking. She had loved him since their very first meeting and, despite their quarrel, her feelings had grown stronger in his absence. She had feared she might never see him again and that had made her realise just how much he meant to her. Rosamunde knew now that she could bear anything other than to be forced to leave him.

'Then we shall arrange the wedding as agreed?' he said.

'Yes.' She caught her breath as he moved in closer. He reached out for her and she gave her lips sweetly, her body melding with his as he held her near and looked down at her. 'It is my true and honest wish.'

'I am glad of it, for I have already spoken to your father.'

'You have seen my father?' she exclaimed.

'I called at your home on my way here, briefly, but long enough to see that all is well. Beth has the house and furniture gleaming with polish, and her husband has acquired pigs, sheep and a cow, besides hens, ducks and geese. Next year the harvest will ensure that there is bread for all, but for the moment he has bought flour and supplies, which are well hidden from the tax collector.' Raphael grinned.

'My father received you?' she gasped. 'Was he well?'

'He was in bed but able to see me and thanked me for sending Beth and Ferdie to care for him and the land. He is well pleased with the promise you made them, and assures me he has no objection to our marriage.'

'How could Ferdie have done so much so soon?' Her eyes narrowed in speculation. 'You gave him money to buy stock, did you not?'

'He has served me well and deserved it,' Raphael

said. 'Had I not given him a start, their first year or so would have been hard indeed. As it is, they are thriving. He has been able to employ more men so that they can protect themselves against the tax collectors.'

'Which means my father is cared for and has no financial worries,' Rosamunde said with relief. 'You have been more than generous, my lord.'

'It would not do to have my wife's father living in poverty,' Raphael said, his expression giving nothing away. 'Ferdie is a strong man and used to fighting. I do not think the tax collectors will rob him, as they did your father. It will not be long now before Richard is home and there is an end to this tyranny.'

'It cannot come soon enough for the people. We have had beggars at our door these past few days. Some of them were freemen who farmed their own strips and paid their dues to their lord in labour two days a week. They could not afford the new taxes the prince imposed and lost everything. One man told me that his wife and young son had died of a fever after being forced to the road in search of work. We gave him food, and a day's work helping the thatcher, but many were too ill to work. We did what we could for them before they travelled on,' Rosamunde told him.

'We shall continue to give where we can,' Raphael said. 'But there is no justice in England and will be none until Richard is home again.'

'I shall pray the King comes soon.'

Raphael bent his head, kissing her softly. 'You must wash your face and then come down, Rosamunde. I would have you meet my friends and celebrate my return. In three days we must begin to celebrate Christ's Mass—and for that we must bring in greenery and make a kissing bough.'

'Yes, that would be wonderful. It is years since I celebrated in that way,' she said excitedly.

'The men deserve a feast and we shall give them one.' He smiled and touched her cheek. 'You will come down and join us?'

'Yes, I shall come in a moment,' she said.

She stood for a moment, staring at the door as he closed it behind him. She was happy to have him back and pleased that they had made up their quarrel, but nothing had changed.

Raphael still wished to marry her, but he needed a chatelaine for his castle and a mother for his sons. He perceived her as worthy to be his second wife, but he had said nothing to her of love.

It might be that he would never love her as he'd loved his first wife. Rosamunde would have to accept what he gave, because she knew now that she loved him too much to walk away.

Chapter Nine

The men were in merry mood that night, singing and stamping their feet in approval when Raphael introduced his friend the Earl of Loxley. Rosamunde was surprised at how simply the earl dressed, but Raphael explained that he had adopted the clothes and lifestyle of a peasant in order to live in the forest and visit Nottingham without being noticed.

'The earl has sent a large sum of money to help meet Richard's ransom, as have others who want him home. Everything is in place now, but we must be on our guard, for Prince John may try to capture or kill Richard as soon as he steps foot on English soil,' Raphael said.

'Would he really dare to raise his hand against the rightful king?'

'No doubt his rogues would be well disguised.

John might even try to blame outlaws if he succeeded.'

'I believe that the common folk would rise to protect their king if they knew he was in danger,' Rosamunde remarked.

'Yes, but they have no weapons and are not trained in warfare. It is men of standing that are needed. Once Richard has an army at his back, the prince will be forced to bend his knee and protest that all he wanted was his brother's return,' Raphael declared.

Rosamunde nodded and Raphael turned to speak to the earl, who was sitting in the place of honour at his other hand. Her eyes travelled round the hall, noting that the smiles were back in place and all was as it had been. The shadow of Sir Edmund's hanging had completely passed.

'My friend has expressed a wish to fly the hawks tomorrow,' Raphael said as he turned back to Rosamunde. 'We may also hunt in the woods with dogs for wild boar. I think that perhaps it is best if you do not come this time. I promise I will take you another time.'

'I enjoyed hawking, but I should not care for boar hunting,' Rosamunde agreed. 'In any case, we shall be busy preparing sweetmeats for the feast. Do not concern yourself on my account, my lord.'

'I have arranged for the banns to be called for the first time this Sunday. After our wedding we could journey to your home to visit your father,' he suggested.

'Yes, I should like that,' Rosamunde said and sipped her wine. Her heart raced but she gave no sign of the turmoil his words aroused in her.

She longed to be his wife and yet she was apprehensive. Just what did he expect of her?

The following day, the women had just finished preparing the little almond cakes that were such a treat at this time, and mincemeat tarts with nuts and dates added to the mixture, when the door opened and Lilia entered. She was clearly anxious and looked from her mother to Rosamunde before speaking.

'My lord and the men have returned from the forest. One of the men has been badly gored by a wild boar and two others are slightly hurt. My lord asks if you will attend them, my lady.'

'Yes, of course I shall,' Rosamunde said immediately. 'Run up to my chamber, Lilia, and bring rolls of linen. We shall need it to bind the injured man's wounds—also balms and moss for healing.'

'I know where the moss grows,' Elspeth said. 'I shall go to fetch what we need, my lady. It is best applied to a wound fresh, especially if the wound has been cauterised.'

'I shall go to my lord and see what has been done,' Rosamunde agreed. 'Bring the moss to me as soon as you have it.'

The three women dispersed, each to their appointed task. Rosamunde discovered the men in the hall. Raphael was bending over one of the men, who lay writhing on the floor. Someone had placed a mattress and linen on the floor and a hot iron had been brought. She heard the patient's scream of agony as Raphael applied it to the wound, burning out the poison from the beast's fangs and sealing the wound. The sound of the poor wretch's screams was pitiful but it was the way such wounds had to be treated and was in the patient's best interest. After a moment or two he fell silent and she knew that he had fainted from the pain.

Approaching, she saw that the man was stripped

to the waist; there was a deep gash in his side where he had been gored, also gashes to his arm and hands.

'Elspeth has gone to fetch moss that will help heal his deep wound,' Rosamunde said. 'If you will allow me, I shall bind the other wounds and apply a healing balm.'

'Yes, that may ease him a little,' Raphael said and made way for her.

Rosamunde knelt by the man's side, applying soothing creams to his arms and hands and binding them with the strips of linen Lilia had brought. As she was finishing, Elspeth came hurrying in with the soft, wet moss she had gathered which Rosamunde then packed around the deep wound. Together, they bound him around his body, their work finishing just as his eyelids fluttered and he moaned in pain.

'Could you lift him for me?' Rosamunde asked and Raphael lifted the patient gently in his arms while she held a small flask to the man's lips. 'Drink a little of this, sir. It will ease you.'

The man's lips parted and he swallowed obediently. He was then allowed to lie back against the straw pillow someone had provided, his eyes closing.

'He will be easier now. Who else needs attention?' she asked.

Two more men came forward. Both had slight gashes, one to his hands, the other to his leg. None were deep, and after balm and linen had been applied they took themselves off to join their comrades.

'What happened?' Rosamunde asked.

It was not often that this kind of accident happened during a hunt. The huntsman was experienced and usually applied a swift blow to kill a wounded beast quickly.

'The dogs cornered the boar,' Raphael said. 'It had been shot by an arrow but was not dead. We thought the arrow had delivered the deathblow but, when the huntsman approached to slit its throat, it got up and attacked him. The other men went to his help but it was too late to save him from being badly injured.'

'Hunting is dangerous,' Rosamunde said. 'I know that a wounded boar can kill. It happened to one of my father's men some years ago, but he was too badly gored to save. I have hope that your man will live.'

'His wound has been dealt with but he may develop a fever.' Raphael frowned. 'The man that shot the boar was certain he had killed it, but he did not hit the right spot. He should have fired again. His carelessness could have led to this huntsman's death.'

'Will he be punished?' she asked.

'I shall have to discipline him,' Raphael said. 'In a hunt we all rely on one another. No man should allow pride to cloud his judgment.'

'No, I suppose not,' Rosamunde said and turned away. She felt that it must have been an accident but would not voice her opinion. It was not for her to interfere with Raphael's decisions.

'If there is nothing more, my lord, I shall return to my chamber. We have been working most of the day and I wish to change my gown.'

'Yes, of course,' Raphael said. 'We both have work to do, my lady.'

'Lilia will watch over our patient. If she needs me she can fetch me, but he will sleep for some hours before he needs to be tended again.'

Leaving the hall, Rosamunde walked upstairs to

her chamber. She wondered what punishment the negligent man would receive and hoped it would not cast a shadow over the castle this time.

'You admit that your careless aim caused Boris to approach the boar too soon?'

'Yes, my lord,' Eric answered, his head downcast. 'I thought it was shot through the eye but I missed and the boar was not fatally injured; my arrow merely went through its ear and pierced its skin at the side of the head.'

'What should you have done?' Raphael asked calmly.

'I should have warned Boris and shot again, or let others shoot it instead of claiming the kill.'

'It is fortunate that Boris was not fatally wounded or your punishment might have been even more severe.' Raphael looked at him gravely. 'What do you think should be your punishment?'

'I should be whipped and dismissed from your service, my lord.'

'How would that benefit Boris?'

'I do not know, sir. It is the punishment men are usually given for making such a mistake.'

'I do not think it would serve anyone in this case.

My judgment is that you shall undertake to feed Boris's wife and family until he is able to work again. You will chop wood for their fire and make sure the family has bread, meat and fish. You will apologise to Boris and pay him one shilling from your wages. Do you accept your punishment as fair?' Raphael asked.

Eric dropped to his knees. He was shaking and it was clear that he had expected an even worse punishment than the one Raphael had indicated.

'I beg your pardon and Boris's pardon, my lord. I will do all that you have ordered—and I will not make such a mistake again,' Eric said hoarsely.

'No, I am sure you will not,' Raphael said dryly. 'Get up and go back to your family until we need you again, but do not fail in your promises or I might change my mind and find a different punishment for you. I will not tolerate any flouting of your duty, Eric.'

'It shall not happen, my lord. I know that my foolish pride almost caused a good man's death and I shall be more careful in future. I am grateful for your mercy.'

'I believe you have learned your lesson. Do not give me cause to doubt you again.'

Once the man had left, Raphael turned to his watching friend with a grim smile. 'How do you manage to keep order amongst your outlaws, Loxley? It cannot be easy, for some of them have no respect of the law.'

'That is true enough. Fortunately, they respect me and the King, and thus far I have not had to hang anyone—but if necessary I would do it, and they know it,' the earl said grimly.

'Yes, one has to make an example sometimes, but I prefer to give a more measured judgment,' Raphael said.

'As you have today,' Loxley agreed. 'I might not have thought of it, but you have both given the man a task he can do and protected the family of the wounded man. I think everyone should applaud your judgment.'

'Not everyone thinks as highly of me as you,' Raphael said and smiled wryly. 'I think supper should soon be ready. I do not know about you, but I am hungry.'

'Forced to pay one shilling, apologise and keep Boris's family in food and firewood until he is able to work again.' Rosamunde looked at Mellors in surprise. 'It is a wise decision. I must admit, I expected the judgment to be harsher.'

'Had Boris been killed it might have been,' the steward admitted. 'I think it both clever and fair. Eric is shamed enough and will not boast of a kill too soon in future.'

'Lilia has been tending Boris since he came to his senses. It may be some months before he is fit to work again, but his family will not starve. I am sure my lord would have taken care of them in any case, but this way it teaches Eric to be more careful in future,' she remarked.

'Yes, indeed it does, my lady,' Mellors said and smiled at her. 'I am glad you approve of Lord Mornay's judgment.'

Rosamunde nodded. Mellors left her to go about his duty and she went downstairs to a small room at the rear of the hall to where Boris had been moved to give him some peace. His wife had been sent for and she and Lilia had rebound his wound and made him comfortable.

Boris's wife curtsied to her, smiling shyly as Rosamunde told her to be at ease.

'Who is looking after your children, mistress?'

'My sister has them for the moment. She told me

to stay with Boris while he needs me, and with your permission I shall sleep here by his side, my lady.'

'Yes, of course. Tell me, how old are your children?'

'Erin is twelve and Harold is ten.'

'Are they in employment?' she asked the older woman.

'There is no work for them other than helping me tend the pig and our vegetable patch.'

'Perhaps we could find work for you all within the castle,' Rosamunde said. 'If you would like to help my women once your husband has recovered but is still unable to resume his position? And your children can be found light work in the kitchens or serving at table. When your husband is well you may return to your home or remain here at the castle, as you choose.'

'My sister would tend the pig,' the woman said. 'It has been in my mind to offer service since Elspeth and her daughters came here. I am well known for my brewing, my lady. Folk say my ale is the best hereabouts and I would be willing to help with cooking or making wine and ale.'

'Then we shall be glad of your services,' Rosamunde told her and smiled. 'For the moment you must help to tend your husband. Lilia need not spend all her time with him now that you are here, and therefore you are already playing your part. You will be paid the same as Elspeth and Lilia.'

'You are gracious, my lady. We are all pleased that our lord is to marry an Englishwoman of beauty and generosity.'

Rosamunde nodded and smiled. It seemed that she was playing her part in bringing the castle back to its proper state.

'Excuse me, I am expected in the hall.'

Christmas Eve was a cold, bright morning, the ground hard with frost. Rosamunde, her ladies, Raphael and some of the men made up the party to gather in the greenery. They picked holly, ivy and mistletoe from the woods, loading the branches onto a cart, which was then driven back to the castle.

'Everyone is looking forward to the feast this evening,' Rosamunde said to Raphael as they walked back to the castle together. 'We have venison, roasting pig and mutton—also pies, preserved fruits and sweetmeats my ladies and I have pre-pared. It will be a merry occasion, my lord.'

'Yes, indeed, it will,' he said. 'I believe we may have minstrels to entertain us this night for they came seeking shelter for the period of Christ's Mass and would pay for their supper with song and music.'

'Sir Jonathan sings sweetly, but it would be nice to have a merry jig so that the men could dance.'

'Dance?' Raphael arched his brows. 'Yes, per-haps. I remember the custom. We used to dance a carol when I was a boy but I had forgotten.'

'That is what I meant. Everyone joins hands in a circle and someone must go to the centre and perform a poem or a trick, then we all dance to-gether, until another takes his or her place,' she explained.

'I remember how much everyone enjoyed such things,' Raphael said and his gaze was warm as it rested on her. 'You will bring the joy back to this house, Rosamunde. It hath too long been absent.'

'It will give me pleasure to make your house a home, my lord,' she said demurely.

'You do that just by being here,' he said tenderly

and reached for her hand. 'It may be that I have a little surprise for you.'

Her heart fluttered. What could he mean?

The hall had been decorated with greenery and there were kissing boughs of mistletoe hanging here and there. Now that there were more women servants in the castle, the sound of laughter as they dodged eager suitors lent an air of excitement and mischief to the night. Raphael had decreed that there were to be games, as well as the dancing and the feasting that night, and during the afternoon they watched an archery contest. The servants played bob-apple and blind man's buff and everyone was given a small gift of money from the lord.

Rosamunde wore her best gown of emerald velvet. She was cheered as she took her place at table and sat beside Raphael. The entertainment began almost at once. The travelling players put on a display of tumbling and a dwarf rushed around the hall hitting people with a pig's bladder filled with air. Then the minstrels began to play.

Food was served to all the tables, course after course of rich meats, worts and sweetmeats, with fresh bread, sweet and savoury pies, nuts, dates and sticky marchpane. Then the musicians struck up and Raphael stood, offering Rosamunde his hand.

She blushed with pleasure for she had not expected that he would dance with her. They took their places to the sound of clapping from the men. Rosamunde was surprised at her betrothed's elegant dancing as they performed a slow, graceful dance. More cheering greeted them as they retook their seats and Raphael invited everyone else to begin dancing.

It was then that the merriment began in earnest. Men who were used to working and training hard relaxed and joined in the dancing, drinking freely of the ale provided. Rosamunde watched and clapped, joining in some of the jigs and carols. Not until the torches began to flicker did she wish everyone good night and leave the table.

She was surprised when Raphael joined her, escorting her to her chamber at the top of the tower. He took her hand and kissed it.

'I wish you pleasant dreams, my lady,' he said. 'Please accept this token as my gift to you this festive season.'

'Oh…' She looked with surprise and pleasure at the small packet he handed her. Inside the square of silk was something hard. When she opened it, she discovered a pendant of silver enamelled with bright colours and set with a garnet and large baroque pearl. 'I have never seen anything this exquisite.'

'It came from the craftsmen of the east,' he said and smiled at her pleasure. 'You can clip it to your tunic at the shoulder or here…' He took it from her and clipped it at the place where her gown crossed over between her beasts.

Rosamunde trembled as his hands just brushed against her cleavage, her stomach fluttering with something she recognised as desire.

'Thank you for my wonderful gift,' she said and looked at him shyly. 'I fear I have nothing to give you.'

'You have already given me more than you know,' he said and bent his head to kiss her on the lips.

Rosamunde felt that she was swooning, her body melting into his, her lips soft and welcoming as she surrendered her being to his. She wanted the kiss to go on and on. She wanted more, far more, from him but he smiled and let her go.

'We shall be married soon,' he whispered, recognising and understanding her frustration. 'I can wait a little longer. Besides, it is nearly Christ's day and we must keep it holy. Sleep well, my lady.'

Rosamunde sighed in acquiescence, then went into her chamber, closing the door behind her. She stood for a moment with her back against it, feeling the glow of happiness surround her. She was so fortunate to have found a man she could love. Her selfish cousin had sent her here as a sacrifice and now she was truly the luckiest of women.

She had all that she could want of life.

The day of Christ's birth was spent quietly. In the morning everyone visited the chapel and a mass was said. Afterwards, the ladies sat at their sewing while the men trained or played games in the courtyard. In the evening they gathered for supper as always, but it was a much quieter celebration without the singing and dancing.

Rosamunde said good night early and left Raphael with his guests and his men, going up the twisting stair to her room. Maire and Elspeth were waiting for her, but Lilia had stayed in the hall.

'I believe she has found a young man she likes,' Elspeth said. 'She will be happier now, my lady. She was a little jealous of Beth, but Eric gave her a gift of cloth and she says they are pledged to one another. She asks that you will speak to Lord Mornay on her behalf.'

'Yes, of course I shall, but she must wait for three months to be certain of her feelings, and then they can be wed,' Rosamunde said.

'She will be happy when I tell her,' Elspeth said. 'Shall you undress now, my lady?'

'If you could help me out of my gown and then leave me—you too, Maire. I shall just sit here and think for a while.'

When her ladies had gone, she sat gazing out at the moon. She had never expected to be so happy, and she couldn't help but be aware of a tiny doubt at the back of her mind. She was almost Raphael's wife but not quite yet. Pray God nothing happened to spoil her happiness.

'It is many years since we celebrated Christ's Mass in the old way,' Mellors remarked when Rosamunde spoke to him about checking their stores the next afternoon. 'I believe we have enough meat and flour to last the winter, my lady, but perhaps we need more spices and sugar. If you wish to give gifts of cloth to the villagers we shall need to purchase more for our own use.'

'I think we must resume all the old customs. The poor of the village must be given cloth and flour or meat as a gift. You will send for what we need from London? The roads are still hard with frost. When the thaw comes, it may be impossible to pass this way,' she said.

'It shall be done now, my lady.'

Rosamunde nodded and walked away to attend to other duties.

Some hours later, as she entered the hall, she saw Raphael and the Earl of Loxley speaking together. She went up to them, for the servants had not quite finished setting out the places at the high board.

'Good evening, my lords.' She curtsied to them. 'I thought I should be late, but it is not so.'

Raphael looked at her, his brows rising as if he wondered what her reaction would be. She smiled and he inclined his head, holding his hand out to her as the horn was sounded.

'I believe you are in good time, my lady. This is Loxley's last night with us, for he must return to the forest.'

'It has been pleasant to make your acquaintance, my lord,' she said to the earl.

'I must tell you that I am glad to see my friend in better spirits. I believe that must be because of you, lady. I hope that we shall meet again in the future,' Loxley replied with some considerable charm.

'When the King is restored and you are no longer outlawed.' She smiled.

'We must hope that justice will prevail.' He grinned.

Rosamunde murmured her agreement and they moved to their seats at the high board. Letting her gaze move round the hall, Rosamunde saw that the men were smiling and jesting amongst themselves. It seemed that the feasting had banished any lingering unease from the men's minds.

'You are thoughtful.'

Raphael's lowered tone made her turn her head to look at him. 'I was thinking the men seemed pleased with life, my lord.'

'Is that not how it should be? I am privileged

to be lord here, and you will soon be my wife, but we should not take advantage of our position. Instead, it is our duty to care for and protect our people—and if that sometimes means we must correct or punish it is a part of the price we pay for our privilege,' he said quietly.

'Yes, I think I understand that now,' she murmured. 'Our duty is to the men we live amongst and the villagers we protect by a show of strength. If you were thought weak, other knights might seek to take what you have, and to terrorise our people.'

'With strength there must also be fairness, but every knight learns to behave with honour and compassion. It is a part of our training. Those that abuse their power, as I fear my father and Sir Edmund did, betray their vows,' he said somewhat sadly.

'I am very glad you are not like your father,' Rosamunde replied, her cheeks slightly warm.

Raphael's hand reached for hers. He held it lightly, but with a look in his eyes that set her pulses racing.

'I think that perhaps we begin to know each

other a little better, lady. We shall do well enough once we are wed,' he said.

'And when is that to be, my lord?'

'In three weeks' time.' His finger caressed the back of her hand, sending little tremors down her spine. 'I would it were sooner but I wish to observe the laws of the church. I would not have your father think I rushed you into an illegal marriage. My sons must know that they were born in wedlock.'

Rosamunde felt a spasm of desire clench deep inside her. Her lips parted and she wished that they could be alone so that he could take her in his arms and kiss her.

'It must be as you wish, my lord,' she said on a sigh instead.

'Must it?' A wry smile touched his mouth. 'You sound exceedingly modest, Rosamunde, but I know that you have a temper.'

'I am shamed that I lost my temper before,' she said. 'A wife should not question or doubt her husband.'

'I would not have you doubt me—for I swear to you that you will have no cause to do so—but you may question me whenever you wish. You are to be my wife, Rosamunde, not my slave,' he said earnestly.

'My father said my mother was constantly nagging him. I do not think you would wish for a nagging wife, would you?'

'I should probably beat you,' he teased, and then laughed as he saw her eyes darken. 'No, my lady, I do not mean it. I speak in jest, but I do not believe you would nag me constantly.'

'I should not,' she said and laughed softly. 'I was testing you a little, my lord. I hope that we shall live in harmony and peace.'

'That is also my hope. I shall do my best to make you happy and content with your lot,' Raphael said and took her hand to raise it to his lips. He dropped a kiss in the palm and smiled as she blushed. 'Have I told you that I think you one of the most beautiful ladies I have ever known?'

'I think you flatter me, my lord,' she murmured and dropped her eyes. Her heart was racing wildly. The heat in his eyes told her that he wanted her in the way a man wants a beautiful woman, but at the back of her mind the warning still lingered. He was marrying her because it was convenient for him to do so, not because he loved her as she loved him.

Rosamunde turned her head away as Sir Jonathan began to sing. Her gaze followed him about the room. He sang of love and disappointment, his song ending with a knight wasting away for a love of another knight's wife.

'I think once Richard returns our minstrel will leave us,' Raphael remarked. 'I believe he intends to seek a place at court. Shall you miss his company, Rosamunde?'

She glanced at him, surprised by the odd expression in his eyes. 'He has a pleasant voice and I enjoy his music. I believe he is a good friend to you, my lord. You may miss him yourself.'

'Yes, I dare say I shall. I have other friends who may choose to settle here when they return with Richard, but that is for the future.' His eyes narrowed. 'You know why Jonathan will move on, do you not?'

'No, my lord. I thought him settled here,' she said innocently.

'He is in love with you. Had you no idea?' he asked curiously.

'None at all!' She gasped. 'I have done nothing

to encourage him, my lord. I would not have it so for I do not wish to cause distress.'

'He knows you have given him no encouragement. Had he chosen to do so, he might have courted you, but he believed you would refuse him. Was he right?'

'I like Sir Jonathan but I could not marry him,' she said bluntly.

'Why?'

Rosamunde was silent for a moment. 'If you do not know the answer, I shall not tell you, my lord.'

'Is it that…?' Raphael broke off as there was a commotion at the other end of the hall. Three guards entered, dragging another man with them. They hauled him in front of Raphael and then forced him to his knees. 'What is the meaning of this?' Raphael rose to his feet.

'This rogue was trying to sneak into the castle,' one of the men said. 'He says he brings a message for you but would not give it to anyone but you.'

'Stand up like a man and speak,' Raphael commanded. 'What do you have to say to me that cannot be said to my men?'

'Baron Sigmund sent me,' the man said, visibly shaken by his treatment. 'He bid me tell you that he has heard the King is soon to land on English soil. He begs that you will join him on the road to London.'

'His Majesty is on his way home to England?' Raphael said eagerly. 'This is wonderful news. When did your lord receive this news?'

'It came a few hours ago. I was sent to warn you but commanded to speak with no one but yourself.'

'You have spoken and your lord will forgive you for disobeying his orders in the circumstances. You may find a place and eat with us.'

Raphael turned to the earl. 'I think we must leave at once, Loxley. We journey in different directions. You must return to your men, but alert those you can on the way. I shall take thirty men and ride for London at once. We shall meet when you bring your supporters to join Richard.'

'I shall leave immediately,' the earl said, rose to his feet and made a sign to the men he'd brought with him. 'My men and I must meet the King and pledge our loyalty.'

'How can you be sure this news is true, my lord?' Rosamunde queried cautiously.

'We cannot be entirely sure,' Raphael said. 'I

shall respond to the summons but I shall not drop my guard either here or on the road. Yet we must leave, for Richard will need all men loyal to him.'

'You will need to make preparations,' she said. 'Is there anything my ladies and I may do for you, my lord?'

'There is nothing for the moment. However, it may be that I shall invite Richard to visit here with us,' Raphael said. 'Be ready to receive him, if he consents to make this his stronghold until he is ready to take the throne.'

'Yes, of course. We shall prepare for a feast on your return. May God be with you, my lord,' she said.

'Go to your chamber now, my lady. I shall come to take my leave of you before I go.'

She inclined her head and smiled. 'I shall await your coming, my lord.'

Rosamunde left the hall, closely followed by Elspeth and Lilia. They went up to the tower rooms where they were housed.

'It is momentous news,' Elspeth said excitedly. 'England will be a better place if His Majesty has returned.'

'Yes, it must be happy news for all His Majesty's loyal subjects,' Rosamunde replied.

She bid her ladies good night, saying that she would send for Maire when she was ready to disrobe. She went to the narrow window of her chamber, looking down at the courtyard. Men were scurrying here and there as horses and armour were prepared. Wagons carrying food and equipment would follow, but the men-at-arms would travel light and fast.

It was a race against time to meet with the King and show support, to protect him if need be against an attempt to murder him. Rosamunde knew that Raphael must leave at once but, remembering the attention he had paid her at supper, she could not help regretting that he must leave before their wedding.

'Rosamunde.' A tremor went through her as she heard his voice. She turned and saw him, something in his gaze telling her that he too was reluctant to leave. 'I wanted to say farewell in private. Last time we parted in anger and I would not have it so again.'

She smiled and moved towards him, her hands outstretched. 'Know that you have my blessing, my lord. I might wish you could stay longer but I know you have your work to do.'

'You are very understanding.' He took her hands, looking down into her face. 'I would not leave you again so soon if it were not of vital importance. I must go to the King to show my support.'

'I know that you must go. I pray that you will return safely to wed me.'

'I long for it,' Raphael said, his voice deep with passion. 'I have come to know myself these past weeks and I want only to live in peace and content with you, my love. This Christ's Mass showed me how much more you bring to my life and the lives of my men. This place hath needed a woman's gentle touch for many years.'

Rosamunde's heart leaped. He had called her his love—but could he mean it?

'I long to be your wife,' she answered tremulously. 'I know that you may be in danger, my lord. I do not seek to cling or to bind you in any way, but you should know that you have my love. I loved you that day you saved my kitten, and I love you now. My love grows stronger with every day.'

'You are as beautiful within as without,' Raphael

replied huskily. He reached out, drawing her close to him, pressing her hard into his body as he bent his head to kiss her lips. 'My sweet Rosamunde.'

She clung to him, giving her lips and her love without reserve. When he'd left her the last time in such anger, it had almost broken her heart, but this time he would take her love with him. He must know that she was his heart and soul so that he would come back to her.

'Return to me safely, my lord.'

'I shall,' he promised and his fingers cupped her cheek. 'How could I fail when I have so much waiting for me?'

Rosamunde smiled and let him go. It was hard to control the tears, and her desire to call him back, but she knew that she must allow him to do his duty. A woman must wait for her husband to return. Life was often harsh and cruel; women died in childbed and men were killed in battle. A woman must not weep and hold her husband back, though she might shed many tears in private.

Surely life could not be so utterly unfair as to take him from her before she had even had the chance to be a wife?

Chapter Ten

'My lord said that we should prepare for a feast on his return,' Rosamunde said to Mellors a week later. 'I know that some of the cattle were killed when we salted the meat for winter, but we cannot serve His Majesty such fare. Have we fatted cattle and sucking pig?'

'Yes, my lady. The wild boar killed yesterday was roasted last evening, but there is plenty of fish in the ponds and we also have duck, geese and capon.'

'It is a pity we have no sheep,' Rosamunde said regretfully. 'A piece of fat mutton makes a tasty stew with onions and worts. Has my lord said nothing to you of purchasing breeding ewes and a ram?'

'He hath not had the time to attend to the lack as yet,' Mellors said. 'Though I believe it his intention.'

'We should send men to market to buy sheep and the kind of luxuries that the King would require. Not lampreys, for they must be fresh and we do not know when my lord will return, but sugar, honeycomb and nuts. My ladies and I will begin to prepare sweetmeats when we have news of Lord Mornay's return,' she said.

'Before he left, my lord instructed me to obey your orders in these matters, my lady. All that you have asked for shall be bought at the markets, and anything that cannot be purchased locally will be sent for to London.'

'Then everything will be as it should be for my lord's return and the King's visit,' she said happily.

'My lord also instructed that silks, velvets and good quality wool should be purchased from the merchants of London. Has my lady any preferences for the colour these should be?' Mellors enquired.

'I believe Lord Mornay's favourite colours are blue, silver and black. I like these colours, but also favour green. For my ladies I should like some lighter materials to make gowns for the spring and summer, and these should be rich brown, grey or a figured damask for best. If you order a selection I shall allow them to choose.'

'Very well. Ethelred, the wife of Boris the huntsman who was injured, told me that you said she and her children could work at the castle if they chose, at least until Boris is well again,' the steward remarked.

'Yes; I thought it better for them to be together as a family. I am sure we can find something for the children to do, can we not?' she said.

'The girl can help in the kitchens, and the boy wants to train as a squire, so for the moment he can be put to cleaning the men's armour and working in the stables.'

Rosamunde smiled. 'That is excellent, Mellors. I think we should encourage more of the villagers to work here, either in the castle or as craftsmen. I am certain that some of our excellent craftsmen need apprentices to help them.'

'I believe that we shall have more people asking for work now that you are to marry my lord. The castle has come alive, and if we have flocks of sheep once more there will be work for both women and children,' he said.

Rosamunde nodded her agreement and they

parted. It was January now and deep winter. Because the morning was bitter-cold with hoarfrost on the ground, she had planned to visit the kitchens that morning to make an inventory of what spices and stores they might need. The weather was too inclement to go foraging with her ladies, but as soon as it cleared a little she would venture to the woods and discover what fresh herbs and roots might be found.

Richard was not yet landed in England. The message had been hasty, but the news was that he had been freed from his imprisonment and might soon be on a ship headed for England.

Forced to kick his heels and wait, Raphael thought with regret of Rosamunde's warm arms. Her image had begun to haunt his dreams and when he woke now it was with a smile on his lips.

At last the grief and guilt he had felt for so long over Messalina's death had eased and he could no longer see the reproachful face of his dead wife when he slept.

It is not that I have forgotten you, he told her in his thoughts. *You were my wife, and I shall always honour your memory, but life goes on and I must find a new way.*

He was beginning to see that his feelings for Messalina had always been protective and chivalrous and he had never truly been in love with her. His feelings for Rosamunde were very different.

Rosamunde was sweet and loving, but she was also both brave and practical, and did not cling or weep as Messalina had when he'd left her. He knew that he wanted to be with her, to hold her in his arms and have her in his bed. He had vowed he would not love again, and yet he found the waiting irksome and wished to be at home with the woman who had unexpectedly filled the empty space in his heart.

Was what he felt for Rosamunde really love? It was so different from the feeling he'd had for Messalina. Instead of wanting to escape for a few hours, he found himself longing to be with her. The need seemed to grow stronger every day that they were apart and he was already increasingly impatient to see her again though they had been apart for no more than three weeks.

Would Raphael never return to her? Rosamunde stared out of her window at the courtyard below. More than eight weeks had passed since Raphael had left to meet the King. They had received but one brief message to say that as yet His Majesty had not landed, and since then no word had come.

She was constantly busy, but sometimes the loneliness was almost unbearable. Rosamunde thought of her father and wondered how he was. Yet she could not leave the castle to visit him because Raphael had asked her to remain until he returned.

Supposing he did not return? The thought filled her with black despair. If she never saw him again, she would not wish to live. She did not even wish to think about what she would do if he were killed in battle.

After a week of bitter frosts the sun was shining at last. The month of February had almost passed and there was finally a touch of spring in the air. Each day Rosamunde looked eagerly for word of Raphael's return, but knew that it might still not come for weeks. It might be that there would be fighting and Raphael would be needed at his King's side. Sometimes she could not sleep at night, tossing restlessly as she wondered if he were in danger, and yet something inside her told her all was well.

They had ordered liberally from the markets, as Raphael had instructed, and the stores were now well stocked with sugar, salt, spices, flour and dried fruits. However, they lacked fresh herbs. Rosamunde had set in order the creation of a herb garden within the castle grounds, but it would take months before she could expect to harvest enough for their needs. So she called Elspeth and Lilia to her and told them to bring their baskets. Taking three of their most trusted men-at-arms, they left the castle well wrapped up in cloaks and shawls to search for herbs, leaves, roots and anything in the hedgerows that would help to bring flavour to their food.

Both Rosamunde and Elspeth had skills at making cures, so they would also take bark and lichens to help in the preparations of their cures.

It was good to be out in the fresh air again, though it was still cool despite the sun.

'We shall pick as much as we can as swiftly as we can and return to the castle,' Rosamunde told her ladies. 'It is pleasant now but there is a hint of rain in the air.'

'At this time of the year a mist can come down swiftly,' Elspeth agreed. 'We should not be wise to stay out too long, my lady.'

They had agreed that they would not go too

deeply into the woods. Many of the herbs they were looking for would grow close to the stream or in the hedgerows, and the lichens they sought grew on the stone walling that separated the lord's demesne lands from the common ground.

Lilia was sent to forage beside the stream. Elspeth knew where the best lichens were to be found, and Rosamunde concentrated on the edge of the woods. It was too early to find violets, but she soon discovered a patch of snowdrops, and then aconite, and knelt to pick the flowers. Seeing a further patch a little deeper into the woods, she decided to venture further than she'd intended. She could see some interesting growths on a clump of trees and suspected they would be useful in making certain cures for a skin complaint the men often suffered with during the long winter. Glancing back, she saw that two of her men were close by, though one had wandered in the direction of the stream where both Elspeth and Lilia were now working.

Intent on her work, Rosamunde took no notice of the rustling in the trees close by. She had loved the woods close to her father's keep and knew that it was probably a small animal looking for food beneath the fallen debris.

When she had filled her basket, she stood up and looked about her, suddenly realising that a mist had started to creep through the trees. She could not see the men-at-arms, who had been close to her when she had last looked, and felt suddenly disorientated and alone, cut off from her friends. In the mist the wood looked unfamiliar and she was uncertain of the way she should go.

'Are you there?' she called. 'Call out to me and tell me where you are.'

She heard a muffled shout and turned towards the direction from where it had come, but before she could call again she was roughly pushed in the back and then a thick blanket was thrown over her head. She screamed but the cloth covering her head muffled the sound. Despite her struggles, she was lifted from the ground and carried away, though she could not tell in what direction. She heard muffled shouts but nothing was clear and she had no idea of what was happening or where she was being taken.

Raphael! The words were in her head but not

upon her lips. *I need you so, my love. Forgive me. I was careless and forgot your warnings.*

Suddenly, she was flung down and felt the blanket being removed. Opening her eyes, she discovered that she had been dumped on the ground. She looked up into the eyes of a man she despised.

'What have you done?' she demanded hotly of Sir Ian. 'My lord will search for me and when he finds me he will punish you.'

Sir Ian sneered at her. 'He may look but he will not find you. You are my prisoner now, lady—and you will discover what the word truly means.'

Rosamunde tried to stand but was thrust back to her knees by a booted foot. 'You are a brute and my lord will make you pay for your treatment of me. If you harm me, he will surely kill you.'

'He may try but I have powerful friends,' Sir Ian boasted. 'Your lord murdered Sir Edmund Roth and he was kinsman to Baron Sigmund. It is to his stronghold that you are bound, lady. Say your prayers, for only God can help you now.'

Rosamunde gasped in horror as the man laughed evilly. Then she lifted her head proudly. 'I am but a woman and cannot defend myself—but Raphael will avenge me. If I am harmed, you will wish you had never been born.'

'Bind and gag her,' Sir Ian commanded his men. 'Save your breath, lady. Baron Sigmund finds you of interest and therefore I shall not give you the beating you deserve. If I bring you to him he will give me service, and soon I shall be wealthy enough to purchase my own lands. I've sickened of bending the knee to more powerful lords. You will buy me the freedom I need.'

His henchmen had bound her wrists behind her back and there was a gag over her mouth. She could not answer him but continued to hold her head high, her eyes showing the contempt she felt.

'We must go quickly. The longer we stay in these confounded woods, the deeper the mist will be and we shall never find our way out,' Sir Ian said urgently.

Rosamunde suffered the indignity of being thrown into a wagon. She lay with her eyes closed, blocking the fear that threatened to overtake her. She must not weep or give way to fear. Instead, she must remain alert and, when the opportunity came, try to escape.

Her only chance lay in Raphael's return before it

was too late. Did anyone yet know that she'd been kidnapped, or would Raphael be told that she had simply disappeared?

'My lady was kidnapped!' Janquil gasped. 'They mean to take her to Baron Sigmund's stronghold. Her captor spoke of her being the baron's prisoner but I do not know if she is to be held for ransom or…'

'Used for his evil purposes,' Sir Jonathan finished, feeling a sick horror. He stared at Janquil hard, a glint of anger in his eyes. 'Why did you not rescue your lady? If you saw what happened, you might have alerted us sooner.'

'I am not a fighting man,' Janquil answered. 'If I had rushed in on them they would have killed me, as they killed one of the guards who were supposed to guard her, and then you would never have known what had become of my lady. The other guard is sorely wounded and, had it not been for the woman Elspeth, he would have died of his wounds.'

'Why was Lady Rosamunde allowed to wander off like that?' Jonathan snapped.

'The mist came down suddenly. She was in full

view of her guards and then she was gone. I alone could see her and I crept closer, following the men who took her so that I could discover what they meant to do with her. There were six of them and I had only a dagger. I knew I could not stop them taking her, so I came here to tell you what I knew,' Janquil said.

'We should take a force and attack Sigmund's castle!' one of the other men cried. 'Lord Mornay will never forgive us if we allow her to become that devil's prisoner.'

'We are not strong enough,' Jonathan responded in angry frustration. 'Raphael took thirty men with him and we must maintain the security of the castle. This could be a ploy to draw us out, leaving the castle vulnerable.'

'What are we to do?'

He paced the room, then turned to look at Janquil. 'You will take a force of twenty-five men, which is all I can spare for the moment. And you will find Raphael—tell him the situation here. He has friends of influence who may aid him. Baron Sigmund has terrorised his neighbours for too long. He must be stopped for good.'

'Yes, lord. I shall do as you ask,' Janquil said.

'I have failed my lord and must pay the price he demands.'

'Raphael has need of us all,' Sir Jonathan said. 'Step forward those who are prepared to fight and die in his service.'

As one, all seventy of the men present stepped forward. Jonathan smiled and shook his head. 'I thank you for your loyalty, but I can spare only twenty-five.'

He walked along the line of men and tapped several on the shoulder.

'You will go with Janquil. The others remain here to hold the castle with me. Tell my lord that if we are attacked we shall not surrender, no matter the odds. We shall fight to the last man until he sends reinforcements.'

There was a murmur of agreement and then the men split into two. Those who were to go in search of Raphael left to mount their horses. Twenty of them would ride swiftly to find their lord without provisions or weapons of war, but these would be made ready, and the other five men would proceed towards the baron's castle. They would remain hidden in the woods until Raphael brought his forces to attack the baron's castle.

* * *

'The people have risen for Richard now that he is back in England. They flock to him from all over the country,' Raphael said, looking in satisfaction at the Earl of Loxley. 'This is a happy day for England. Prince John's tyranny is finally at an end.'

'He has not yet come to surrender his power as regent and make his peace with his brother,' the earl warned.

'It is surely only a matter of time. I have offered my support to the King, and he accepted my promise if he should need it, but he has released me to return home. He is to make a progress throughout the kingdom so that the people see him and know he is returned. I have invited him to Mornay and he has promised to visit in the next few weeks. Therefore I shall return home and await his coming,' Raphael said.

'My men and I have received a royal pardon,' the earl told him with a smile. 'Some of them have already returned to their homes, but those who wish to serve with me when my manor and lands are returned to me will stay with His Majesty, as

I shall for the moment.' He offered his hand. 'You may see me sooner than you imagine, my friend.'

'You have yet to wrest your manor back from those who stole it from you,' Raphael said. 'I have a lady I care for waiting for me at home and must return to wed her—but should you need my help, you have only to send word.'

'I thank you, but Richard has promised to attend to this matter personally. Know that I would come to your aid should you…' Loxley broke off as he saw something. 'Is that not your servant?'

Raphael looked in the direction he indicated and frowned. 'Something must be wrong. Janquil would not come in search of me if he had not good reason. Excuse me, I must speak with him.'

'I shall come with you,' the earl said. 'My promise holds true. If you need me, I shall bring as many men as I can muster to your aid.'

'I thank you,' Raphael said and moved his horse through the press of knights, men-at-arms and squires who had gathered to show their support for the King. 'For the moment your duty is to Richard, but if I need help I shall send word.'

Loxley inclined his head and they parted.

Raphael felt ice at his nape as he rode towards his servant, and saw there were more of his men here than there should be, mingling with the crowd. From the expressions on their faces, they were searching for him.

Rosamunde! He was gripped by a terrible fear. He knew that only if something had happened to her would Sir Jonathan send so many men in search of him. Something terrible must have happened. He cursed the crowd that prevented him from reaching Janquil more quickly, but held the urge to thrust his way though. The worst thing he could do now was to lose his head.

At last Janquil had seen him and pointed away from the press of the crowds milling about the King and his knights. Raphael turned his horse and saw that others of his men were now following him. It took a few minutes but at last they came together at the edge of the meadow where the King had set up his standard.

'Janquil—why have you come? Is the castle under attack? Is my lady ill?' he asked anxiously.

'Forgive me, my lord,' Janquil replied, his eyes cast down. 'Sir Ian has abducted the lady Rosamunde. He has taken her to Baron Sigmund's stronghold. Sir Jonathan bid us find you. There are twenty-one of us, and another five have taken the engines of war to meet with you outside the baron's castle. Sir Jonathan remains to guard Mornay. It may be a part of the baron's plan to split our forces and make us vulnerable to an attack.'

'Sir Jonathan swore that they would hold Mornay until the last, my lord,' interjected another of his men.

Raphael inclined his head. 'Yes, that is like him. I know that he will keep his word.'

'What are your orders, my lord?' Janquil asked.

'We ride for the Dark Towers immediately. Gather the men and give the word to move out,' Raphael ordered.

He was frowning as he spoke. For the moment he had work to do, plans to make, but he knew that soon the torture of his imagination would begin. Rosamunde was at the mercy of men steeped in evil. He could hardly bear to think what might happen to her.

God protect her until he could reach her side.

Rosamunde was hauled from the wagon and thrust to her knees. She struggled to stand, but with her ankles and hands bound it was impossible. Her angry words of protest were lost beneath the gag they had tied so tightly that she felt she would choke. During the journey here she had swooned and been mercifully unconscious for a time, but now she was aware of the perilous situation in which she stood, and her heart was beating madly.

'What is this? Why are you treating the lady so in my castle?'

The voice was loud and booming. Looking up, Rosamunde saw the flowing red locks and beard of the man she'd glimpsed briefly at Mornay. He was a large man with coarse features and eyes that looked more green than blue. As he bent down to help her rise, she noticed his hands were large and powerful, and looked capable of breaking a man's neck with ease. Taking a long, thin dagger from his belt, he sliced the bonds that held her hands and then bent to slash those binding her ankles. Rosamunde was already busy untying the gag that had almost choked her.

'How dare you have me brought here like this?' she demanded. 'My lord will surely come in anger against you for this outrage.'

'It was not done by my order,' Sigmund protested. 'I admit that I have a score to settle with Raphael de Mornay, but I do not hide behind a woman's skirts. I was told that you would come willingly to me!'

'Why should I leave the protection of my betrothed?' Rosamunde demanded proudly. Inside she was trembling, but instinctively she felt that this man would respect her only if she showed courage. 'My lord went to meet the King but when he returns we are to be married.'

The baron's eyes narrowed as he looked down at her. 'Was this by your consent, lady?'

'Yes. I gave my promise willingly. I love him and wish to be his wife.'

'Indeed? Then it seems that I've been lied to!' he roared and turned on Sir Ian. 'You are a liar and a cowardly knave—what else have you lied about, sirrah?'

'Nothing. She was a prisoner. I heard she had quarrelled with Mornay and…'

'He stole me from my lord!' Rosamunde cried. 'He and Sir Edmund planned to rob my lord and to abduct me.'

'Hold him,' the baron barked at his men.

'No. You wanted her—I brought her to you,' Sir Ian cried. 'You owe me…'

'Silence!' the baron roared again, turning to him for a moment, eyes glittering with anger. 'Take him to the dungeons. I shall discover the extent of his lies later.'

As Sir Ian was dragged away screaming and struggling, Baron Sigmund turned back to Rosamunde. His face gave no indication of his thoughts as he studied her in silence for a moment.

'Your beauty makes you a prize most men would value highly,' he said greasily. 'Forgive me for allowing that fool to treat you so ill. Sir Edmund was a kinsman and I am pledged to avenge his death. However, I would not have had you harmed, lady. You will allow me to show you the hospitality of my home. You shall have food, clothes and anything else you desire while you stay here.'

'I demand that you give me an escort and return me to Lord Mornay at once,' she said, not trusting him or his supposedly pleasant words an inch.

'Forgive me, lady, but that I cannot do. Whatever my kinsman was, he should have been given a fair trial and accorded the honourable death a knight deserves,' the baron replied.

'Sir Edmund tied me up and then basely tried to kill Lord Mornay. He also planned to abduct me. How can you defend him?' Rosamunde accused.

The baron looked taken aback by her directness. 'It seems as if he had behaved in a manner I should not tolerate amongst my own men, yet Sir Edmund was my blood, and a man has no choice but to defend his blood kin. Lord Mornay must answer to me. We shall settle this man to man in the old way. In the meantime, you will remain as my honoured guest.'

'Your guest or your hostage?' Rosamunde asked bitterly. 'Why is it that men always fight and women are used as bargaining tools? I do not deny you the right to settle your blood feud, if that is what you must do, but why may I not return to my home?'

'And where is your home, lady?'

'My father is Sir Randolph Meldreth and I am Rosamunde, his only child.'

'Sir Randolph?' the baron said and frowned

fiercely. 'I know him of old. Long ago we were friends. Hmm; this alters things somewhat, lady.'

'You will let me go after all?' she asked hopefully.

'Forgive me. In other circumstances I should escort you to your home, but I fear I must tell you that your father is dead. Prince John's tax collectors were angry when they could find nothing of value. They ransacked the house, dragged your father from the house and beat his servants half to death.'

'My father is *dead*?' Rosamunde's eyes filled with grief-stricken tears. 'How wicked these men are. My father was ill; he gave all he had to help others and now he has been foully murdered. How did he die?' she choked out.

'He was alive when the rogues left, but I have heard that he died soon after in his bed. The shock was too much for him,' the baron replied. 'I am sorry to give you this news, but it means that for an old friend's sake I cannot let you go home. There is nothing for you there. Fear not, lady; I shall protect you. In time, when your grief is done, we shall speak of the future.' He did a poor job of hiding his satisfaction; she could see it gleaming in his eyes.

'Lord Mornay is my betrothed. If I cannot return to my home, let me return to him. I beg you, sir. Do not force me to remain here as your hostage,' she pleaded.

'Your lord must answer for my kinsman's death,' the baron insisted stubbornly. 'It will be a fight to the death, single combat. If Mornay wins he may claim you, but if I win you will become my property.'

'No!' Rosamunde shrank away from him. 'Please let me go! I love Sir Raphael. I belong to him. I can never be yours.'

'Never is a long time, lady.' He turned and beckoned to an old crone, who came hobbling towards them. 'Griselda, take this lady to the tower. She is in your care until I have time to speak with her again.'

Rosamunde looked at him and saw that he would not be swayed. He was insisting on defending the so-called honour of his blood kin, regardless of the truth. When Raphael came to find her, he would be forced to fight this man—a man so strong and powerful that she doubted any one knight could defeat him.

Tears burned behind her eyes as she was led away. She held them back, because she must not allow Baron Sigmund to see her as a weak woman. He spoke of friendship towards her father but he would not let her go home. She was but a woman, and as such the property of any man who cared to take her.

Her throat tightened as she realised that in truth she no longer had any home but Mornay Castle. Her father was dead and she was a woman alone. She had no powerful relatives to defend or claim her. No one but Raphael—the man she loved.

He had never told her that he loved her, but she believed he cared for her as much as he was able. When he learned she was being held hostage here, he would come to try and wrest her from the baron. A terrible price would be demanded of him, because she was sure that he would accept the baron's challenge; no knight of honour would refuse. Raphael would fight to win her back and there was a good chance he would be killed.

The tears that she'd held back earlier trickled down her cheeks. Her father was dead and soon the man she loved could also be dead. If that happened, she would be alone and at the mercy of Baron Sigmund—but not for long.

Rather than wed him she knew she would take her own life. She would rather join those she loved in the grave than live with a man like the baron.

Chapter Eleven

Standing at the window of her chamber at the top of the west tower, Rosamunde looked down at the courtyard below her. She could see that preparations were being made for a siege and realised that Baron Sigmund must have received word that Raphael was bringing a force against him.

'Do not let him fight single-handed,' she whispered, her lips moving in prayer. 'I would not have him die for my sake.'

'Your prayers will do little good in this godforsaken place,' a voice said behind her.

Rosamunde turned to look at the woman who had served her since she was brought to this room two days earlier. She was in truth a prisoner, seeing no one but Griselda. Unlike Raphael, her gaoler had not invited her to dine in his hall.

Indeed, she'd seen nothing of him since that first meeting.

'Is there nothing I can do to move the baron?' she asked, her throat tight with emotion. 'I would do anything to save Lord Mornay's life. I would rather die than be the cause of his death.'

'If you gave your honour it would not suffice. The baron would lose all respect for you and, once he tired of you, would give you to his men. I have seen it many times, lady. It was only your pride and your courage—and your father's name— that kept him from using you as he has so many others,' the old crone said.

'Then there is nothing I can do,' Rosamunde said hopelessly. 'Yet I would rather die than submit to him. I shall not wed him.'

'You will have little choice once your betrothed is dead. The baron will wed you, and if you please him he may keep you until you give him a son. He has three wives already in the grave. Two died in suspicious circumstances after giving him only daughters,' Griselda told her.

Rosamunde closed her eyes, shudders of revulsion sweeping through her. 'Then I shall take my own life. When I know that my lord is dead, I shall not be long in joining him.'

'You might escape if you have the courage to try.'

'What?' Rosamunde thought she had misheard. 'How could I escape? There are always guards, and my door is locked.'

'I could unlock it at night and show you a way out,' the old lady offered gleefully.

'Why would you do that?' she gasped.

'The baron killed my son,' Griselda replied. 'I have hated him from that day to this, waiting my chance for revenge.'

'You would help me because of what Sigmund did to your son?'

'And others—friends who died because of his brutality.' Griselda nodded.

'Why have you waited until now?'

'Because I am too weak to kill him and there is not a man in the castle that would risk it. I would have used poison but everything he eats is tasted first. I have decided that my only hope of revenge is to take from him something he truly covets—and that is you, my lady.'

'When? It must be soon, for if we delay it will be too late,' Rosamunde urged.

'I shall come tonight. I can release you and show you the way to escape, but you must go on alone. I am too old to run and hide and I should only slow you down. You must get to your lord and warn him not to accept the challenge,' Griselda said.

'Yes, I shall,' Rosamunde replied eagerly. 'But what of you? Will the baron not punish you?'

'He can only take my life. I shall give it willingly to know that I have thwarted him. It will be sweet revenge, lady. I am nothing, less than the dirt beneath his feet. To see his face when he learns that you are gone, and it was I that set you free, will be sweeter than honey,' the old lady crooned with satisfaction.

'You are brave,' Rosamunde said with admiration. 'Will you not come with me? I could find you a place in my household. You would be fed and cared for until you die.'

'No, I shall not run from him. My time is close and I would sooner meet death swiftly than linger. Death will be welcome to me, lady.'

'Then I can only thank you—and remember you in my prayers,' Rosamunde said gratefully.

'Light a candle for me,' Griselda said and gave her a toothless smile. 'Your prayers may light the path to heaven and I shall see my loved ones again.'

'Listen—someone is coming,' Rosamunde warned. 'Be careful.'

The door was flung back and Baron Sigmund appeared in the opening, his eyes narrowed as he saw the two women.

'What goes on here?'

'I came to bring the lady water, for she had none,' Griselda said. 'I was about to leave and lock her in, lord. Do you wish me to wait?'

'Go.' He dismissed her, then held her arm as she would have passed. 'Give me the key. In future a guard will accompany you when you visit her.'

'Yes, my lord.' Griselda handed him a large, black iron key, then shuffled off, closing the door behind her.

Had he heard them discussing her escape? Rosamunde's heart sank painfully as she saw the baron pocket the key without glancing at it. Griselda would not be able to help her now. She was truly the baron's prisoner and there was nothing she could do. She faced him proudly, waiting for him to speak.

'The castle is preparing for a siege; your lord is coming. He thinks to take you back, lady, but you are under my protection and I shall issue my challenge. When he is dead, you will be mine. If you behave as you ought, I shall wed you, but if you remain proud and stubborn I shall give you to my men as a plaything.'

'If you mean to frighten me you waste your breath,' Rosamunde said, pride making her strong again.

'By heaven, you tempt me sorely, wench. I think you would fight like a cat but I would risk your scratches to taste that sweetness at your core.' He moved towards her as if he intended to make good his promise. Rosamunde tensed, prepared to fight to the last for her honour, but the sound of running feet up the stone steps halted him and he turned as the door was once more flung open. 'What is it, man?'

'Lord Mornay's forces have been seen beyond the village, lord. He could be here within the hour.'

'He will send a messenger to negotiate. It is but an hour to sunset; he would not risk an attack before morning. Go down and tell the men to double the guard. I shall be with you in a moment,' the baron ordered.

The man departed and Baron Sigmund turned back to Rosamunde. 'I shall allow you to watch the fight between us. You will know when you see Mornay dead at my feet that I am the better warrior and more fitted to be your husband.'

Rosamunde did not reply; far better to give him a proud, haughty stare. He looked at her in frustration for a moment, then turned and walked away. She heard the sound of a key in the lock and sank down on the edge of the bed in despair.

There was nothing she could do but wait.

'Take my message to the gates of Sigmund's stronghold,' Raphael said to his knight. 'He must honour a flag of truce, and I believe he will do so, for it is obvious he wants something of me. Had he wanted money, he would have simply tried to take Mornay while I was absent.'

As the man rode away with his white banner, Raphael looked at Janquil. 'It is my intention to go in alone and challenge Baron Sigmund to armed combat. If he believes he has a score to settle with me I would rather meet him face to face than risk the lives of others. I need someone to accompany me and carry my pennant. Will you be that man?'

'You know the answer, my lord,' Janquil said. 'I would lay down my life for you—but surely another knight might be of more use in a fight?'

'Your task is to find my lady. It is my hope that, while the assembled company is busy watching the fight, you may be able to spirit her away. I know there is not a lock you cannot open, and you have a clever, devious mind. If there is a way to rescue her, you will find it. There is but a slim chance of success but I know you would do anything to save her,' Raphael said.

'There might be a way,' Janquil said thoughtfully. 'But it will only work if you win.'

'Tell me what is in your mind,' Raphael said. He listened as Janquil outlined his plan and then smiled. 'Yes, my friend. It is dangerous, particularly for you, but it might work.'

'My life is not important. Had I been a warrior, I would have given it the day they took her, but I knew I could not hope to rescue her and it seemed best to bring the news of her capture.'

'You did well, my friend. I think your plan will

work, but if it does not know that I shall not blame you. I alone am to blame for this,' Raphael stated grimly.

A key was turning in the lock. Rosamunde stood up, tensed and ready for whatever would happen next. She stood bravely, waiting. When the old woman entered the chamber alone, she was so stunned she could not move for the moment.

'Does the guard wait outside?' she gasped.

'I am alone. Come, my lady. Most of the men are on the ramparts. A messenger has arrived from Lord Mornay under a flag of truce. The baron is talking with him and this is our chance to leave,' Griselda urged.

'How did you get the key?'

'I had two keys with me, one to the chapel; it is my duty to clean the altar and the chalices. I gave him that key and he did not glance at it, for he had left his own key in the lock of the door,' the old crone said triumphantly.

'That was clever and well done,' Rosamunde said with approval. 'I believed all help of rescue was gone. Yet how shall we pass the guards unseen?

The drawbridge is raised. I do not see how we can leave the castle without being noticed.'

'I came here as a child, when the old baron's father was lord here. When I grew up he fell in love with me. He never thought of marriage, but he loved and trusted me, and I became his mistress. I had his son. Before he died, he showed me a secret passage that leads below the castle and out to the ruins of an ancient church. The ruins are half a mile from the village and it is somewhere close by the village that you may find Lord Mornay's camp,' Griselda explained.

'A secret passage?' Rosamunde felt icy cold. 'Have you ever used it?'

'I showed it to my son once and begged him to escape. Baron Sigmund knew that Robert was his half-brother. He feared his father's men might rise for him and so he murdered him before he had the chance to use it.'

'It is little wonder that you hate him,' Rosamunde said, but Griselda put a finger to her lips.

'No more now,' she whispered.

They crept down the stone steps leading to the tower room. At the bottom, Griselda whispered that she should wait in the shadows for a moment.

The old woman shuffled off and she heard an argument ensue, then she returned and beckoned to Rosamunde.

'I have sent the guard on an errand. Come quickly, lady, for he was suspicious and will not be long.'

They fled through the shadows in the large hall. Torches were flaring in sconces but because the men were on the battlements many had not been lit and the hall was empty. At this hour the men would normally be eating supper, relaxing at the end of the day.

At the end of the hall there was a heavy tapestry. Griselda moved it aside, her fingers exploring the thick, stone walls until she found a lever which she pulled sharply. There was a loud noise as a segment of the wall slid forward, and a black hole appeared.

Rosamunde hesitated, knowing that in such darkness she might encounter rats, spider's webs and other creatures. Her courage almost failed her, but the thought of the alternative made her step forward.

'Wait, mistress. You will need this.'

Griselda had fetched a torch of flaming pitch

from its sconce on the wall and passed her the tapering handle.

'It will show you the path you must follow and scare away the rats.'

'Thank you; the torch will make it easier,' Rosamunde said through fear-numbed lips and stepped into the darkness, feeling the chill begin to eat into her bones. 'Are you sure you will not come with me?'

'No, I must remain to close the passage or they will know where you have gone,' Griselda said. 'May God protect and bless you, lady.'

'And you,' Rosamunde replied with sincere gratitude.

She walked into the darkness. The torch showed her a passage leading on a downward slope, taking her below the castle walls and beyond. Behind her the wall had shut. She was alone in this horrible place and now her fear was very real, almost suffocating. Her heart raced as she took another step, her mouth dry as the terror swept over her.

'I am not afraid.' She spoke the words aloud to comfort herself. 'There is an end to this tunnel and I shall come to it if I have courage.'

She had never felt so alone, never been so terrified, but one thought drove her on: she must reach the end and find Raphael before he accepted the baron's challenge.

'God be praised, you have returned unharmed.' Raphael clapped the brave knight that had carried his message on the shoulder. 'I prayed that Sigmund would honour the flag of truce but I could not be certain.'

'He came to the gates himself and spoke with me, my lord. He bade me tell you that this is a matter of blood feud, and you must give your word that this must be settled between the two of you. Sir Edmund was his kinsman and he believes you executed him on a trumped-up charge.'

'Is that what this is all about?' Raphael frowned. 'Did you give him my message? If he will allow Rosamunde to go free, I will accept a truce and leave in peace—but if he refuses I shall fight to the death.'

'He says he will fight you for her. If you kill him, his men will allow you to take her, but if you lose she belongs to him.'

'How can I agree to such a bargain?' Raphael said, flinging away with a cry of despair. He stood in the darkness, his back towards the knight. A feeling of despair and anger swept over him. 'I have a plan, but if it does not work she will be at his mercy.' He shook his head. 'Leave me, sir. I would be alone to think on this. If I give my word… No, I cannot let him have her.'

'We could take the castle by force, my lord?' his man suggested.

'Perhaps, but men would die—and the baron might make her suffer for it. Leave me now. I shall think on this for a time before you take my answer.'

Raphael felt the pain twist inside him. It was unthinkable to leave Rosamunde to the mercy of Baron Sigmund. He was prepared for single combat and hopeful that he would prevail—but supposing he failed? If he gave his word to the baron that this matter would be settled between the two of them, he could not in all honour allow Janquil to spirit her away as they'd planned.

Be damned to his honour! As a young squire, and then when he was knighted, Raphael had sworn before God always to behave with honour. To give his word and break it was a foul trick and would be a stain upon his reputation for ever—yet the alternative was not to be thought of.

Rosamunde could not be left to that devil's mercy. Raphael would sacrifice not only his life but also his honour to see her safe.

His mind made up, he summoned his messenger.

'Go back to Baron Sigmund. At the hour of ten bells tomorrow morning, my squire and I will enter the castle alone under a flag of truce. I shall meet the baron and the winner will win the hand of the lady Rosamunde Meldreth.'

'But my lord,' the knight said, somewhat startled, 'the men are ready to storm the castle and take her.'

'I have a plan to bring her out,' Raphael replied. 'If I fail, you have my permission to do as your hearts dictate. Take revenge for me and rescue my lady if you can for love of me.'

The knight looked puzzled but inclined his head and turned away to where his horse stood ready, a squire waiting to assist him to mount.

Raphael looked back at the camp, where his men were sitting by a fire roasting meat in the flames. They were talking and laughing, seemingly filled with confidence. He could not face them at this moment. Walking into the darkness, he sought solitude and a chance to reflect.

Where was Rosamunde at this moment? He felt that she was in trouble and afraid. Of course she must be, knowing that she was a prisoner of the baron. He might already have harmed her, forced her... No; even the thought was too painful. He could not bear it and thrust it from his mind.

Rosamunde was his. He wanted her more than he had ever wanted a woman in his life. He loved her, loved her passionately with all his heart and being, in a way that he had not dreamed he could ever love anyone.

As the realisation swept over him, he was filled with a sense of joy mixed with despair. Rosamunde had completely taken away the pain of his first wife's death and in its place had come a deep, warm and abiding love that he believed would last his whole life. He had never realised that he could love like this. Rosamunde had showed him his true nature and if he lost her now his life would not be worth living.

'I vow I will not fail you,' he said, and fell to his knees beneath the branches of an ancient oak. 'If God grants me victory, I shall show you how much I love you—and if I die I pray that you will be safe.'

Tears slipped down his cheeks in the darkness. He had learned to understand himself and his feelings for Rosamunde—but was it too late for the two of them to find happiness together?

'I cannot lose you. I cannot let you suffer at that beast's hands.'

Rising to his feet, he steeled himself, shutting off emotion as he had so often in the past. He must be strong. Nothing mattered but the woman he had come to love. All his hopes rested with Janquil. His servant was slight, his shape almost womanly. It was his plan that he change clothes with Rosamunde once they were inside. As they had entered under a flag of truce, Rosamunde— masquerading as Janquil—would be allowed to ride out and take Raphael's fallen body back to his men, if the absolute worst happened.

If Rosamunde had the courage, she could take Janquil's place and escape to freedom—but would she? Raphael remembered her declaration of love and feared that she would lose her head and give in to her grief.

He must kill Baron Sigmund. It was the only

way to be certain of securing her freedom. He knew without boasting that he was an excellent fighter, but all the reports of the baron said the other man was truly fearsome in battle. Raphael had to prepare himself for it to be an even fight, with perhaps only an even chance of triumphing.

Once or twice the air in the passage had become very stuffy. Rosamunde had feared that her torch would go out and she would be forced to continue in the dark. She'd heard scuffling in the darkness and knew that there were some kind of creatures here. Once a furry body brushed her ankle and she gave a scream of fright. Would the rats attack her?

Whatever it was she had disturbed, it went running off, probably as frightened as she. She breathed deeply, her throat tight. How long had she been in this terrible place? It felt like the end of the world, as if she were dead and searching like a lost soul for the way across the River Styx.

The walls of the tunnel had been damp at one stage, water trickling down the walls. However, for a while now the air had been better and the rock on either side of her was dry. She noticed that she appeared to be climbing upwards and her spirits lifted. Surely she must be coming to the end of this foul journey? Soon she would be out in the fresh air—and then what?

Griselda had told her she would come out in some ancient ruins. From there she needed to find the village, because Raphael's camp would not be far away.

She might soon be with him. Her pulse raced and her pace increased. What time was it? She had no idea whether it was night or morning. Would she be in time to stop the combat between Raphael and the baron?

Ahead of her she could see a glimmer of light. Running towards it, she began to realise that the entrance to the passage stood open, covered only by living vines. Thrusting them to one side, she emerged into the fresh air and looked about her.

She was clearly in what had once been a chapel and she could see the shape of a stone cross lying amongst the rubble. What had happened here? For a moment she seemed to hear the cries of terrified priests as invading hordes cut them down and she shivered. The entrance to the passage was guarded by the ghosts of long ago, keeping away curious villagers. She ran through the fallen stones and stood on the grassy bank that rose above the surrounding countryside. Away to her left was a flickering light that gave a red glow to the night. The glow must be the fires of Raphael's camp; it was no more than half a mile distant.

Her torch flickered, spluttered and went out. Throwing it down, Rosamunde began to run towards the glow of the campfires.

Raphael sat with his back to the tree. He knew that he must rest. He had no appetite for food, yet he ought to eat if only to remain strong for the next day. Baron Sigmund had agreed to meet him in single combat the following morning at ten.

'Rosamunde, my love,' he whispered into the darkness. 'If I could but look upon your face once more…'

Thrusting aside the thoughts that could only make him weak, he rose to his feet. He must rest if he were to be strong enough in the morning. To think of her now would drive him mad.

He stared up at the sky. The moon was full, shedding its silvery light over trees and bushes, the road leading to an early Christian church that had been razed to the ground in the ninth century by invading Vikings. Someone was running from the ruins—a woman. Something about the way she moved drew his gaze, holding it, his heart beginning to drum so it became thunder in his ears. 'Rosamunde…' He could not see her and yet his senses drove him forward as he began to run. 'Rosamunde, my beloved!'

She had seen him and she cried out something. He increased his pace and then she was close enough for him to see her face.

'It *is* you—my dear one! Rosamunde, they told me you were his prisoner—how came you here?' he cried out.

'Raphael!' she cried and threw herself into his arms, a sob in her voice as he held her close. 'I was locked in the tower but escaped with an old lady's help. She hated the baron passionately because he killed her son—his half-brother, baseborn out of wedlock.'

'My love.' He clasped her to him, holding her close as if he hardly dared to believe that she was here in his arms. She could hear his heartbeat, feel her own racing wildly as he gazed down at her, his look so wild and passionate that it sent shivers through her. 'You are safe. God has answered my prayers. Now I can meet my fate with a brave heart.'

She looked up at him, close to tears. 'No, you must not meet the baron in single combat. No one has ever beaten him. He is bigger and heavier than you, Raphael. There is no need to fight him now. I am free; let us return to the castle and be safe together.'

'My word is given,' Raphael said and looked down at her, a smile of understanding on his lips. 'You must not be afraid for me, my dearest one. I have fought many warriors as brave and fierce as the baron. Now that I know you are free, I can fight with a free heart. Have courage, my dearest, for God is with me and I shall prevail.'

'Please, I beg you, do not fight him,' she pleaded. 'I escaped so that you would not have to give your life for mine. The baron never meant to set me free. Had he killed you, he would have taken me as his whore, or his wife if I pleased him.'

'That was my fear and will remain so if we leave now. You will never be safe unless I fight him and win,' Raphael said, and his arms tightened about her. 'You must not be anxious, Rosamunde. Now that I do not have to worry for your sake, I shall be stronger.'

'Please, no…'

He closed her mouth with a passionate kiss, his lips so tender that she near swooned against him. She clung to him but held back her tears, knowing that his mind was set and she must not continue to beg.

'Hush, my love. I must fight, for this score remains unsettled between us. If it is not settled now we shall none of us be able to rest in peace,' he said gently.

'If you die I shall not want to live. I have no one but you. My father is dead and I will not return to my cousin's service,' she said brokenly.

He drew back and looked at her. 'Your father lives and I have already made arrangements for your future. He will have money enough to employ men to defend you both and to give you a dowry, should you choose to marry another.'

'Baron Sigmund told me my father was dead!' she exclaimed.

'He lied. You are not alone, Rosamunde. Besides, I truly believe that I shall prevail,' he said determinedly.

'Will nothing sway you?' She would not beg and yet she truly feared that she would lose him if he fought, for the baron was so strong.

'Nothing you can say will change what must be,' Raphael reiterated and smiled at her reassuringly. 'Fear not, I shall not fail you. Now, I shall take you to the camp. When I ride to meet the baron, six of my men shall take you back to Mornay. You will wait there until I come for you.'

'And if you do not return?' she whispered.

'Then you must go to your father.'

'If it is your command, my lord.'

'Not my command—my wish. I would not have you come to harm, dearest one,' he said tenderly.

'I shall do as you bid me, my lord.'

How could she say otherwise? She loved him so, but it would break her heart to lose him.

A tear trickled down her cheek. Raphael frowned and smoothed it away. 'I must see you safe and then I should rest. I need my strength for the morning and if I spend the entire night with you I should be too weak to fight,' he teased gently and was rewarded with a wan smile from her.

Chapter Twelve

'My lady, forgive me for not saving you from this ordeal,' Janquil said as he brought her food and wine. 'Alone that day, I could do nothing when you were captured by Sir Ian, though I would gladly have given my life for yours. I knew I should be killed and then no one would know where you were. It was my duty to let my lord know what had happened.'

'Had you not returned to the castle to inform them of my capture, my lord would not have been here to rescue me now. I escaped the castle, but had I been forced to find my own way to Mornay I might have been recaptured or starved to death before I reached safety,' she acknowledged.

'Tell me, lady,' Janquil said as he squatted on the earth beside her. 'How did you escape? My lord did not tell us.'

'Through a secret passage that leads from the ruins to the great hall of the castle. An old woman showed me the way but would not come with me. She wanted to see Baron Sigmund's face when he discovered that I escaped.'

'He will kill her.'

'She knows that but does not care,' she said sadly.

'She must hate him very much,' he commented.

'Yes, I believe she does.' Rosamunde looked at him. 'You know my lord well. Is there no way we can prevent him from fighting the baron?'

'At the moment he is sleeping,' Janquil said. 'In the morning I shall tell him of the secret way. By such a means we could let our men into the castle. Tell me exactly where the lever is to be found, my lady. I begin to see what we might do.'

'I know my lord is a brave fighter, but I fear treachery,' Rosamunde said. 'When Sigmund discovers I am not there, he will be angry. Raphael will be alone. If the baron chooses, Raphael may be taken prisoner and slain without a chance to fight.'

'This is what I have always feared,' Janquil told her. 'My lord is too stubborn. He might have deceived the baron for your sake, but he is a man of honour, and now he will keep his promise to fight—but there *is* something we might do…'

'Be of good heart, my love,' Raphael said and gazed down into her face. His fingers trailed her cheek and her white throat. Her body felt as if it were melting. She wanted to melt into him so that they need not be parted—for if he died what was there in life for her? 'If God is on my side I shall win this day and then we shall be wed. I swear that we shall never be parted again while I live.'

'I love you,' Rosamunde said, head high as she smiled bravely. The time for begging was past but now she had a plan to save him if the baron betrayed him. 'You have my love and my prayers.'

He bent his head and kissed her softly, incredibly proud of her bravery. 'Keep that in your heart until we meet again.'

Rosamunde nodded and stood back, watching as Janquil mounted and rode off with his master. He turned once, making a slight movement of his head, as if to indicate that all would be well.

Rosamunde blinked and looked at the men waiting to escort her back to Mornay. She walked towards the horse that she was to mount and then stopped, shaking her head.

'I want to go with the men,' she said. 'I want to go back through the passage with you into the castle. I must be there. I cannot ride to safety when my lord may lose his life.'

'Raphael would hang us all if we allowed you to do that, lady. We must obey his orders,' said one of the men in dismay.

'You may, but I shall not,' Rosamunde said forcefully and turned. She ran up the slight incline towards the ruins. Raphael had no idea what Janquil and the rest of his men had plotted together, but already she could see the knights and men-at-arms preparing to enter the tunnel. Behind her, the men detailed to escort her had paused, unsure of what to do.

Rosamunde saw the last of the men enter the tunnel and went in after them. Three had flares held aloft but the darkness held no fears for her this time. She was determined to see what happened. Raphael's men would not dare to interfere if the fight took place, for his fury would know no bounds—but, if the baron betrayed him, they would fall upon them and rescue him. The baron's men would not expect an attack from within and the attackers would have the advantage.

Hearing a sound behind her, Rosamunde looked over her shoulder and saw that her escort had decided to follow after all. They made no attempt to drag her back, and she smiled, knowing that all the men felt as she did: they wanted to be there in case the baron reneged on his word. They all knew Baron Sigmund was not to be trusted in the slightest. Raphael was in more danger than he imagined.

'What?' Baron Sigmund glared at the old woman as she stood before him. 'Why can you not bring Lady Rosamunde to watch the combat?'

'Because she has gone.' Griselda cackled, a look of wild glee in her eyes. 'I helped her to escape and she went last night.'

'Damn you!' He struck her across the face, knocking her off her feet. Towering over her, he swore furiously. 'If this is the truth, you will suffer the torments of the damned.'

'Nothing you do now can harm me,' Griselda said defiantly as she rose to her feet and stood before him once more. 'You killed my son, your

half-brother. When you did that I vowed revenge—
and this day I have it.'

'Damn you.' The baron caught his sword but
even as he lifted his arm a fanfare drew his attention. 'You will keep. I have more important work
for my sword,' he snarled.

He strode away, watching as two men rode into
the courtyard. Seeing that Raphael had brought
only a puny squire with him, he smiled. The fool
was unprotected. He had planned to fight man to
man in order to show the woman he held hostage
that he was invincible in battle and was deserv-
ing of her as a prize, but now there was no real
purpose to the fight. He had the son of a hated
enemy at his mercy. He would hang him and be
done with it.

Striding towards Raphael, he saw the squire fall
back, and then turn tail and run in the direction of
the hall. He laughed, because the man was clearly
terrified.

'Let the rabbit run,' he said as one of his men
moved, as if to stop him. 'He can do us no harm.
He will be caught and dealt with later. He cannot
escape.'

'My squire is here under a flag of truce,' Raphael said coolly. 'He must be allowed to leave without harm, whatever the outcome.'

'I find I am not minded to fight this day,' the baron drawled. 'You are a fool, Mornay. You are completely at my mercy. I do not know why you rode in here without an escort to see fair play, but since you have I shall accept the gift you offer. I hated your father and now I have a score to settle with you. Sir Edmund was my blood kin and his death must be avenged.'

'We shall settle this by combat as we agreed,' Raphael said firmly.

'That was before the wench managed to escape me.' Sigmund scowled. 'I see no reason to waste my breath fighting you when I have you at my mercy. Once you are dead, I shall take all that was yours—your lands, your castle *and* your woman.'

'You are a coward and a fool, sir,' Raphael retorted. 'I have come with all honour to fight you. Let it be done according to the rules of chivalry and retain your own honour.'

'I have none to lose,' Sigmund said with a sour twist of his mouth. 'My father wanted to put his bastard in my place. I killed them both and took what belonged to me. Why should I give you the chance to kill me?'

'You swore that you owed loyalty to King Richard—was even that false?' Raphael asked heatedly.

'If Richard comes here I shall bend the knee. I am no fool, but I serve only myself. Richard will not remain in England for long. He loves war and the chance of glory. Besides, he will be too busy holding his throne to bother about my business.'

'You are a knave and without honour. Your blood would taint my sword,' Raphael said grimly. 'I was warned not to trust you and I should have listened.'

'Take him!' the baron yelled to his men. 'Drag him from his horse and bring him here.'

For a moment the men were too stunned to move. They were rogues who lived by the sword, but a flag of truce was sacred, and so was the promise Baron Sigmund had given to fight in single combat.

'Damn you, do as I tell you!' the baron roared. 'Or I'll hang the lot of you.'

Galvanised into action, four men moved towards Raphael, trying to grab him and pull him from his horse. He drew his sword and slashed at them, cutting into the light armour of chain mail they wore.

'Pull him down. What are you—weaklings? He is but one man.'

'One man too many for you,' Raphael cried and dug his spurs into his horse's flanks. The beast snorted and leaped forward, shaking off the men on the ground. Raphael rode at the baron, who drew his sword and prepared to defend himself. 'Will you fight me now? Call off your dogs and fight like a man?'

The baron lashed out at the horse, causing it to shrill, rear up and almost unseat Raphael. He clung on, bending low in the saddle to sweep down with his sword arm and strike at the baron's arm.

Sigmund gave a scream of anger or pain and struck again, his sword striking the metal guards that protected the lower half of Raphael's leg.

His men were watching the battle, looking uneasily from one to the other. Then the sound of blood-curdling cries alerted them and suddenly thirty or forty men were pouring out into the courtyard. They wore the same colours as Lord Mornay and charged towards him as Raphael whirled on his horse and then rode at the baron once more.

Men-at-arms, who had been trying to decide how best to help the baron, were suddenly under attack themselves. They called for help, and their comrades who had been watching from the battlements began to make their way down the stone steps, but there was room for only one or two at a time.

Raphael had dismounted and was now engaged in hand to hand combat with the baron. Outside, the sound of a fanfare could be heard. Some of the men on the ramparts looked down at the huge company of knights that had gathered below their walls. Suddenly, a cheer came from every throat on the battlements and someone gave the order to lower the drawbridge.

Raphael and the baron fought on, but the rest of the men fell silent and put down their swords, disengaging as the fanfare sounded again and they saw the advance party of knights. They carried the King's standard and, as they saw it, man after man took up the cheering! Then they threw down their swords and one by one fell to their knees as a tall man rode forward.

'God save His Majesty! God save the King!'

Gradually becoming aware of what was happening, Raphael stood back, lowering his sword. He would not fight in the presence of his king, for all men must bend the knee. In that moment, the baron struck a terrific blow against his shield and sent him staggering back. The baron stood over him, his sword hovering as Raphael fended his shield and struggled to rise.

A woman's scream was heard and suddenly Rosamunde came from nowhere; racing towards the baron, she flung herself on his back and put both hands over his eyes, blinding him. He had been so intent on his kill that he was taken aback, and turned round and round in a circle, trying to shake her off and roaring in frustration. Her nails scratched across his face, poking at his eyes and making him yell out in pain. In seconds Raphael was on his feet. He picked up his sword and struck at the baron's legs, which was the only place he could strike without injuring her. Rosamunde fell off and lay on the ground, winded and shaken, until Janquil rushed to pick her up and carry her to safety.

'Enough!' the King cried. 'The next man to use his sword in anger will be hanged by my order.'

Baron Sigmund's head swivelled. He saw Richard's face and his own fell, his mouth opening in shock. He stood back, finally dropping his sword. Then he went down on one knee, leaving Raphael and the King the only two men still standing.

'Well, my old friend, it seems that I am in time,' Richard said and smiled. 'Though from what I could see you were well on your way to victory before I arrived.'

'It seems someone else had less faith in me than you, sire,' Raphael said, and looked angry. Across the compound Janquil was trying to control Rosamunde but she broke from his hold and ran to Raphael's side. 'That was the most foolish thing I have ever seen. I sent you home. Why did you defy me and come here?' he asked furiously.

'We all came through the secret way,' Rosamunde explained. 'We feared treachery from the baron—he might have killed you had the men not come to your aid.'

'Go back to Janquil at once,' Raphael ordered, his lips white.

'You are angry because I tried to help you.' The

colour drained from her face. 'You were down. I thought he would kill you before you could rise.'

'I should not have allowed that to happen, lady,' the King said and smiled at her. 'Your action was brave but unnecessary. Your lord was in command of the situation.'

'How could he…?' Suddenly realising who she was addressing, Rosamunde's cheeks flooded with colour and she sank into a curtsey. 'Forgive me, sire. I meant no disrespect.'

'Go with Janquil, as your lord requested,' Richard advised her. 'Yet I would not have you leave us too soon. Your lord hath told me of his intention to wed, and you have proved yourself worthy of our respect. It is in my mind that I would speak with you later in private—after I have dealt with the situation here.'

'Yes, sire.' She glanced at Raphael but his expression was icy cold. 'Forgive me.'

Rosamunde bowed her head and returned to Janquil. She knew from Raphael's manner that he was very angry indeed with her.

'I have offended my lord,' she said dismally to Janquil. 'He was so angry with me. What have I done that was so very wrong?'

'You have made a fool of him before his men,' Janquil explained. 'It was clear that you imagined he needed help, and that shames him.'

'But the baron stood over him. He would have killed him.'

'He was in no way finished,' Janquil argued. 'The baron struck a foul blow after Raphael put down his sword because he was in the King's presence. However, I have seen him down, without either shield or sword, and yet winning the contest. My lord is a mighty warrior indeed. You should not have acted as you did, lady.'

'Then why did you open the secret way for the rest of us?'

'Because the baron is an evil man who would not have stuck to his bargain. He reneged on his promise to meet Raphael in single combat. Had the men not disobeyed his orders and entered the castle, Sir Raphael might have been hanged in revenge for Sir Edmund.'

Rosamunde bit her lip. She looked across the compound, wishing that she could be there and hear what was going on.

'What will happen now?'

'The King is mediating between them,' Janquil

said. 'It might be that he will decide they should settle this by combat.'

'No!' Rosamunde caught the sob that rose to her lips. 'My lord may be killed after all.'

'No, look—the baron is on both knees before the King.'

'Now he has risen to his feet.' Rosamunde wrung her hands in distress. She dared not disobey either the King or Raphael by approaching them and she could only watch as the King began to speak.

'Oh…' she gasped. 'The baron is picking up his sword. What is going to happen?'

Janquil placed a warning hand on her arm. 'Stay here, lady. My lord will not forgive you if you interfere now.'

'They *are* going to fight again,' Rosamunde said, her eyes stinging with tears. 'I cannot watch this…'

'You must, unless you wish to shame both yourself and your lord,' Janquil said. 'Your King is here. The fight will be fair, because the baron knows that if he tried treachery he would be severely punished.'

'Yes.' Rosamunde lifted her head, holding back the tears. Her heart was beating wildly but there was nothing she could do other than stand and watch. It was unbearable but she must bear it because she had no other choice.

The fight was fast and furious but over very quickly. Rosamunde could scarcely believe what she was seeing. The baron was a huge man and must have been tremendously strong, his blows enough to send any foe to the floor, but to her surprise Raphael was more than a match for him, meeting blow with blow and seeming faster and more skilled. For what seemed an endless agony for her, they thrust and parried, but finally the baron's sword went spinning and he dropped to his knees.

Rosamunde was too far away to hear what was being said, but she saw Raphael look at the King. Richard inclined his head and Raphael held his sword to the baron's throat, but then he said something and dropped his sword. Baron Sigmund bowed his head, then rose to his feet. The King stepped forward, indicating that the two men should make up their quarrel. The Baron offered his hand; Raphael took it and a sigh of relief went through the assembled watchers.

'What has happened?' Rosamunde asked Janquil.

'My lord has shown mercy. He has given the baron his life and in return received his homage. Raphael is now lord of this manor and its demesne, but he will allow Baron Sigmund to remain as the lord here—providing that he gives allegiance to the King. The baron must hold the castle in the King's name, and come when my lord commands, but otherwise he is his own man. My lord asks nothing more than his allegiance.'

'I do not understand. How do you know this?' she asked, bewildered.

'I am able to read expressions and words,' Janquil explained. 'It is one of my skills that my lord prizes. I am not certain of it all, but I have seen this kind of surrender before at Acre.'

'Do you think the baron will keep to his bargain?'

'He must. If he does not, his life is forfeit. My lord would need only to say the word and he would be outlawed.'

Rosamunde bowed her head, saying nothing more. The baron was offering hospitality to the King. Servants were scurrying here and there.

Raphael sent one furious glance towards her and then strode past her into the hall with Richard.

Feeling unsure of what she ought to do, Rosamunde followed at a distance. The baron had ordered food to be brought and the hall was a hive of activity.

Raphael was ignoring her. Rosamunde felt hurt and angry; did he not understand that she'd acted impulsively out of love for him? She had not meant to embarrass him before his men—indeed, she saw no reason for him to be humiliated by what she'd done. The baron had struck a foul blow and she'd gone to his assistance. How could that be so very wrong?

Tears pricking her eyes, she turned and fled from the hall. There were men everywhere and she did not wish to be seen weeping. In despair she fled to the tower room where she had been held captive by the baron, took the key from its lock and locked it on the inside before throwing herself on the bed to weep.

It was perhaps an hour later when someone knocked at the door. Rosamunde asked who it was and Griselda answered her.

'Your lord sends for you to come down, lady.'

'I do not wish to come,' Rosamunde replied dully.

'A meal has been prepared. Everyone is waiting for you. If you keep them waiting, both Lord Mornay and His Majesty will be angry. You have no choice. I have brought you a clean gown to wear.'

Reluctantly, Rosamunde answered the door. Her tears had dried and now she was angry too. It was on the tip of her tongue to refuse, but she realised such behaviour would seem childish. She would not give Raphael an excuse to treat her as a naughty child, but would instead treat him with cool dignity. She had had enough of his coldness. Now he should see that she too could be proud.

Some minutes later, dressed in a gown that the party from the castle had brought with them, she went down to the hall. Everyone turned their heads to look at her as she entered and stood hesitating, uncertain of her place here. Then the King walked towards her, a smile of welcome on his face.

'Come, my lady,' he said kindly. 'I would have you sit at my left hand. 'I thought your action brave, if foolhardy, and would not have you hang your head in shame.'

'You are generous, sire,' she murmured, her cheeks pink.

Rosamunde took his hand and let him lead her to her place beside him at the high table. Since Raphael sat at his right hand, she was spared the necessity of looking at him or speaking to him.

'Now, my lady Rosamunde, tell me how your father fares. I have heard that he has been ill-treated in my absence and it is my intention to make recompense as far as I am able,' the King said.

'Baron Sigmund told me my father was dead, but I have since heard that he lied. I would like to go home and see for myself, sire,' she said.

'Then I shall arrange an escort for you,' Richard said. 'Tell your father that I am mindful of all he has done for my cause in the past and will do what I can to help him. I return to debts and turmoil, but something will be arranged as soon as it can be managed. I do not forget my friends.'

'I thank you with all my heart,' she said, smiling at him.

The servants were bringing dishes of rich meats, soups, stews and roast boar to table. As always, a page first tasted everything the King ate, but nothing untoward happened, and the atmosphere was a merry one.

Gradually, Rosamunde felt some of the tension leave her and she ate a little of the food placed before her, particularly the soft cheese, figs and dates. She drank sparingly of the wine, for though it was sweet and fruity it was also very strong.

As the company ate and drank, minstrels sang songs of brave deeds and lovelorn knights to entertain them. There was also a juggler, and a dwarf who did acts of tumbling and buffoonery.

Now and then the King spoke to her, but most of the time he was talking with Raphael in a low voice. She caught snatches of their conversation and knew that it concerned Prince John, who had presented himself to his brother with alacrity once he had heard that the people had flocked to the King's standard.

'My brother blames his council and bad advice for the evil that has taken place here,' Richard was saying. 'I know that he lies, but he is my brother and carries the same blood. If I exacted a cruel punishment, my soul would carry the stain of his blood. I am minded to be lenient on this occasion.'

Rosamunde could not hear Raphael's reply but

the King nodded, obviously pleased with what was said. When the evening was well advanced, she asked the King if she might be excused. His permission given, she rose to her feet, curtsied and then walked away. She did not dare to glance at Raphael for fear of what she might see in his eyes. He had promised to wed her, but that had been before she had humiliated him before his men.

Griselda had waited to help her undress, but she sent her away and sat on a deep stone window-ledge recessed into the thick walls, brushing her long hair as she gazed out at the night. The sky was dark, but a crescent moon was behind the clouds, and now and then its silvery light brought a glow to the darkness.

Hearing the knock at her door, she stiffened, then got up and went close to it, asking who was there.

'It is Raphael,' he said. 'Please allow me to come in and speak with you, Rosamunde.'

She hesitated, then sighed and turned the key, standing back as he entered and then turning away. She went back to her window and continued to look out at the night.

'Richard tells me he has promised you an escort to your father's home,' he stated.

'Yes.' She did not turn to look at him. 'My father is ill and I would care for him.'

'I told you that he is well cared-for by Beth and Ferdie and lacks for nothing. Did you not believe me?'

'I would see him for myself,' she said stubbornly.

'Very well, I shall take you there.'

'A small escort is all that is needed. I dare say you are too busy to concern yourself with such things,' she said coolly.

'Have you learned nothing?' Raphael's voice grated and she heard the suppressed anger in it. 'Do you not know that you will never be safe unless you marry? Your husband must be strong enough to protect you or others will seek to steal you away for their own ends.'

'Perhaps you would have me retire to a nunnery?' she shot back. 'If I shut myself away from the world I shall cause no more trouble—for you or anyone.'

'Foolish woman!' She felt his hands on her shoulders. A shiver ran down her spine and for a moment she felt as if she would faint from desire.

He turned her to face him. 'Look at me and tell me you wish to become a nun.'

His eyes blazed at her passionately. Rosamunde's gaze dropped from the heat in his. She could not lie to him. All she wanted was to be his wife and lie in his arms the night long.

'I have caused you so much trouble. I do not wonder that you hate me,' she said brokenly.

'I could never hate you,' he said huskily, giving her a slight shake. 'How could you think it?'

'You do not love me. I know your heart lies in the grave with your first wife.'

'I cannot deny that I did care for her,' he said, and a nerve flicked in his throat. He hesitated, then spoke again. 'She was a sweet child and did not deserve to die so foully. But you must know that I care for you deeply,' he continued awkwardly. He'd never avowed his love for any woman before and he was suddenly uncertain of what to say to her.

'No. I thought… I did not know.' She spoke the words so softly that he hardly heard her. She saw him frown and took a deep breath. 'I thought it would be enough for me to be your wife without love, my lord—but I find it is not.'

'What do you mean?' His question was swift and angry, but also uncertain.

'I want to be loved passionately,' Rosamunde said earnestly. 'I know that you cannot give me the love I desire and so it will be better if I go to my father.'

'You are renouncing your promise to wed me?' he asked in disbelief, stung by her rejection of him.

'I… No…' she faltered and the tears trickled down her cheeks. 'Yes, perhaps. I must have time to think. I am no longer sure what I want.'

Raphael stared at her in silence for what seemed an eternity, then he bowed his head grimly. 'Very well, if that is your wish. I shall take you to your father.'

'Raphael, I didn't mean…' The words died on her lips as he turned and walked out, closing the door hard behind him. 'I love you.'

She sank down on the edge of the bed, lowering her head into her hands as the bitter tears came. Raphael cared for her, and would wed her with all honour, but he did not love her as she wanted to be loved—as he had loved Messalina.

Chapter Thirteen

They left Baron Sigmund's castle the next morning. Rosamunde did not know what had been said to him, but he begged her pardon before she mounted her horse and asked what recompense he could make for his ill-treatment of her.

'You will forgive Griselda for what she did,' Rosamunde said. 'Let her live out her life in peace and comfort and ask her forgiveness so that the quarrel between you may be at an end.'

The baron's eyes flickered, as if he disliked her request, but he merely inclined his head and murmured something she could not hear.

'You need not be concerned for the old woman,' Raphael said as he helped her to mount her palfrey. 'I have arranged for her to be taken to Mornay, where she can sit by the kitchen fire and dream away her days.'

'My lord is generous,' Rosamunde said, her lips stiff. She felt numbed all over. The night had been long and restless and she'd hardly slept.

Why must they always quarrel when all she wanted was to be his, to know the sweetness of his loving and surrender herself to his dominion?

'I would be more so if you would let me,' he said bitterly and moved away to mount his own horse.

For a while they rode in silence. Rosamunde did not dare to look at him, because she was afraid that she might weep. Why had she been so foolish? It was true that she wanted to visit her father, but she did not wish to stay with him. If Raphael rode away and she never saw him again it would break her heart. She could not bear to lose him now.

She wanted him to love her with all his heart but she knew that was impossible. However, he did care for her, and he wanted her. He had shown desire and caring too many times for her to believe him indifferent to her.

Surely it must be enough for her? Yet she wanted more, so much more. If she could not be satisfied with less she might lose all, and yet there was something within her that would not let go of her need and desire to be loved to distraction by him.

'Richard bade me tell you he will give your father a pension of one-hundred silver crowns every six months. Do you think it will suffice?' Raphael said quietly.

'It is more than I had hoped,' Rosamunde said and felt puzzled. 'I did not think the King had money to spare. He spoke of debts and turmoil to be settled before he could think of such things.'

'His Majesty received a substantial donation to his coffers,' Raphael said evasively. 'I dare say he decided to use some of it to reward men like your father who had done much for him in the past.'

'Who made the donation to the King's purse?' she pressed.

'I believe it may have been Baron Sigmund. We found a large amount of stolen gold and jewels in his stronghold. Shall we say that he was persuaded to part with a generous portion of his wealth?' Raphael said with a grim smile.

'*You* commanded him to make the gift! He will hate you even more,' Rosamunde pointed out agitatedly. 'You know he is your bitterest enemy now? He may be forced to accept you as his over-lord, but he will be no true friend.'

'Perhaps. It hardly matters. I have decided I may

return to France and spend most of the year there. Jonathan has no land of his own and he *is* a true friend. He would protect Mornay and its people with his life.' Raphael shrugged off her concerns. 'I shall not lose sleep over the baron or any other man—but I must confess that I did not sleep well last night.'

Rosamunde stared at him in confusion. 'Why was that, my lord?'

A teasing smile flickered in his eyes and he arched his right eyebrow. 'You do not know? I fancied you too might have spent a restless night, but perhaps I was wrong. Perhaps you slept like a babe?'

Rosamunde blushed and looked down. She sensed that he was teasing her and the dark cloud that hung over her eased a little. This was the man she loved, the man she'd feared had gone for ever.

'I think I spoke in haste, my lord. I was hurt and angry—too proud, as usual.'

'Perhaps we have both been hasty. I too was hurt and my pride was touched, Rosamunde, but pride is one thing and affairs of the heart are another,' he added, then spurred his horse and rode on to speak with one of his men.

Did that mean he was no longer angry with her? Rosamunde knew that she must find the courage to tell him that she loved him, and wanted nothing more than to be his wife as soon as possible, but it would not be easy unless she could put away her pride and accept whatever Raphael could give her.

Raphael was laughing with his men, riding ahead of her. Rosamunde let him go. She had learned that it was best to wait. In time he would tell her what was on his mind—and perhaps in his heart.

That night they made camp in the clearing of a wood. The servants put up a small pavilion for her so that she might rest on a soft mattress with pillows for her head. Raphael and his men were to sleep on the hard ground. She asked him why he did not have a pavilion of his own.

'Surely the men could provide a pavilion for you?' she asked before they said good night.

'When in the open I prefer to sleep as my men do, on the ground,' he said and smiled at her wickedly. 'Unless you wish me to share your bed, Rosamunde?'

His words made her cheeks burn and she turned

away without giving him an answer. Her heart was racing and she knew that she *did* wish him to lie with her. Had she been sure of his love for her, she would have shown her willingness to lie with him, but she was still uncertain.

Yet she lay there awake, listening to the sounds as the darkness deepened, wishing that she had found the courage to answer his teasing. It was so foolish to have this barrier between them. Soon she would be at Mornay and then perhaps they would be married, despite their quarrel. Why did she need to preserve her pride when her body cried out for his?

She toyed with the idea of going in search of him but still her pride would not let her beg.

When she heard the sound of a knife slitting the cloth of her pavilion, she tensed, alert and anxious. Who amongst Raphael's men would do such a thing? The answer was that none would, and she threw off her covers and jumped up, ready for the attack she was sure would come. When the man put his head through the slit he had made and crawled in, she screamed and seized the nearest thing to hand, which was an iron peg that had been left lying inside the pavilion and not used to secure it. She struck the intruder on the back of the head.

He gave a shout of pain but the blow was not sufficient to knock him out and he climbed to his feet, albeit a trifle unsteadily. She saw it was Sir Ian. He had kidnapped her once before, but this time he was alone.

'You little witch,' he muttered and lunged at her. 'I'll make you pay for that!'

'The baron locked you in his dungeons,' Rosamunde gasped, staring at him in disbelief. 'I thought you dead.'

'Now you see that you are wrong.' His fingers curled about her wrist and he started to drag her towards the entrance of the pavilion. 'I dare say you have woken the entire camp with your screaming, but if they try to take you I'll slit your throat.' He thrust her through the entrance of the pavilion in front of him, still holding the fleshy part of her upper arm.

Rosamunde found herself grabbed by someone else and pushed out of the way. As Sir Ian followed, his arm was taken and he was wrestled to the ground, where he lay glaring up at a furious Raphael.

'Damn you,' he spat. 'If the wench had not woken, I should have had her and been away with none the wiser.'

Raphael reached down and hauled the man roughly to his feet. 'You speak of my lady, dog. Have some respect or I shall have you whipped to an inch of your life. Richard should have left you where he found you.'

'The King freed me,' Sir Ian whined. 'I have the royal pardon. Kill me and he will punish you.'

'Do you imagine I would waste my time on a runt like you?' Raphael said through clenched teeth and forced the man to his knees once more. 'I shall send you in chains to London. There you will await your fate in Richard's dungeons. This time I do not think you will find him so lenient. May God give you time to reflect on your sins before you die.'

At his signal some of his men came and led Sir Ian away. Raphael turned to Rosamunde, looking at her in concern.

'Has that brute hurt you, my lady? I heard you scream but it took me a minute to reach you.'

'I do not know what he meant to do but I heard

him slit the cloth with his knife and was ready for him. When he entered, I hit him.'

'Not hard enough, unfortunately,' Raphael said with a grim look. 'Thank God I was awake and close enough to hear your scream.'

'Could you not sleep, my lord?' she asked pertly.

Raphael looked at her, his mouth softening with amusement and something more—something that set her pulses racing. 'No, I could not. Were you also sleepless, my Rosamunde?'

'Yes, my lord.'

She moved towards him, a little smile on her lips. 'Do you not think it strange that we were both restless this night, my lord?'

'I do not think it strange at all.' He took two steps towards her, reaching out to draw her hard against him. 'Sweet jade. You have kept me awake these many nights. I have burned for you. Do you truly not understand what you mean to me, my love?'

She hesitated, eyes wide with wonder. Her heart began to beat faster, her lips parted on a shuddering breath of need. 'I thought you felt something—but I thought you still in love with your first wife.'

'Although I did care for her, I never truly gave

her my heart,' he admitted. 'It was only when they told me you were taken by the baron I finally understood what love truly was, and now I know that without you my life means nothing. You have brought light to my darkness and made an empty house live again. I do not believe that I could bear to lose you again, Rosamunde,' he said tenderly. 'I would have told you this in your chamber at the baron's castle, but I was hurt and angered by your wish to break your vow to wed me and was not thinking clearly. I was stupidly proud in leaving you without telling you how I truly felt about you.'

'Say it,' she whispered, leaning into him, looking up into his face. Her whole body cried out for his, and she felt an answering need in him, but still she wanted more. 'Say the words I need to hear, my dearest one. Tell me that you love me—as I love you with all my heart.'

'I love you with my heart, my body, with every breath I take,' he murmured fervently and bent his head. Softly, he caressed her lips and, as her mouth parted, he explored it, the tip of his tongue touching hers.

Rosamunde moaned softly, her body melding with his as she seemed to melt into him, on fire with desire and need. She was trembling, heat pooling low in her abdomen as she felt the moistness between her thighs and understood the raging need within. She wanted to be his, to belong to the man she loved so completely.

'I do not think I shall rest alone this night,' she whispered, her lips soft and moist as they parted on a sighing breath. 'Will you not stay with me to protect me?'

'Is it only my protection that you want?' he asked gruffly, his brows arched. She shook her head, reaching up to touch his cheek and run her thumb over his sensuous mouth.

'No, I want you to love me,' she said honestly. 'I want you to lie by my side and teach me all the things I must know to please my husband. Show me how to make you happy, Raphael, how to be the woman you want in your bed.'

'You please me just by being here,' Raphael replied with a groan and held her close. She could feel the hardness of his need through her fine gown, and the throbbing urgency of his desire. He wanted her as much as she wanted him. He laughed softly in his throat. 'Yes, my beloved. I shall lie with you this night. We shall be man and wife before the priest gives his blessing and no one shall ever part us again.'

'Yes.' Rosamunde gave him her hand. 'I would have no more misunderstandings between us.'

They walked into the pavilion and let the flap fall. Taking his hand, Rosamunde led him towards her pallet. She knelt down on the softness and he knelt with her. They kissed tenderly and then he helped her to lift her fine tunic over her head. Beneath her shift, her breasts were peaked and pouting, evidence of her own arousal. As he bent his head to push away the silk and gently stroke them with his tongue she shivered and moaned, her body pliant and inviting.

They lay down together at last, naked, flesh to silken flesh, warm despite the bitter night, wrapped in the heat of sweet desire.

Afterwards, they lay side by side, their limbs entwined. Raphael's hand stroked the satin arch of her back as he held her close.

'I never believed that I could find such happiness,' he said softly. He held her close, his breath warm against her throat. 'You have chased away the shadows, my dear one. I am whole again.'

She snuggled up to the smooth firmness of his

body, her fingers moving through the cluster of hair on his chest, stroking him gently.

'I did not know loving could be so beautiful,' Rosamunde sighed. 'I have heard the servants speak of their lovers when they did not know I listened, but I did not know that I could feel this way.'

'You are more than my lover; you are my soul,' he murmured and kissed the side of her neck. He nibbled at her, inhaling her perfume as his hand move idly over her silky thighs. 'I have never been this close to a woman before, I swear it. You are so brave and beautiful, my Rosamunde. When you attacked the baron, I feared you might be killed and I lost my head.'

'Is *that* why you were so angry with me?' she asked incredulously.

He looked down at her, stroking her face with the tips of his fingers. 'Did you not realise that he might have killed you? In his bloodlust he might easily have thrust his sword through you.'

'I did not stop to think,' she said and gazed up into his face. 'All I thought of was my love for you. If he had killed you, then I should have wanted to die too.'

'Promise me you will never do such a thing again?' Raphael begged seriously.

'I did not mean to make you look foolish before your men. Janquil explained that my actions had caused you to lose face,' she went on, when he raised a brow in query at her.

'Janquil is my trusted servant and friend, but he cannot know my heart. Only you will ever know that, Rosamunde. My anger was not due to hurt pride, or because I felt humiliated, but simply a reflection of my fear of losing you,' he explained.

'I thought…' She shook her head as the tears trickled down her cheek. 'I was foolish and I too am proud, my lord. I shall never doubt your love again.'

He kissed her and drew her close, desire raging between them once more. They kissed, touched and sought each other, discovering the pleasures of true love, her body arching beneath his as he thrust into her warmth again and again. She moaned with pleasure as her inner self reached out to him, and he groaned in response and spilled himself inside her.

After a while they began to talk again.

'We shall visit your father together—and I wish

to speak with your cousin too. Then we shall be married and you will always be protected. No man shall ever threaten you again while I live,' he said sternly.

'Do not talk of these things now,' Rosamunde whispered. 'I know that we cannot wrap ourselves in silk and be protected from the harshness of a world that is often cruel. I am strong enough to face whatever life brings if I have you at my side.'

'I shall never leave you,' he vowed. 'Until death do us part.'

* * * * *

Afterword

'So, daughter, this is finally your wedding day,' Sir Randolph said. He had risen from his bed that morning in March and looked better than when she'd visited him before, though still a little frail. 'I shall be glad to see you wed to a good man who will care for you and love you.'

'Raphael does truly love me,' she said with satisfaction and took his arm as they walked towards the chapel where she was to become her lover's bride. 'I am happier than I ever expected to be, Father.'

'You know that I would never have sent you to your cousin had I known how she would treat you. Everything has turned out well, but it might have been very different. Her father is angry with her, and he has told her that she must apologise to you, for he owes Lord Mornay a debt. Had Sir

Raphael not given Count Torrs his freedom, the prince might have taken his life,' her father said.

'Angelina was selfish but she wanted to marry Sir Thomas. I know she loves him and I understand why she could not bear to take the ransom herself. Besides, I had to pay the debt you owed her family.'

'She lied to you, Rosamunde. There was no debt. It was cruel and despicable and I for one shall not forgive her—or myself, for placing you in such danger,' he said.

'You were ill, Father. You did not know that I was in danger, and in the end I was not. Had it not been for my cousin, I might never have seen Raphael again. I forgive her because I am happy,' she replied honestly.

Her father leaned down to kiss her cheek. 'You look beautiful, Rosamunde. Your mother would be proud of you. Take my arm. We do not want to keep Lord Mornay waiting.'

'I am ready,' she said and smiled.

'So you are wed to him.' Angelina looked at Rosamunde, a glint of envy in her eyes when they met in the hall as the guests mingled for the wedding breakfast. 'You know that you owe your good fortune to me. Had I not sent you to him, you would still be my servant.'

'I know that I owe my good fortune to the bargain we made,' Rosamunde said, looking her cousin directly in the eye. 'But do not pretend that you did it for my sake. You believed that Lord Mornay was an evil man and sent me to pay the price he demanded in your stead.'

Angelina looked uncomfortable. 'Had I known the old Lord Mornay was dead, I should have gone myself. You do not know how fortunate you are, cousin. Your husband is rich, while mine...' She stopped and pulled a wry face. 'You still owe me money. You had the other half of the ransom money and my horses.'

'Raphael holds the money for your father,' Rosamunde said firmly. 'As for the horses—I think there was a little matter of fifty gold talents that *you* promised to pay *me*. If you pay me what you owe me, I will return the horses.'

'You know I cannot,' Angelina said with a sour look. 'You have so much—surely you could give me what is mine?'

'The horses belong to Raphael now. He is my

lord and everything I have is his. You may ask him for them, if you wish,' Rosamunde said without feeling any pity for her selfish kinswoman.

Angelina turned away. She had already tried to charm her cousin's betrothed and the cold, withering look Raphael had given her had made her flinch.

'I wish I had never taken you in,' she said spitefully. 'I should have sent you back to your father at the start. I gave you gowns and food, and how have you repaid me?'

'You treated me as a servant. I shall gladly return the gowns you gave me, for I never wear them,' Rosamunde said placidly.

'I suppose he gives you all you want,' Angelina said bitterly and looked for her husband. 'I am leaving now. Do not come to me if things go wrong for you.'

'No, cousin, I shall not.'

Rosamunde watched as her cousin walked from the hall, then turned to look out of the window at the gardens.

'Has she gone?' Rosamunde turned to see Raphael looking at her. 'I heard what she said to you, my love. Was she always as unkind to you?'

'Yes. I think she is jealous. Sir Thomas may not be all she thought him.' She smiled.

'She has only what she deserves,' he stated. He walked towards her and took her into his arms. He gazed down at her, searching her face for signs of distress. 'Has she upset you?'

'No. Nothing Angelina could say would hurt me now,' she assured her new husband.

'I am glad,' he said and bent his head to kiss her softly on the lips. 'Are you ready to go home, my love?'

'Oh yes,' she said and smiled up at him. 'My father is as well here in his own bed as he would be with us. I know he is being cared for and all he wants is for me to be happy.'

'It will be my privilege to see that you are happy now—and for the rest of our lives,' he said fervently, then he kissed her passionately.

HISTORICAL

Large Print

SEDUCED BY THE SCOUNDREL
Louise Allen

Rescued from a shipwreck by the mysterious Captain Luc d'Aunay, Averil Heydon is introduced to passion in his arms. Now she must return to Society and convention—except Luc has a shockingly tempting proposition for her…

UNMASKING THE DUKE'S MISTRESS
Margaret McPhee

At Mrs Silver's House of Pleasures, Dominic Furneaux is stunned to see Arabella, the woman who shattered his heart, reduced to donning the mask of Miss Noir. He offers her a way out—by making her his mistress!

TO CATCH A HUSBAND…
Sarah Mallory

Impoverished Kitty Wythenshawe knows she must marry a wealthy gentleman to save her mother from a life of drudgery. Landowner Daniel Blackwood knows Kitty cares only for his fortune—but her kisses are irresistible …

THE HIGHLANDER'S REDEMPTION
Marguerite Kaye

Calumn Munro doesn't know why he agreed to take Madeleine Lafayette under his protection, but finds that her innocence and bravery soothe his tortured soul—he might be her reluctant saviour, but he'll be her willing seducer…